"A JAPANESE TEAMED UP WITH ARAB TERRORISTS?"

Hal Brognola's skepticism showed on his face. "I'd have a lot of trouble swallowing that one."

"Let's suppose for just a moment that Shukan has betrayed the United States and is a high-ranking member of the Aum Shinrikyo. In order for him to be effective, he's going to need to find help from outside sources. But I doubt he is up to the task of seizing an entire aircraft carrier. Besides, he needs someone to execute the operation because he's on board the *Stennis*. So he reaches out to a group that has experience in attacking American military targets, and makes them some kind of offer they can't refuse. And I believe that group was Ansar al-Islam," Price told him.

"Then we have to figure out what Shukan could have offered the Ansar al-Islam that would have made them agree to such a coalition."

"It could be something as simple as hatred of a common enemy."

"Maybe. And just maybe it's something with higher stakes."

DON PENDLETON'S

STONY

AMERICA'S ULTRA-COVERT INTELLIGENCE AGENCY

MAN®

VANISHING POINT

A GOLD EAGLE BOOK FROM

WORLDWIDE®

TORONTO • NEW YORK • LONDON
AMSTERDAM • PARIS • SYDNEY • HAMBURG
STOCKHOLM • ATHENS • TOKYO • MILAN
MADRID • WARSAW • BUDAPEST • AUCKLAND

First edition April 2006

ISBN 0-373-61966-9

VANISHING POINT

Special thanks and acknowledgment to
Jon Guenther for his contribution to this work.

Printed in U.S.A.

VANISHING POINT

PROLOGUE

North Island, San Francisco, California

He watched the harried activity around him with a mix of amusement and mild interest.

His blue eyes, like twin points of cold steel, settled briefly on a group of uniformed Navy officers huddled around a coffeepot and then moved to the shapely backside of a civilian clerk bending to pick up the pencil she'd dropped. The clerk happened to notice she had the man's attention, but he didn't avert his eyes. When she realized the reason for his appraisal, she smiled at him. He winked and then watched her appreciatively as she continued about her business.

He'd been cooped up too long in this building, polishing a chair with his behind, waiting. He knew the call would eventually come, but many of the military and civilian personnel around him were anxious, and they showed it. He just wanted to be somewhere he could stretch his legs. He wasn't used to this length of inactivity and his toes were starting to fall asleep. But he knew until they heard something he wasn't going any place, and that didn't sit well with him. He wasn't so anxious that he *wanted* something to happen. In fact, he would have preferred a peaceful resolution, but then he didn't get to make that call. In his line of business, action was always preferable to reaction.

The phone on the desk next to him rang and the place went quiet. He studied the faces gaping at him for a moment and then grabbed the receiver midway through the second ring. "Yeah."

"I will not waste time asking your name," the caller replied in a heavily accented voice. "Since I know you were informed to expect my call, I will assume that you are authorized to make any decisions necessary."

"I am," the man said.

"Then listen carefully to me. I represent the Supporters of Islam. Dr. Jin Shukan is our prisoner. You will pay us one billion U.S. dollars for his return. If you do not, we will kill him."

"I'm afraid not," the man replied.

"What?"

"My government doesn't negotiate with terrorists."

"Then your government will have to make an exception," the caller said. "Otherwise, we will deliver your precious scientist to you a few pieces at a time until our demand is met. Do you have something to write with?"

"Yeah."

The caller gave him a phone number. "You will call

this number within four hours to let us know that you have the money, and we will give you instructions on where it should be delivered. Don't bother asking for more time. If you attempt to retaliate against any of our associates, Shukan dies. If you attempt a rescue, Shukan dies. If you do not pay, Shukan dies. Is that clear?"

"It's clear," the man replied, but he realized that the caller had already hung up.

He replaced the receiver quietly and then reached to a cellular phone on his belt. He spared another glance at the eyes fixated on him as he flipped open the front panel of the phone and pushed a button on it. By the time he'd brought the special phone to his ear, the line was ringing.

A deep, booming voice answered. "Yes?"

"Did you get it?" the man asked.

There was a pause before he replied, "You bet. The call originated from a triangulated point in South San Francisco, near Oyster Point. We're still getting the exact coordinates. I can send them to you by clear-text via this link."

"Good enough," the man replied. "Call me back when you have it. We'll start heading that way."

He disconnected the call and then turned in his chair to look at the other two men who had accompanied him to San Francisco less than twenty-four hours earlier. Both men were relatively the same height, but one was slightly heavier. His hair was combed back, and his eyes seemed to be as black as tar. He sat on a nearby desk with his arms folded.

The other man stood next to him. He was a bit leaner, with brown hair, a mustache and muscular forearms. He splayed his hands and said, "Well?"

Carl Lyons smiled and replied, "We're in business."

CHAPTER ONE

South San Francisco

As promised, Stony Man Farm computer expert Aaron Kurtzman had transmitted the coordinates to Carl Lyons's cellular phone as Able Team was disembarking the ferry from North Island to Oyster Point Marina in Northern California. A government sedan awaited them and the threesome headed for Nectar Gardens, a condominium complex only about five blocks off the main road bordering the marina.

A flash of forged FBI credentials got Rosario "The Politician" Blancanales the information he needed from complex security. Lyons now watched the front door and windows of an upstairs unit through binoculars as Blancanales returned to the sedan and gave them the lowdown.

"A security guard at the front gate remembered passing through an SUV early yesterday morning with

several Middle Eastern men in front. Said he understood that the Arabs were new residents, but he didn't
recognize the Chinese—" Barncanales made quote
signs "—guy with them."

"Sounds like Shukan," Schwarz remarked.

"Sounds like the guard doesn't know a Japanese
person from a hole in the ground," Lyons added, not
taking his eyes from the unit.

"He's kind of an old fart, just doing his thing and
minding his own business," Barncanales said in defense
of the guard. "What're you thinking, Ironman?"

"That if we're going to do this, we'd better get a
move on," Lyons said, looking at his watch. "Hal will
be getting impatient."

"Don't you mean the Man will be getting impatient?"
Gadgets Schwarz asked.

"He's always impatient," Blancanales reminded his
friend.

"And Hal isn't?"

"Let's go," Lyons cut in.

Blancanales went EVA first to open the trunk, and
was followed by his teammates a minute later.

John Kissinger, the Stony Man armorer, had packed
in the top-of-the-line armament. For starters, there was
a brand-new SG 551, test-fired only once. A carbine
version of the SG 550, the Swiss-made assault rifle
held a 30-round detachable box magazine that was
designed to allow clipping of two more magazines to
it, one on either side. At a cyclic rate of 700 rounds per
minute, the weapon would prove formidable in capa-

ble hands. Hermann "Gadgets" Schwarz, the team's electronics expert, snagged the weapon from the trunk and immediately checked the action before loading a magazine.

Blancanales reached in and handed Lyons an Italian-made RS202 M-3 combat shotgun. Designed by Armi Beretta, the RS202 chambered two-and-three-quarter-inch 12-gauge shells in under-barrel, tube-fed magazines. Lyons popped open the breach and quickly spied the first shell, smiling with satisfaction when he noted its special markings. The shotgun had been loaded with Lyons's favorite shells, a mix of No. 2 and double-aught.

Finally, Blancanales procured an H&K MP-5 40 for himself. The weapon was identical to the 9 mm MP-5 A-3, with the exception that this one was chambered for the .40 Smith & Wesson cartridge and had a sloping magazine versus the signature curved one. Additionally, these weapons had been modified for single-shot, 2-shot and full-auto.

He closed the trunk and Able Team walked across the street in very nonchalant fashion, keeping their weapons concealed as much as possible. When they reached the sidewalk that ran parallel to a vine-covered wall bordering Nectar Gardens, Schwarz boosted Lyons up the wall, followed by Blancanales. The plan was for two to converge on the room, while one man remained to watch the perimeter for problems and to pick off any potential escapees.

Once his teammates were clear of the wall, Schwarz trotted down the sidewalk to the complex entrance and quickly contacted the guard inside the small, cramped shelter nestled between the gated entrance and exit lanes. The guard was an older guy, and his eyes went wide when Schwarz suddenly stepped into the building with an assault rifle in his grasp. It was a natural reaction, and one the Able Team commando wanted to let play out. He didn't expect any trouble but the sudden shock of seeing someone carrying an assault weapon in this sleepy neighborhood would have the desired effect. What he couldn't afford was the guard warning the police, because that just attracted crowds, and crowds meant innocent bystanders in the way.

"W-who are you?" the guard asked.

Schwarz noted the guard was unarmed, and then flashed his FBI credentials. "I'm a federal officer."

"I knew it!" the guard shouted, slapping his knee. His reaction took Schwarz a little off guard, but before he could reply the security guard continued, "I knew when that guy came by earlier asking questions that something was up. Finally! We're going to get some action around here!"

"Yeah," Schwarz replied, unable to repress a grin at the man's enthusiasm. "Sure."

The Able Team warrior turned and risked sticking his head out of the guard shack long enough to confirm that Lyons and Blancanales had reached the stairs leading to the upstairs unit where they believed the al-Islam terrorists held Dr. Jin Shukan hostage. Lyons turned and gestured a thumbs-up to Schwarz before he and Blancanales started slowly up the steps.

Schwarz ducked back into the guard shack, whipped out his cellular phone and checked his watch as he put the phone to his ear. The original caller had told Lyons three hours. It had been three hours and twenty minutes since they'd left North Island—forty minutes to spare. With any luck, and if the terrorists had actually been stupid enough to call from the same location where they held their prisoner, Shukan was still alive.

"Yes?" a tense, heavily accented voice answered.

"I have an answer for you regarding your demands," the electronics expert said.

"And what is that?"

"Up yours."

Through the earpiece, Schwarz made out shouting, gunfire and then what sounded like the phone being dropped. He disconnected the call, returned the phone to its holder on his belt and prepared for action.

OUTSIDE THE DOOR to the condominium, Lyons rendered a silent three count once he heard the ringing telephone, and then kicked the door six inches below the lock. It swung violently inward and the Able Team warrior was thankful the terrorists hadn't engaged the dead bolt.

Lyons quickly spotted his first target. The terrorist had the telephone receiver pressed to his ear; he turned with a shocked expression as Lyons and Blancanales came through the door, weapons held at the ready. The terrorist whirled to his left and reached for a machine pistol on a nearby table, but he was a heartbeat too late. Lyons leveled his shotgun and fired a lethal blast of No.

2-shot and double-aught, which took the terrorist in the chest just as he reached for his weapon. The receiver flew from the terrorist's fingers as the close-range force lifted him off his feet and slammed him into a wall.

A second terrorist rushed from the hallway entry on the opposite side of the room, a pistol clutched in his grasp, but Blancanales was ready for him. He swung the muzzle of his MP-5 40 in the terrorist's direction and squeezed the trigger. The weapon was set for bursts, and he used it effectively. The first .40 S&W shell hit the enemy gunner in the stomach, ripped through his liver and exited by way of his right kidney. The second round caught him in the sternum and spun him into a table covered with papers. The lightweight coffee table upended from the deadweight, and scattered the papers through the air.

The sound of an opening door and rapidly receding footfalls echoed into the living room from the hallway. Lyons and Blancanales exchanged looks before traversing the hallway, one on either side. Lyons stayed slightly ahead of the pair, acting as point. Obviously someone was escaping but neither cared to die by not proceeding with caution. For all they knew, it was a ruse to lure them into an ambush.

It was a fate neither one of them envisioned for themselves—at least not this.

Blancanales took a closed door with his shoulder and went low while Lyons covered the high ground. They exploded into an empty bedroom. The bedsheets were rumpled, stained with what looked like blood, and there were what looked like the remnants of medium-fiber rope hanging from the bedposts.

The pair whirled and proceeded down the hallway until they found a back room with a door that led to the outside. Lyons cursed himself for not doing a more thorough recon first.

"Dammit!" he snarled.

"What's wrong?"

"I didn't know there would be a back way," Lyons said as he pushed through the door and the pair began to rapidly descend the stairs. "I wasn't thinking outside the box."

"Don't sweat it, Ironman," his partner said as he reached for the communications unit attached to his belt. The device was one of Gadgets Schwarz's best inventions, a wireless transceiver that used microwave signals bounced off an "always-on" satellite link. Capable of a range approximately the area of L.A. County and using burst-mode transmissions to provide security, the device was efficient and effective for communications during sensitive operations.

"Politician to Gadgets."

"Go."

"Watch for bogies coming your way, buddy. One may be our special little package."

"Roger."

Blancanales ended with, "Out here."

As they continued down the metal frame steps, he told Lyons, "Schwarz will be watching for them."

The Able Team leader only grunted in reply and

slowed purposefully as they reached the bottom of the steps. Once more, it was time to proceed with greater caution. The steps terminated at a wide flagstone path that opened onto a common area with patio tables and chairs. There was no swimming pool here—there was one in front of the complex—but there was plenty of ivy covering the walls and more than enough bushes to provide adequate concealment.

Lyons kept moving in a zigzag pattern with Blancanales behind him doing the same pattern in an opposing direction so that, in effect, they passed each other while maintaining forward motion. It was an excellent way to proceed through an area like this while keeping any potential snipers busy with crossovers. It was difficult enough to hit a moving target, but when forced to attempt to hit one target moving in tandem and coordination with another could become quickly disorienting, even for the most skilled snipers.

They covered the entire distance of the broad courtyard unchallenged. Lyons released a pent-up breath when they reached the opposite wall, relaxing his body and mind. He moved to the wrought-iron gate that exited onto the parking lot. He quickly scanned the area and it only took a few seconds to spot their quarry. Two more terrorists were headed toward the far side of the lot, using the pool area as a shortcut, half dragging their prisoner with them.

From that distance, Lyons couldn't tell if their hostage was Shukan, but he had to assume that it was unless they were using some clever ploy. Lyons keyed the transceiver and called for Schwarz, who responded immediately.

Lyons said, "Package is in sight, plus two enemy."

"Acknowledged."

Lyons and Blancanales sprinted across the parking lot and made it to the pool area just in time to see their enemy reach the opposite end. They were fumbling with a gate that led to what looked like a bush-lined walkway. While one of the terrorists kept trying to open the gate, the other stood behind the hostage, using him as a shield as he cut loose with his machine gun.

The Able Team commandos dived away from each other, preferring the hot, rough concrete of the pool deck to being ventilated by the storm of lead that burned past their heads. A few rounds ricocheted off the deck, sending concrete chips flying, a few nicking Lyons's face. Several more slugs zinged off the decorative wrought-iron fence surrounding the pool, charging the air with sparks and the sounds of metal on metal.

Lyons leveled his weapon, but realized that a shotgun blast at that range wouldn't do the hostage much good. He laid the shotgun flat on the ground in front of him and rolled onto his back so he could draw the Glock 26 pistol from the shoulder leather beneath his jacket.

It obviously took Blancanales only a moment to realize Lyons's dilemma, and he picked up the temporary slack by leveling the MP-5 40 three-dot sights on the terrorist trying to open the gate. He took a deep breath as he closed one eye and pressed his cheek against the stock, pulled the butt tightly against his shoulder, and thumbed the selector to single shot. He let out half of the breath before squeezing the trigger. The S&W .40-caliber bullet landed spot-on, punching through the terrorist's spine and slamming him into the gate. The man's body bounced away with equal force, but his sleeve snagged on one of the decorative spikes emerging from the top of the gate. The gate came free of the latch and the remaining terrorist fired another rapid volley in their direction even as Blancanales put a second round into the first terrorist whose upper body was suspended from the free-swinging gate.

Lyons and Blancanales leaped to their feet and continued the pursuit. As they reached the gate and merged onto the walkway, they heard an engine start. They sprinted toward the end of the walkway and came out on the far side of the parking lot in time to see a Toyota SUV rocket from a covered space and head for the front gate. Lyons reached for the transceiver on his belt.

"COMING YOUR WAY, Gadgets." Lyons's voice echoed static-free in Hermann Schwarz's ear. The microphone on the transceiver was so sensitive that he could hear the roar of a vehicle's engine in the background. It sounded powerful enough to be that of a truck or sport utility vehicle. That would match with what Blancanales had told them earlier about the security guard waving through an SUV.

The warrior turned and motioned for the security guard to get on the floor. The man moved slowly, but he obeyed as he wasn't obviously in a position to argue about it.

Once he was on the ground, Schwarz said, "That SUV you told my associate about that passed through yesterday. What color was it?"

"Maybe silver or gray. Yeah, silver I guess."

Satisfied that the description was solid enough that he wouldn't be gunning down some poor innocent schmuck who was just late for an appointment with his plastic surgeon, Schwarz stepped from the guard shack. There was a squeal of tires as a silver SUV rounded a curve and barreled toward the gate in the entrance lane. The electronics wizard had insured both gates were closed and secured, which minimized the risk to outside traffic against what he was about to do next.

Schwarz raised the SG 551 to his shoulder, sighted on the driver's-side windshield and triggered a short burst. The rounds peppered the window, but it didn't pebble, as he had supposed it would, nor did it appear the vehicle was slowing. Schwarz let loose with another short burst, which appeared to produce the same null effect.

The glass was heat-tempered and bulletproof! The Able Team commando cursed as he lowered the muzzle and went for the engine block. He fired a sustained burst this time, confident that if the vehicle slammed through the gate and managed to escape, it wouldn't get far. At the last moment, the SUV swerved, bouncing over the wide curb that separated the two lanes and barely angled its way between two miniature palm trees planted in the median for decoration.

The SUV was now headed for the exit gate. Schwarz

realigned his sights and squeezed off two more bursts, going for the tires. The Able Team warrior's aim paid off as steam suddenly erupted from the grille and the vehicle swerved violently out of control. The sudden turn was too much for the top-heavy SUV and it flipped onto its side before spinning and skidding and finally grinding to a halt a few inches from the gate. Schwarz waited a moment before lowering his assault rifle and stepping toward the vehicle.

The driver's-side door suddenly swung open and a dark-skinned man popped his head through the opening, a machine pistol clutched in his fist. Schwarz realized his mistake a moment too late, and even as he raised the SG 551 he knew the driver was a second ahead of him.

A shot rang out, but Schwarz didn't feel the burning of hot lead through his body, nor did he see his life flash before his eyes as he'd heard so many times. Some unseen force had decided that he should live another day as the round missed him by a fraction of an inch, burying itself into the dirt of a flowerbed instead of his tender flesh. Schwarz took the blessing and brought his rifle into play. He was about to depress the trigger but quickly realized it wasn't needed as the terrorist's head exploded in a wash of red and gray, and then his body dropped from sight.

Schwarz turned in time to see Carl Lyons lower his Glock 26, smoke still curling from the barrel.

He waved at Lyons. "Damned glad to see you, Ironman!"

CHAPTER TWO

Hamid Adil hated America. As he stood on the balcony of his hotel suite and watched the waters of San Francisco Bay crash against the beaches, he smiled at the thought of her inevitable demise. If all went as planned—and he was confident it would—he would soon have control of the most technologically advanced aircraft ever conceived by the human mind. And he would use it to decimate the Americans.

Adil's hatred of America had been bred into him. So many wanted to blame the Arab world for the conflicts in the Middle East, but Adil's father had taught him the truth. He'd taught him of the oppression of the Islamic people by America and her allies. It made little difference whether it was the Turkish looking to destroy the northerners of Iraq, or the Israelis trying to commit a form of "legalized" genocide under the guise of antiterrorism, when Adil considered the totality of circumstances. Moreover, he didn't care about Islam as a religious right of passage into Paradise. He'd fallen from the pure faith long ago when he watched as his parents had been gunned down in cold blood. No, Adil's only paradise was seeing the destruction of his enemies, and he would go anywhere and do anything to achieve those ends. That was because Hamid had fought for his people, and as a true patriot he was deserving of his position as leader of this cell of the Ansar al-Islam.

In fact, his particular group occupied a special place in the hierarchy of the jihad, and they had earned the respect of the Islamic world for their successes. Adil's group had been instrumental in the bombing of the U.S.S. *Cole* in Yemen, as well as the embassy bombing in Kenya. They had also done significant work to facilitate their major victory against the Americans on September 11, 2001. But even through their victories, it wasn't enough. The American response to those attacks had been admittedly impressive, and the increased security in their airports and government facilities had made another such attack fairly impossible.

But Adil was an educated man. He'd graduated with honors from some of the finest schools in the Middle East before his father sent him to Afghanistan and a new kind of university. It was there that Adil had learned of the rules of Islam and the war against America and her allies. What Adil had learned at the secret camps of al Qaeda was different from anything they had ever taught him in school. But it was the American invasion of Afghanistan and wanton, unwarranted violence against its people—and what caused his people to ultimately turn against one another—that left Adil convinced that he had a higher calling.

His support of Ansar al-Islam against the Kurdish terrorists in northern Iraq during the U.S. invasion had left him with all of the skills necessary to fight his enemies. He would fight them in their own streets and alleyways, and he would prey upon their worst fears and insecurities. And he would do it in a way previously unfathomable.

There was a knock at the door of his suite, audible through the open sliding-glass patio door, but he didn't answer it. A quick look at his watch told him who it would be. He heard a second knock and then detected the door being opened. Adil whirled and reached beneath his loose-fitting shirt that concealed a .380 pistol, but he relaxed when he saw it was only his personal assistant.

The man, who was more of a boy than a man, had only poked his head through the door. He looked carefully in every direction, and looked as if he were about to call Adil's name when he spotted his leader and master coming in from the balcony. "I am sorry to disturb you, master. I did knock, but—"

Adil waved him in. "Come, Nabish, don't be afraid. I've been expecting you."

Nabish entered, quietly closing the door behind him as he replied, "You have?"

"Yes, I'm certain that you bring news of the Americans and their attempted rescue of Shukan."

"Y-yes," Nabish stammered. "I am afraid that the news is not good, master."

"Tell me," Adil said, bracing himself. He'd been standing on the porch, meditating as he awaited the news, and he was confident that he would hear what he expected.

"The, uh, well—"

Adil quickly grew impatient. "Out with it!"

Nabish began speaking rapidly. "The Americans somehow found out where our men were holding the prisoner, master. They put together a rescue operation and hit our people before we knew what had happened. We lost our men and they recovered our hostage. We believe Dr. Shukan is now missing, presumably in the hands of the Americans. There were no survivors."

A slow, purposeful smile played across Adil's face, and he could see that Nabish was shocked by his reaction. Hamid Adil had a reputation as a hard taskmaster who instilled discipline in his men. He didn't participate in any of the Islamic rituals himself, and while he didn't force his men to follow those antiquated practices, he did encourage them if they chose that path. He didn't want his men to lose those things they had inherited from their families. Some of his men came from the lineage of Islamic imams, and so they ministered to the rest of the men. But their first duty was to God, and in that they served Adil and Ansar al-Islam.

"This is excellent news," Adil finally replied after savoring the moment. He clapped Nabish on the shoulder and gripped it firmly. "This is *most* excellent news!"

"I…" Nabish began, but he shut his mouth.

"Yes, Nabish, what is it?"

"I thought you would be angered to hear this news, master."

"Under normal circumstances I would have been very angry," Adil said as he moved to the refrigerator and removed a pitcher of ice water.

If there was one tradition that Adil held, it was abstinence from alcohol. In fact, he neither drank nor smoked, as he considered them pollutants to God's temple, and he rarely allowed the audience of women. They were tools of satisfaction, nothing more, and they served their function best in the home. Adil thought of his wife waiting for him in their village. She'd been waiting for him to come home since his departure to the camps, but he'd elected instead to carry out his missions in America. He missed her, and his firstborn—a young healthy boy—but his cause took precedence right now. Fayah understood that, and she understood that they could never expect to live in peace until he'd accomplished his mission.

Many of his men had made similar sacrifices. He wasn't about to ask them to do something he hadn't done himself. It was these convictions and his example in leadership that had won the hearts of his men. They would go anywhere he told them and do anything he commanded. Such loyalty was rare in organizations, but he didn't ask them to be more than human. He was hard but he was fair, and he kept a distance with his men that made it easier during those times he had to dole out discipline.

"Yes, I would normally be quite upset," Adil continued as he poured himself some ice water. He offered some to Nabish, but his aide declined. He wouldn't have dared drink or eat in front of his master. Nabish was a faithful servant, but there were times when Adil wondered if he was too hard on the young man. He didn't want it to turn into his undoing.

"You mean, this was planned, master?"

"To the last detail," Adil replied. He took a few swallows of water, then continued, "I am saddened by the loss of our brothers, but their sacrifice will not be in vain. They will have their just rewards in due time."

"But why did you want this to happen?"

"That is something I cannot tell you, Nabish," Adil said, wagging his finger as he walked from the kitchenette to the couch and sat. "You will understand in good time. But there is a time for everything, and your time to understand has not yet come. Neither has it come for the men, so you will not speak of this outside of me, because to do so would mean the loss of your tongue. Do you understand?"

"I understand, master," Nabish replied quickly.

"Fine. Now I want you to go find Budai and send him to me."

Nabish bowed and left the hotel room with a noted hurriedness in his step. Adil couldn't contain another smile.

Yes, I'm too hard on him, he thought.

BLANCANALES COULD TELL that Carl Lyons had just about had all he could stand.

Since they had returned and safely delivered Dr. Jin

Shukan into the NCIS, Able Team had been forced to listen to one bureaucrat after another drone on endlessly about more joint cooperation from the civilian law-enforcement agencies, and how they took a terrible risk and should have waited for the assistance of local law-enforcement or state agencies. Now Lyons and his teammates were seated in the office of the North Island naval base commander, Admiral Harold Pacheco, listening to what Lyons knew was more crap.

"Gentlemen, I must say that your efforts were impressive," Pacheco began as he closed the case file that contained a report on the rescue. He folded his hands on his desk and continued, "And I'm *very* glad that you were able to facilitate the return of Dr. Shukan in one piece. You have the gratitude of the Pacific Fleet and the United States Navy. But I have to protest this latest turn of events."

"Blah, blah, blah…look, Admiral, we're not asking you," Lyons said. "This is the way it's going to be."

Pacheco started to open his mouth and Blancanales decided to step in and wield the scepter of reason and diplomacy. "With all due respect, Admiral Pacheco, I think what my partner is trying to say is that these orders come directly from the Oval Office. Now both our boss and yours think this is a good idea, and there's really nothing more to it than that."

Yeah, it was a big scepter.

Pacheco's resolute expression began to falter. "Your point is well taken. But I'm not sure that you understand the circumstances of secrecy here."

"We know how to keep secrets, Admiral," Blanca-nales countered. "Believe me."

Pacheco sighed and sat back in his chair, placing his hands behind his head and exchanging glances with each of the Able Team warriors. They knew the guy was caught between a rock and a hard place, and it wasn't difficult to have sympathy for him, at least not for Blancanales. He couldn't speak for team-mates, but from experience he'd have guessed that Schwarz would be easier to sway toward that view than Lyons. Oh well, he would do what he could when he could to save them all from Lyons's almost boyish impatience.

"I walk a fine line here, gentlemen," Pacheco said. "But then again, I guess I've been there before, so what the hell. In less than twenty-four hours, the *John C. Stennis* will be leaving this port and headed for a nice, easy cruise across the Pacific."

"What's our destination?" Schwarz asked.

"That's classified," Pacheco responded.

Lyons started to open his mouth, but again Blanca-nales cut in. "Fine, Admiral, but once we're under way you'll have to tell us. Fair enough?"

"Seems so."

"What's the purpose of this mission?" Lyons asked. "The details my people had were sketchy."

"I'm not surprised," Pacheco replied with a grin. "Some of the details have been sketchy even for me. The official story is that we're taking the *Stennis* on a sixty-day float for maneuvers with some other ships from

Pearl Harbor, primarily for the purpose of testing her combat readiness following a recent retrofitting."

"How much of that do you think will actually wash with the press if they get wind of *that* cockamamie story?" Lyons asked.

"Quite a bit, probably, seeing as the *Stennis* did in fact go through a recent retrofitting."

"And one that I imagine you made sure was highly publicized," Schwarz concluded.

Pacheco nodded. "Now, I'll tell you the other half. The man you rescued today is more than just any scientist. He happens to be one of the smartest men on this planet."

"Yeah, I've met a few others like him," Lyons replied. "I have yet to be impressed."

"Oh I can assure you that this man's impressive, Agent Thompson," Pacheco replied. "Jin Shukan is the chief designer and architect of the X-51."

"And that is?" Blancanales asked.

"Perhaps the greatest aerial combat vehicle ever created in the history of the U.S. military."

"An airplane?" Schwarz asked.

"Not just an airplane, gents. An unmanned plane, capable of performing heavy bombings, missile delivery and advanced aerial reconnaissance missions under the control of technicians from more than two thousand nautical miles away. In short, the X-51 is a modern marvel of technology."

"We've had unmanned bombers for some time, haven't we?" Schwarz asked.

"Yes, but nothing like this," Pacheco replied. "Dr. Shukan could explain all of this to you so I think I'll leave it to him. After all, he designed the aircraft, and he could give you much more quantifiable information than I could. Very few of the Navy's people were involved early in the project. We only got the go-ahead to participate when DARPA and the Air Force realized that for the X-51 to be fully effective and reliable that they had to be able to launch it from an aircraft carrier as much as from dry land."

"Well, that's all very interesting," Lyons interjected. "But I don't see what any of this has to do with our mission."

"You weren't given any guidance from your people?"

"We weren't told any more than you were," Lyons said. "We were to stay on here at North Island, or wherever, and provide security for him and his operations."

Pacheco sat forward and looked at the Executive Order on his desk. "Yes, that's effectively what I was told of your mission. And it was signed by the President."

Schwarz grinned and replied, "Well, he handles booking for most of our events. He's kind of like our business manager."

Blancanales fixed his friend with an expression of combined shock and embarrassment.

"Listen, Admiral," Lyons said, "we're not looking to cause you any grief. But we do have our orders, and they *are* from the President, and as such we mean to carry them out."

"And since the security of any civilian employee of

the DOD or other military defense agency falls into the purview of Homeland Security," Blancanales added, "with whom our task force is attached, we naturally become involved."

"I understand everything you're saying, men," Pacheco replied. "And frankly, I agree with you, particularly given recent events. Under the circumstances, I'll be happy to have you along for the trip."

"Then we can expect your full cooperation?" Lyons asked.

"As long as I can expect yours," Pacheco replied.

"It's a deal."

With that, Pacheco adjourned the meeting and three Able Team commandos left the headquarters offices and headed for the billets where Jin Shukan was currently under guard.

"Frankly, I'm a bit surprised that Hal chose to communicate like this with us," Schwarz said. "I mean, what's all this going through official channels and the issuance of an Executive Order? Why not just call us?"

"He's protecting our role," Lyons said. "He didn't want to compromise the position we'd established for ourselves here."

"Ah, I guess I hadn't thought of that."

"Well, the good thing is that Blancanales covered nicely for us with that little speech about Homeland Security and all that jazz." Lyons directed his voice toward the back seat as he said, "That was good work, buddy."

"Well, I don't think my performance would win an award, but thanks anyway," Blancanales replied.

"What worries me most is this new plane they're going to test," Lyons continued. "I know Hal could have at least called us on the side and told us about it."

"Maybe that was part of the ruse," Schwarz replied. "We all know how often the big muckety-mucks in Wonderland like to treat their underlings like mushrooms."

"Yeah, keep them in the dark and feed them bullshit," Blancanales stated.

Schwarz grinned. "Precisely."

"Something still bothers me about this whole thing," Lyons said.

"You know, I do believe Ironman's just afraid of boats."

"Sounds like it to me," Schwarz agreed.

"Yeah," Lyons said, getting in on the action. In a pirate's accent, he added, "And me first act once aboard is to have ya scrubbin' the decks, ye swabs. Aaargh!"

They burst into at their leader's rare wisecrack laughter, which seemed to relieve much of tension from the day's activities.

Hal Brognola had sent them to North Island to accomplish a mission, and Blancanales felt they had operated admirably, despite what some of the boys with the Navy might think. That was one nice thing about their position with Stony Man. With the authority of the Oval Office, they could throw their weight around when absolutely needed, although they didn't abuse the privilege. It was more important to keep up appearances in whatever cover roles they were assigned.

"I'm not going to sweat it for now," Lyons said. "But

I have a bad feeling about this whole blasted thing. I'm certain we haven't heard the last of the Ansar al-Islam."

"They could try something else before it's over," Schwarz said. "Ironman makes a good point."

"We'll just have to keep our eyes open," Blancanales said.

"No worries," Lyons added. "If they try anything, we'll be ready."

CHAPTER THREE

Stony Man Farm, Virginia

Bureaucratic red tape aggravated Harold Brognola, especially when it tangled up his teams in the field. The men of Able Team and Phoenix Force had a tough enough job without someone adding problems. This kind of thing lessened effective communications between Stony Man and its people, and it could get someone killed.

"It doesn't make any damn sense," Brognola told Barbara Price.

Price nodded with a sympathetic expression. "I understand how you feel, Hal, but we've been here before and you know it."

"That's not the point," Brognola replied, yanking an unlit cigar from his mouth. "It's tough enough just keeping track of our people and making sure we get them back in one piece. I'm all for protecting their cover, but I'm *not* for keeping them out of the loop on matters of international security. I have a good mind to put Phoenix Force on a plane right now to California."

While it made sense and it made Brognola feel better to say it, he also knew that wasn't completely his call. He wouldn't have dared activate Phoenix Force unless Price agreed with such a move. He was the head of Stony Man, sure, but she was the mission controller and as such that gave her carte blanche where sending the teams into action was concerned. Brognola was more of a figurehead and liaison with the Oval Office than he was in control of actual operations. Missions were left to Barbara Price. She gave out the assignments, she gleaned the intelligence and she made decisions based on the logistics. Brognola tended many times to become overly emotional about certain issues, so he deferred to her judgment, and it was rare for him to supercede anything once she'd laid out a game plan.

"Okay, I'll agree that it was short notice," she agreed, resting a hand on his forearm while maintaining a level gaze. "But Able Team can handle it. We both know they've been here before, and they're professionals who are able to adapt very quickly to the situation. There's no reason to get Phoenix involved, because I'm sure they'll have something to chew on soon enough."

Yes, Price made sense as usual, and it was just about the same speech he'd gotten from the President. Ultimately, Stony Man served at the pleasure of the Oval Office, and it was only through some miracle that they hadn't been exposed or disbanded long before this. Sending additional support was an option but a last one.

"All right, I'll concede the point for now. But any more surprises like this one and I *will* order Phoenix Force to assist."

"Let's hope it won't come to that," Price replied.

"Agreed," Brognola said with a nod to indicate the matter was closed.

Price smiled and then rose from her chair and stepped out of the conference room. A moment later she returned with Aaron "The Bear" Kurtzman in tow. The broad-shouldered, burly physique may have been confined to a wheelchair, but the mind was another story entirely. A single bullet in the spine had turned Kurtzman's life upside down, and while he could have lain down and wallowed in self-pity, the Bear chose instead to trade his physical shortcoming for the development of a far more powerful weapon: knowledge. Kurtzman's work and the work of his cybernetics team kept Stony Man one step ahead in the technological game, and gave them a tactical advantage over America's most sophisticated enemies.

"What's the story, Bear?" Brognola asked as Kurtzman wheeled to a computer station.

The cybernetic systems wizard grinned broadly as he typed information into the computer system. The lights dimmed quickly and a picture of a short, thin man with closely cropped black hair and a beard was displayed on the screen. The man wore the garb of an Arab guer-rilla fighter, and posed boldly with an assault rifle while a dozen or so men in similar garb stood behind him and looked on.

"The man you're looking at was recently identified by Homeland Security as a possible leader of the Ansar al-Islam, which as you know took credit for the kidnapping of Dr. Shukan."

"Charming-looking fellow," Brognola said after a close study of the man's hardened features.

He looked at Price and asked, "We have a name to go with the face yet?"

Price shook her head. "He doesn't appear on any of the FBI's or CIA's lists, and my contacts at the NSA don't have a matching profile through any official channels."

"What about the unofficial channels?" Brognola asked.

"Nothing has come by field agents, either by coded communications or word of mouth, but that doesn't mean anything. There's a rumor floating in the intelligence community abroad that says this same picture was shown to informants in a number of different countries known to support Ansar al-Islam, and every single one of them swore they didn't know who he was."

"However, we do have reliable intelligence that he fought against our Special Forces team during the early stages of Operation Freedom, so we're checking leads with former CIA intelligence analysts that worked in-country during that time," Price added.

"Is the CIA cooperating with us?"

"As well as can be expected," Kurtzman replied with a shrug. "A good part of what I learned about out mystery man here came through the DIETS."

Brognola nodded. He was familiar with the devices Kurtzman referenced. The Digital Information Extraction Tool System was a significant enhancement in information retrieval. DIETS could crack a network, enter databases of any type, and secretly transport the information contained within those databases back to Stony Man's computers under the nose of its owners. The system was virtually undetectable by any network analyzer or intrusion detection system available to the commercial market, and if they were ever caught Kurtzman had made sure the source was untraceable by spoofing the transmissions with server addresses all over the globe. Once in Stony Man's possession, Kurtzman's team unencrypted the data, and Kurtzman and Price then deciphered and cataloged the information for future use.

"So I would have to assume that there's some reason you think he's behind this," Brognola said.

"We're not a hundred percent certain that he's involved," Price replied. "But since intelligence leads us to believe he's the current head of Ansar al-Islam, we figured it was a place to start."

"Do we know where he is?"

"We don't have any solid leads, but we have to consider he could be operating here in the U.S."

"Okay, so let's assume that he's here in the country and that he may have support from a small force, given what we know from Able Team's encounter with Shukan's kidnappers. What about motivations? Is this a typical operation for Ansar al-Islam?"

"Up until recently, we could have refuted any evidence that Ansar al-Islam had the money or resources to operate within the United States or its protectorates, but that view has changed," Price replied. "Since the invasion of Iraq, their group has continued to receive increasing support from the al Qaeda network. Bin Laden apparently supported them when their efforts were focused on fighting the Patriotic Union of Kurdistan, but since that time they've apparently proven their usefulness in other venues."

"So their terrorist sister groups figured investing in their operations was worth the risk," Brognola concluded.

"Naturally," Price said.

"What about tactical and technical resources, Bear?"

Kurtzman shrugged. "It's still too early to tell. From the standpoint of nonconventional weapons, they've rattled a few cages over the years. At one point, word got through to the worldwide press that they were experimenting with biotoxins and poison gas."

"Have we investigated any of these possibilities?"

"We looked into it, but again we don't have any substantiated evidence to think such an attack against the U.S. is in their plans."

"And why is that?"

It was Price who answered. "Well, we investigated claims that Ansar al-Islam was testing biotoxic weapons and discovered they were focusing their research on poisons extracted from the castor bean. Are you familiar with it?"

Brognola shook his head.

Price sighed, sat forward and folded her hands on the table, then said, "The castor bean plant has seeds that contain a protein called ricin. It's a potent cytotoxin that inhibits the ability of red blood cells to synthesize proteins. In fact, it's been said that if a child of six or younger were to ingest a single seed, they'd be dead in less than a day."

"Sounds like nasty stuff," Kurtzman remarked.

Price nodded as she replied, "It is that. Severity of the effects depends on the type of exposure. Injection or inhalation works about ten to twelve times faster than absorption through the skin or ingestion. Symptoms include everything from diarrhea and vomiting to rapid fluid loss, drop in blood pressure, and eventually death."

Brognola shook his head and furrowed his eyebrows. "None of that makes sense. From what I know of Jin Shukan, he doesn't possess a lick of expertise in that area. He's an aeronautics engineer, not a chemist or biologist."

"No, but he does possess undisputed expertise in weapon delivery systems," Kurtzman said. "Maybe Ansar al-Islam grabbed him because they're planning to distribute this ricin by some type of air-based weapons system."

"Seems like a reasonable hypothesis," Price said.

"But then, why demand a ransom?" Brognola asked.

"True," Kurtzman replied. "I hadn't thought of that."

"So aside from this mysterious unnamed player who may or may not be the leader of Ansar al-Islam, and may or may not be in the country, it sounds as if we know little else," Brognola concluded.

"Unfortunately, that's about the size of it," Price said.

"What about approaching this from the other end? Have we considered taking a closer look at Shukan to see if something in his background might give us a clue as to the motivation for his kidnapping?"

"He's fairly clean," Kurtzman said, typing more information into the computer and projecting a new picture onto the screen.

"Jin Shukan, age, thirty-five," Kurtzman began. "He was born into a poor family and grew up in Tokyo. He probably wouldn't have gone anywhere, or ended up utilizing his talents for more nefarious purposes were it not for Japan's compulsory education laws, which are stringently forced.

"At age fifteen, he'd already surpassed everything in the general studies of other children and was reading third-year college physics books. He was quickly identified as a child prodigy, and by sixteen he was in the Tokyo Metropolitan College of Aeronautical Engineering. He completed their degree in just less than two years and then moved on to the University of Foreign Studies, also in Tokyo. Eventually he wound up at MIT, and that landed him a position with the U.S. Air Force on a work visa, once they saw his talents."

"Impressive," Brognola said. "What about his political affiliations? Anything there we should be concerned about?"

"Nothing too radical, although we do know that he marched in the Japanese student protests of the late seventies."

Price shook her head and chuckled. "Just about everyone marched in a protest in the seventies."

"I can't argue with that," Brognola replied.

"In either case, he has no known political dependencies. When his work visa was up, he returned to Japan and worked there for eight years," Kurtzman continued.

"So how did he get back here?" Brognola asked.

It was Price who said, "Well, American contractors were exclusive to the X-45, which was the first in a series of our joint projects in unmanned air combat systems. Then there was the X-47, which involved contractors from a number of different countries, including Australia and the UK. When the idea for the X-51 came along, DARPA and the Air Force were looking for someone who possessed both the brains and talent to head up the project. Naturally, Shukan was suggested and after DARPA had seen his earlier work with the Air Force, all agreed to sign him up. The State Department pulled some strings to get him back in the country and he's been here ever since."

"What was he doing in Japan so close to the launch of the X-51?" Brognola asked. "That's where he was coming from when al-Islam snatched him, wasn't it?"

Price nodded. "As far as we can tell from the Navy, he was on leave in Japan seeing his family. He's not married and has no kids, but his mother and sister are both alive and still live in Tokyo. He probably wanted to see them before they leave."

"The U.S.S. *John C. Stennis* will be at sea for almost a month during these early trials," Kurtzman offered in way of explanation. "Only official communications will be permitted during that time."

"Yes, I heard from the President that the military's explained this as a training run for the *Stennis*."

"To test her new retrofitting," Price added.

"And apparently, this was thought out well in advance," Kurtzman said. "Apparently, when the Air Force and DARPA knew the approximate time frames for their first trial runs, they coordinated with the Navy, which would be providing the aircraft carrier. Once the *Stennis* was selected, they knew it would need a few modifications so they brought it into dry dock and took out a big press release."

"They also conducted tours for both the press and public, and even did some publicity work with that famous military techno writer, that what's-his-name—?"

"Dan Fancy?" Brognola offered.

"Yes, him."

"At any rate, they made a big to do," Kurtzman continued. "They talked about how they were going to clean her up, refit her engines, all of this great stuff, but they really did very little. Most of the work was conducted at night, away from sight of the regular crews."

"They did do full inspections, repainted her and some other things to pretty her up, but mostly it was a sham job," Price said.

"So now it's equipped to launch the X-51," Brognola said. "That's good. What about the exercises? They must be planning quite a bit if they're going to be out of the loop for that long. I'm not sure how well Able

Team will fare. You know, Ironman's not real big on boats."

"Well, from what we can muster, they'll start with a standard reconnaissance operation," Kurtzman replied, tapping a key and replacing Shukan's picture with that of a full topographic map of the Pacific Ocean. "The *Stennis* will depart port at 10:00 a.m., tomorrow, and head to this point, in grid Alpha Seven, which is approximately 180 longitude by 60 latitude. At about 7:30 a.m. their local time on day two, they'll launch the X-51 remotely, and control and monitor its flight path from that location to the Marianas Naval Air Station."

"Will it land there?" Price asked.

Kurtzman shook his head. "No, the plan is for them to set up some simulated laser-guided bomb strikes. The Navy wants to test its strike capability, which is the first of its kind anywhere in the world. Incidentally, it was Shukan who designed that system."

Price looked at Brognola and said, "A system with that kind of accuracy, targeting a friendly target and delivering a bio-toxic weapon would be a victorious blow for the Ansar al-Islam and al Qaeda."

"Maybe, but they won't be able to access control of the weapon as long as Able Team's around, since they'll be Shukan's shadows for nearly a month," Brognola replied. He winked, adding, "And God help anyone who tries to sabotage the *Stennis* while they're on board."

Price couldn't help but smile at the almost boyish faith that Brognola had in his people. Not that his position wasn't well-founded. The men of Able Team and Phoenix Force were some of the bravest Price had ever known.

"What happens after the demonstration, Bear?" Brognola asked.

Kurtzman replied, "After the bombing run, the X-51 will return to the *Stennis*. After that, the ship is expected to conduct additional maneuvers from other locations within the Pacific, and aside from one day of refuel in Hawaii, she'll be operating on her own."

"They won't even be flying escorts?" Price asked.

Kurtzman shook his head emphatically. "Nope, these operations are strictly classified. When she docks in Hawaii, she'll only be there a few hours, and nobody will be permitted off the ship. They're not kidding around about this thing."

"What about the X-51. Is there only one?"

"As far as we know," Kurtzman said with a shrug.

"Well, all we can do is hope Able Team's little cruise is uneventful," Brognola said.

He looked hard at Price and said, "Effective now, Phoenix Force is on full alert."

CHAPTER FOUR

North Island

Much to the chagrin of Carl Lyons and his colleagues, the questioning of Dr. Jin Shukan revealed little.

"I have no idea why they would want to kidnap me, gentlemen," the astute little man had told them. Shukan stood barely five feet tall, with dark eyes and hair that was neatly trimmed and slicked back in manner that would have only been in style during the 1950s. Combined with his pencil-thin mustache and bifocals, the scientist looked more Hispanic than Japanese.

"They didn't ask you any questions?" Blancanales asked.

"They didn't speak to me at all, other than to tell me to sit or stand or remain quiet."

"So you didn't make any deals," Lyons stated more than asked. "You didn't offer them any money or plead for your life."

Something went hard and cold in Shukan's expression. "Of course I pled for my life, sir. Wouldn't you? But they told me to shut up and so I did, and that was the extent of the conversation."

"Please don't take offense, Dr. Shukan," Blancanales said, "but I'm sure you can understand we have to ask these questions."

"I understand that these operations are a matter of national security, Agent Rose. And I also understand that if I *had* made a deal with these men, that it would compromise everything. But surely you can understand that this is my life's work. I've dedicated the better part of my career to military defense development of your country, sir. I would think that deserves some level of commensurate courtesy. I do not enjoy being interrogated like a common criminal."

Before Blancanales could concoct a reply, Lyons interjected, "Look, Doc, nobody here's questioning your loyalty. But we're dealing with some very nasty individuals. You ever hear of the Ansar al-Islam?"

"Thompson, I don't think we should—" Schwarz began.

"If we have a sworn duty to protect him, then he has a right to know from what," Lyons said, "If he wants courtesy, I'll give him courtesy." He looked at Shukan and added, "That's okay with you, I assume?"

Shukan nodded curtly at Lyons, but the increased tension was apparent in his posture. "Of course."

"Ansar al-Islam claims responsibility for your kidnapping. Are you at all familiar with this group?"

"I would not claim to be an expert, but I know of them. Being in my line of work, I was required to have some familiarity with these kinds of security threats. They are terrorists, I assume, and while I have no idea what they might have wanted with me, I do know that they hate anything American, and would go to any means to see her destroyed."

Lyons smiled, and it wasn't a friendly smile. "Then you must also know that for them to grab you and then ask for a ransom isn't typical for such groups. They could have benefited from your knowledge, or they could have dealt the U.S. a nasty blow by killing you. But to snatch a prominent aeronautical engineer and scientist for nothing more than money makes no sense."

"And do you know why it makes no sense, Agent Thompson?" Shukan asked.

"No. Why don't you enlighten us?"

"It makes no sense because you seem to assume that if you had paid the money, these terrorists would have returned me unharmed. I don't think you're that foolish." He looked at the other two men and added, "Any of you. In fact, I'm sure that they would have killed me as soon as they had the money. Fortunately, you three arrived before that could happen. And for that, I'm grateful."

Lyons studied the man a moment longer and then called a quick sidebar with his friends in the hallway just outside Shukan's new temporary quarters. They hadn't returned him to his apartment, instead choosing to let SPs move his personal belongings to this new location.

The billets were reserved for visiting military personnel only, and as such they seemed the least likely place. As the men in charge of Shukan's security, Lyons had insisted on the move.

"So what do you think?" Lyons asked his teammates. "Is he telling the truth?"

"I think so," Blancanales replied.

Schwarz shrugged and said, "Maybe…probably. Hell, I don't know. I mean, they didn't have him very long, and it doesn't look like they tortured him. He's no worse for the wear anyway."

"That's what bothers me," Lyons said. "Here they had him for almost seventy-two hours and yet they didn't torture him for information. That doesn't seem strange to you guys?"

"Well of course it's strange, Ironman," Blancanales replied. "But maybe they had orders to keep him alive. We didn't find any ID on those guys we pasted, but none of them looked like leadership material to me."

"How do you know that?" Schwarz asked.

Blancanales looked at his friend a little smugly and said, "What, do you want a free lesson in antiterrorism? When we hit that place, those guys ran like a group of chickens. Nobody was in charge, nobody was giving orders, and nobody was in control. It was just run away and hope for the best."

"He's got a point," Lyons said when Schwarz looked at him for confirmation.

The man shrugged, apparently accepting the explanation.

"So what's next?" Blancanales asked.

"Well, I'd like to know more about this X-51," Lyons said. "Let's see if we can get a tour."

THAT HAD BEEN the extent of their interrogation of Jin Shukan. Now the trio rode with Shukan in an unmarked military sedan driven by an SP as it pulled up in front of the X-51 hangar's rear door. At first, Admiral Pacheco had insisted on a military police escort wherever they went, but Lyons squashed that quickly enough. The last thing Able Team needed was military police units getting in the way.

"I want a wide berth for us where Shukan's concerned, Admiral," Lyons told Pacheco.

Lyons had agreed to let one SP chauffeur them wherever Shukan might need to go so that they could concentrate on providing security. While Lyons would have preferred to leave this kind of detail to U.S. Marshals, he understood the President's reasons for wanting Able Team to handle it. First of all, they had done this kind of thing before. Second, there weren't really any FBI agents or U.S. Marshals with high enough security clearances to provide such protection. Finally, Stony Man obviously felt that it was worth Able Team's time, otherwise Hal Brognola would have argued the point with the Oval Office until he was blue in the face.

Lyons exited the rear of the sedan, followed by Shukan and then Schwarz. Blancanales climbed from the front seat where he'd been assigned shotgun.

"If you'll follow me, gentlemen," Shukan replied, straightening his tie.

The trio surrounded him, keeping their bodies close as he entered his pass code into the numeric touch pad. The door clicked open slightly, then Shukan pushed it aside slowly and entered. As they passed, Lyons noted that it wasn't a standard door, but rather one like those found on steel vaults. While the hangar exterior looked exactly like all of the rest lining the air field, the interior of the corrugated tin shell was lined with one-inch steel plates and cross-braced with titanium alloy rivet strips.

Lyons pointed this out to his teammates, and said, "They're not kidding."

The pair nodded their agreement as they passed through the coded door which closed slowly behind them. It locked with a metallic clang that reverberated through the cavernous interior of the hangar.

Directly ahead of them, its flat-black metal hull illuminated by high-watt bulbs overhead, stood one of the most unusual-looking aircraft they had ever seen. It wasn't that big—it stood maybe a little taller than Lyons—but its sharp aerodynamic lines and sleek exterior made it formidable. There were no real wings on the craft. It was almost diamond-shaped, although the single engine protruding from its rear center made the stern taper at steeper angles. It stood like a great shadow, immediately demanding the attention of the eye as if commanding it above all other objects in the room.

"Gentlemen, I give you the X-51 UAV," Shukan said, sweeping the plane with a bony hand.

"It's not as big as I thought it would be," Schwarz remarked.

"True," Shukan said. "In comparison to say your F-117 stealth, it is about half the size. It is 27.4 feet in length and has a twenty-seven-foot wingspan. It was built in a joint venture by Northrop Grumman, Boeing and Pratt & Whitney. Empty, it weighs a mere 1.639 tons, can cruise in excess of Mach 2 at an altitude of thirty-five thousand feet, and has more than four-and-one-half thousand pounds of thrust."

Schwarz could feel his breath catch in his throat as he very slowly and purposefully murmured, "Oh my God."

"Bear in mind, that it doesn't require a pilot. There's no real weight to speak of, so its range is much farther than any conventional vehicle, almost two thousand nautical miles. It can carry a payload of about twenty-five-hundred pounds. Because it's smaller and agile, it has a far superior turning radius, which makes it very difficult to shoot down."

"How long did it take to build, Doctor?" Blancanales asked with sincere interest.

"About four years," Shukan said, adding, "That was after I joined the project, of course. DARPA and the Air Force had been working on the vehicle for some time. It was part of the JUCAS program."

"Which is?" Lyons asked.

Shukan seemed unable to resist from grinning at Lyons as he said, "I see your people have not kept you as well-informed as maybe you should be."

"They tell us enough," Lyons shot back. "We have

the intelligence we need to protect you. That's our job, and that's all we're supposed to do."

Shukan shrugged. "Fair enough."

"You were telling us about this JUCAS program?" Schwarz prompted, attempting to sway the conversation back to matters less sensitive.

Shukan looked at him and replied, "Yes. It stands for Joint Unmanned Combat Air Systems. Conceptually, it is little more than the development of highly technical aircraft. Let's call them 'drones' for simplicity's sake, although I wouldn't use the word too loudly around my colleagues. They are quite typically American in their sensitivity toward semantics."

Lyons wanted to kick the guy in the teeth for *that* little dig. He wasn't sure what had him so edgy about Shukan, but he didn't like the guy, and years of experience had taught him to rely on his instincts. There was just something about Shukan that bothered him. Actually, Lyons did know what about Shukan bothered him so much: the man's story hadn't entirely convinced him that the secret of the X-51 and its maiden voyage remained secure. Not to mention the fact that the scientist simply made his skin crawl. He'd have to keep a watchful eye on the guy for the next few days.

"But as to the main objective of the program, I intend to demonstrate the X-51 can expand tactical mission options by providing new air power and superior intelligence surveys. By virtue of the fact that we can significantly reduce loss of human life in the combat is only the beginning. The X-51 represents a new paradigm in air combat systems, gentlemen. I will show your countrymen that not only can they increase the chances of successful air strikes by fifty, perhaps a hundredfold, but they can exploit the simplicity of the aircraft's design to reduce maintenance costs and costs in pilot training."

"You're talking about a fleet of drone warships then," Schwarz said.

"I'm talking about much more than that, sir. I'm talking about creating a war machine unparalleled in human history. I'm talking about putting the most advanced and powerful unmanned aircraft into the hands of America. The United States would become unchallenged in air superiority."

"Careful, Doctor," Blancanales said with an uneasy smile. "You're beginning to sound a bit like a fanatic."

Something went a little cold in Shukan's eyes and he returned the Able Team commando's attempts at diplomacy with a penetrating stare. "You mistake fanaticism for passion, Agent Rose. I would think what I say would be good news to you. Don't be so hasty to reject the idea. Your President certainly hasn't rejected the thought, and neither have the majority of those directly involved in this project. I've offered your country the chance to become the greatest power on Earth!"

"We already are the greatest power on Earth," Lyons reminded him.

"I think you misunderstand me," Shukan replied. "I hold no grudges for the past."

Lyons shrugged. "I never said you did."

"All I'm telling you—" he looked at each in turn

"—all of you, is that the X-51 presents the greatest chance of securing your country's place in the history of aerodynamic combat." He raised a finger, wagging it slightly at them as he continued, "Imagine just for moment that a hostile country determines to launch an air assault against the country or, forbid the thought, an attack by intercontinental weapons of mass destruction. With no risk of lost lives, your country could launch an entire fleet of X-51s in a counterblow."

"It sounds impressive," Schwarz replied.

Shukan smiled, seemingly prideful of the man's response. "It's one of a kind, gentlemen. We've never built anything like it before. In fact, we've never even designed anything like it before. Sure, my predecessors have come close, but not like this. It can take off and land on its own with very little programming effort, strike targets with pinpoint accuracy, and avoid land- or satellite-based detection systems unlike any conventional aircraft that has come before it."

"Will it make dinner and let the dog out, too?" Lyons cracked.

Shukan shot him a level gaze and replied, "It will do whatever I tell it to do. The X-51 is more than just an unmanned airplane, gentlemen. It is a strike, counterstrike and reconnaissance aircraft that will render its enemies helpless and boggle the minds of the most brilliant men on Earth."

"I thought you were one of the most brilliant men on Earth, Doctor," Blancanales said.

Shukan looked at him with a smile and a bow, and replied, "Your compliment is humbling."

The look in Shukan's eyes bothered Carl Lyons. The problem here seemed less with Ansar al-Islam and more with Shukan. Lyons had seen firsthand what could happen to guys like this. After a while, they began to believe their own press, consider themselves indispensable. That building of a monstrous ego in the average person was bad enough, but when the government—any government—began to build that kind of egocentricity in geniuses, it became another game entirely. Things like that made men like Shukan dangerous.

And that made Carl Lyons nervous.

"Well, I think we've seen enough," Lyons said, making a show of looking at his watch. "We appreciate the tour, Doc, but I think it's about time we get you back to your quarters."

"But I thought you wished to—"

"To learn more about the X-51," Lyons finished. "Yes. And we have, but now it's time to get you back to your quarters."

Shukan offered no further protests and the foursome left the hangar and the X-51 to the quiet of the night.

"HONEST TO PETE, Ironman," Rosario Blancanales said. "What's with you tonight?"

"Nothing," Lyons mumbled as he flipped through basic television channels.

"Who's Pete?" Schwarz asked in his usual attempt at wry humor.

The three sat in their sparse, simple and very typical military quarters that Pacheco had arranged to be set up next to Shukan's. At first, Lyons had considered putting one of them right inside Shukan's billet, but he didn't want to completely intrude on Shukan's right to privacy, so they took an adjoining four-man room and arranged for two SPs to stand post at his door, and a heavily armed Hummer to cruise a thousand-meter perimeter around the building.

"What's your problem?" Blancanales asked. "Really, I want to know."

"My problem is Shukan."

"And what's wrong with Shukan?"

Lyons sighed, turned off the TV and replied, "Everything. And maybe nothing."

"Well, that's as clear as mud," Blancanales said with a shrug, turning to Schwarz for some help.

"And there you have it," Schwarz said as he shook his head.

Lyons began to pace the room. "This guy gets taken by terrorists and gets away without a scratch."

"And the problem is…?" Blancanales interjected.

"The problem *is* just that. Not a cut, not a bruise. And another thing that's got me a little curious is all that blood we saw on the mattress."

"You're wondering if it wasn't his, then—"

"Who did it belong to?" Lyons finished. "Exactly."

"Well, it's not really that important now. Is it?" Schwarz asked.

"Maybe not now, but it could be down the line."

"But some unidentified blood is hardly enough to

suspect the guy of collusion," Blancanales finally said. "Surely you can't tell me that's what you're basing your whole theory on."

"That's just scratching the surface," Lyons said flatly. "Have you guys forgotten just how easy it was for us to pull his ass out of the fire? Or how few terrorists there were actually guarding him? Or even how easy it was for us to find him?"

Blancanales fixed Lyons with a serious expression. "I haven't forgotten any of it. All I'm saying is that it's not concrete evidence. Schwarz, what do you think?"

"I don't want it to seem like I'm taking sides here, but I sort of agree with Ironman. There's something too weird about Shukan. Did you see the look in his eyes when he was talking about the X-51?"

Blancanales returned his gaze to Lyons who had stopped pacing and was now looking at his teammate with hands on hips. The three Able Team warriors were rarely at odds with one another—aside from a little playful banter—and even less in disagreement on mission tactics. But this was one of those rare occasions where Blancanales just wasn't ready to buy into Lyons's theory, and it was driving him nuts.

"All right, Ironman, all right. I've learned to listen to your instincts before, so I'm not going to argue with them this time. But let's not aggravate the situation. For now, I think the best thing we can do is keep our eye on things and wait."

"For what?" Schwarz asked.

"For Ansar al-Islam to try again," Lyons answered.

CHAPTER FIVE

Pacific Ocean

None of the men of Able Team was exactly sure how it had gone hard real quick, but they were sure it *had* happened.

The first two days of their trip had been relatively uneventful, but when they reached the target on day three, things changed and not for the better. Shukan had been the perfect host, along with Pacheco and Rear Admiral Buford Capp, the commander of Carrier Group Seven. Unfortunately, Able Team had no reason to believe any of these men were still alive, although as Schwarz Schwarz had pointed out, "that was unconfirmed."

They had been watching the action down on the flight deck from a forward observation tower. The X-51 was ready to launch when Shukan was urgently summoned to report to the bridge. Lyons had chosen not to accompany the scientist, and less than a minute elapsed before it happened. It started with popping sounds followed by what seemed like a minute of silence, and then Lyons and his fellow warriors watched with amazement as the sky suddenly darkened, although they couldn't really tell what was causing it.

Schwarz looked skyward. "What the hell's going on?"

"I don't know," Lyons replied, "but I don't like it. Come on!"

The trio turned and headed in the direction of the bridge. There were more popping sounds, and then every visible light winked out. The droning sound of the screws abruptly winding down followed the seeming shipwide blackout. The noises of men moving suddenly could be heard coming from every part of the ship within earshot, the crew chiefs shouting orders at the yeomen while the officers shouted orders at the crew chiefs.

I knew it, Lyons thought. I freaking well *knew* it!

He had no proof that this sudden turn of events was the machinations of Jin Shukan, but he wasn't doubtful that they would find out soon enough what was happening. Lyons stopped at the stairwell leading to the upper deck and the bridge. He was mystified at the site. There were large tubes, which looked like nothing more than six-inch water pipes, aimed skyward with smoke belching from their mouths. Lyons could only guess they had been the sources of the popping noises. Seamen and a few Marine roving guards were rushing toward them. The Marine guards had their hands on their side arms, but they hadn't drawn them yet.

The next moments seemed to go in slow motion as from somewhere below the railing there erupted the sounds of assault rifles being fired. The firepower was mercilessly accurate, and Lyons watched helplessly as the Marine guards and some of the deck personnel fell under the autofire in a spray of blood.

"Holy shit," Lyons whispered. He turned to his teammates. "Get down there and take care of business! I'll keep heading for the bridge!"

The pair nodded as Lyons turned and took the steep incline three steps at a time, his powerful legs propelling him upward at a fast. The Able Team warrior hit the top of the stairs and immediately dived for cover as a hail of bullets filled the air where he'd been a heartbeat earlier. Lyons rolled in the direction from which he'd come, making the relative safety of the stairwell precious milliseconds before another volley zinged past him.

Lyons drew his Glock 26, confirmed a round was in the chamber and then risked a glance around the corner. Two Marines in battle dress fatigues trotted toward him, but they weren't wearing side arms—they were toting MP-5 Ks. Not exactly standard military issue. These weren't Marines. They were terrorists as sure as the nose on his face. Lyons knew his enemy when he saw them. In fact, he could practically smell bad guys and these were definitely two of them.

He raised his pistol and fired as they leveled their subguns at him. The first two 9 mm Parabellum rounds punched through the point man's chest, driving him backward into his partner, hindering the guy's movement. The second gunner managed to get himself clear and was about to do the same with his weapon when Lyons hit him with a well-placed shot to the cheek. The impact snapped the enemy gunman's head and his body followed with the force, collapsing to the deck plating of the catwalk.

Lyons waited a moment, clearing the catwalk both ways before risking exposure. He advanced on the position of the now deceased pair and quickly frisked them for identification: nothing. He then snatched their MP-5 Ks, slinging one on his shoulder and trading the other for his Glock. Pacheco had agreed with the ship's captain, Monty Augustine, that Able Team be permitted to retain their side arms given their protective duties, but they hadn't been allowed to bring any other weapons or equipment aboard. These machine pistols would come in handy.

Lyons continued toward the bridge, reaching an area where the main lights had been replaced by the reddish hues of the auxiliary lighting. This part of the catwalk was well lit in contrast to most of the ship, but Lyons couldn't see more than ten or fifteen yards ahead. Something had totally blocked the sun, and he couldn't tell what had happened. It wasn't an eclipse and as far as he knew the Martians hadn't invaded so that left few other options. One thing was sure: the terrorists—whether the Ansar al-Islam or some other group—had made their move. And they had made it right when he'd expected them to, and still he hadn't been ready. Well, it was no time for would've, should've, could've—he had business of the dirtiest kind with these newcomers.

Lyons advanced quickly but carefully, machine pistol held ahead of him. He had his body angled to one side as he walked, intent on making himself as narrow a target as possible. He pushed aside thoughts of what might be happening to his comrades on the lower decks as he heard a fresh outbreak of weapons fire.

Give 'em hell, boys, he thought.

Lyons reached the entryway of the bridge and found the door shut and secured. He began beating on the door. "Hey! We've got a problem out here. Give us some help!"

Lyons pounded on the door a couple more times and then stepped backward and waited patiently. He couldn't hear any movement inside, or sounds that indicated someone was going to open the door. This didn't make a bit of sense, so either they weren't buying it—which he doubted—or there was nobody on the bridge. And if it were the latter scenario then they had bigger problems than terrorists trying to hijack a U.S. aircraft carrier.

For all he knew, they were on a collision course with hell and nobody was steering.

BLANCANALES AND SCHWARZ encountered the enemy as soon as they reached the lower deck.

At first, Schwarz was convinced he and Blancanales were victims of mistaken identity when the Marines started shooting at them. It didn't take him long to realize that *they* were the ones who had mistaken the identity of the terrorists, taking them for Marine guards instead of their enemy. When they realized it, they were quick to respond.

Schwarz dropped to his belly, wishing he could melt into the deck as he drew his Glock 26 and opened up. His first round struck home, ripping through the stomach of his target and dumping the man on the deck. The electronics wizard didn't wait for him to fall before taking a second one with a clean shot to the knee. The man's scream was audible even above the cacophony of weapons reports. His submachine gun flew from his fingers and skittered across the slippery deck.

Sailors could be seen visibly running for cover, risking only occasional exposure long enough to get shot at by unseen terrorists above and ducking back behind cover. What surprised Schwarz was the number of personnel on the deck. The majority were obviously still below, and Able Team had no intelligence on their status or condition. He also didn't know how determined their enemies were. Not that it mattered because whoever these terrorists were, Schwarz knew they had encountered a much more determined trio of bad-asses who were willing to kick enough tail to go around.

Blancanales proved that nicely by pumping two rounds into another terrorist's chest. The impact spun the gunner into a nearby pole, and he collapsed to the deck. Three more Marines appeared to their right, but they weren't firing at the Able Team commandos. Instead they began firing on the remaining targets. Obviously these were the real good guys. But while they put up an admirable fight, they had exposed themselves and were armed only with pistols. The combination proved deadly as the terrorists dropped them with a merciless hail of autofire from their Spectre M-4 SMGs.

Schwarz and his partner couldn't do a thing about the Marines now dying under the horrible onslaught of terrorist fire, but they could use the diversion to neutralize the four remaining gunmen. Blancanales took the closest terrorist with a headshot, the 9mm Parabellum round cracking the terrorist's skull and spraying his comrades with gray matter. The second terrorist met a similar fate as the next shot struck him in the chin with bone-crushing force and nearly severed his head from his body.

Schwarz took the third terrorist with three shots to the gut even as the target's comrade dived away from the melee. The surviving terrorist obviously realized that he was now outgunned and outmanned, but it was also obvious that he had nowhere to go. One of the surviving guards took vengeance for the death of his fellow Marines by putting a well-placed shot in the terrorist's back.

The Able Team warriors realized they still had other unseen gunners to deal with, but for the moment they had neutralized the immediate threat. Schwarz and Blancanales remained behind cover and motioned to four Marines to join them. One man didn't hesitate to immediately rush to their position. When he was close enough Blancanales noticed that he wore the rank of a gunnery sergeant on his lapel. He was taller than either of them, maybe twenty-six years of age, and beads of sweat glistened off his black skin, shimmering even in the dim light of the carrier deck.

"I don't know who you guys are," the man said, "but I sure am glad you're on our side."

"We were part of the team assigned to protect Dr. Shukan," Blancanales replied.

"And it would seem we're not doing a very good job at the moment," Schwarz added.

"Well, either way, I'm grateful because you guys just saved my ass."

"What's your name, soldier?" Blancanales asked.

"Hearst," he replied extending a hand. "Mason Hearst."

"It's a pleasure," the Able Team commando said, returning the handshake. "Although I'm afraid we're going to have to skip the niceties for now. What's your assessment of the current situation?

"I'm not sure what the hell's going on," Hearst stated. "I had just come on shift. They doubled the roving guard for the actual launch of that plane, so it didn't surprise anyone to see so many of us on deck. I didn't have the first clue some of them weren't friendly."

"Understood." Blancanales jerked his thumb in the direction of the sailors still visible on the deck and asked, "Any idea where the rest of the crew might be?"

"Belowdecks, maybe," Hearst said with a shrug.

Blancanales looked at the catwalk above their heads and said, "Okay, here's the story. There are still enemy above us, and although they're not shooting I'd bet they're watching the decks very carefully. Anybody so much as exposes a hair and they stand a pretty good chance of getting it shot off."

"Agreed," Schwarz said.

Hearst merely nodded.

"That means we're going to have to find them and neutralize them. Hearst, do you know of any way we could get our hands on some explosives?" Schwarz asked.

"Not on the flight deck," Hearst replied. "They keep all ordnance belowdecks for safety reasons."

"That figures," Schwarz said. "We never seem to get a break."

"Well, we're not out of the game yet," Blancanales replied.

He said to Hearst, "You're going to be on your own. We need you to get those other Marines to a safe place. Understood?"

Hearst nodded.

"So what's *our* next move?" Schwarz asked his teammate.

"We have two things at the top of our list. The first is to find Ironman and get his status. The second will be to navigate our way back to our quarters where we've got that communications equipment stashed. It will be a whole lot easier for us to break up operations if we can communicate with each other remotely."

"That's easier said than done," Schwarz replied.

"If you have another suggestion, I'm open to hearing it."

"No, not really. I'm just saying that it's not going to be easy. You know, like we might get killed."

"We've been there before," Blancanales pointed out.

"I would say it's safe to assume that they've taken the bridge," Schwarz said.

"I'd say that's about as safe a guess as any. It might also explain why we haven't heard or seen anything of Ironman yet."

"Well, we aren't going to find him with a crystal ball, so we'd best get moving."

The two Able Team warriors nodded at Hearst, then turned and fanned out to pick the bodies clean of any additional weapons and ammunition they could carry. After they had collected their spoils, Blancanales turned to see that Hearst was still standing there with his pistol and covering their backs while they acquired the additional hardware.

"You know something, Hearst? You're one sharp customer," Blancanales said as he tossed one of the Spectre machine pistols at the Marine.

"Are you ready to go, Pol?" Schwarz asked.

"About as ready as I'll ever be.'"

The pair made one last acknowledgment of Hearst, then proceeded for the companionway leading to the upper decks. There was no question in either man's mind that their friend was somewhere above, and they had no idea if he was dead or alive. The only thing they could count on at this point was each other, and if the terrorists had managed to kill Lyons, there was going to be hell to pay.

Schwarz was glad that they'd been able to lift the Spectre M-4s off the terrorists. While it was an unusual weapon, the Spectre submachine gun was a rock-solid ally to have in a situation like this. The weapon had first been introduced in 1984, and worked by closing a bolt over the cartridge but leaving a separate hammer unit cocked. This allowed the submachine gun to be carried in safety, but also permitted rapid firing by simply pulling the trigger. And unlike most 9 mm Parabellum machine pistols of this type, the magazine had a 50-round capacity versus 30-round.

But all of that mattered little to the terrorists they encountered on the next upper deck. The able team warriors were outgunned two to one, but they took some solace in the fact that the terrorists were now occupied with them and not with shooting at the unarmed seaman on the deck below. They could only hope that Hearst used this reprieve to evacuate those men to a safer location.

Still, the fun was just beginning. And Schwarz couldn't help but wonder what had become of Carl Lyons.

CHAPTER SIX

Carl Lyons had known better days.

His failed attempts at gaining access to the bridge didn't bother him nearly as much as the commotion on the decks below. The terrorists, whoever they were, had obviously been mopping up any of the last resistance, which had Lyons extremely concerned for the welfare of his comrades. There was also Shukan to consider. He hadn't seen or heard anything of the scientist since this party had begun, and it was becoming obvious to him that he may have failed not only his friends but the man he had been assigned to protect.

Hal Brognola wasn't going to be happy if Shukan bought the farm.

Not to mention what it would mean to the United States Navy and the X-51 project. Whether Lyons wanted to admit it or not, Shukan was a valuable part of the American military community. If he died, a great deal of his knowledge would die with him. Lyons intended to make sure that didn't happen under any circumstances if the man was still alive.

What bothered him most was the thought that he might have sent his friends to their deaths. It sounded as though the terrorists had a number of guns, and just the fact that Pol and Gadgets would do their job—never to go down without a fight—didn't leave him much in the way of comfort.

Come on, Ironman, snap out of it, he thought. You don't need to worry about those guys…you need to focus on the job at hand.

And the job at hand involved finding Shukan at whatever the cost. After his original ruse hadn't worked, Lyons was presented with a new dilemma. His only other way to get a grasp on the situation was to risk a view through the ports of the bridge. The main challenge there was to avoid getting his head taken off by a volley of well-placed rounds through his skull.

Lyons took a deep breath, gripped the handle of the MP-5 K more tightly and risked a glance through a lower corner of the large viewing window. To his surprise, neither his head nor the glass was shattered by autofire. In fact, the place was empty. The sight wasn't simply surprising to Lyons, it was downright disturbing. All of the computer consoles were dark. Radar was dead, and none of the electrical or communications systems appeared to be functioning. Even the lights were off.

At first Lyons thought that perhaps he made a mistake. But then, as he revisited the thought, it started to become clear that there was much more going on here than he had originally thought. Someone was playing a very dangerous game, and Lyons was willing to bet that someone was Jin Shukan. What didn't make any sense to him was why the bridge was empty. Everything on the *Stennis,* as far as he knew, was controlled from the bridge. However, if it were possible for anyone to control the ship from a remote location it would be somebody like Shukan. After all, the guy was an expert in unmanned systems. Using his knowledge to take over a ship, even one as advanced as this one, would have been child's play.

"Are you actually going to help out here, or you just going to stand around and let all of us do the work?" a familiar voice asked.

Lyons whirled to find Rosario Blancanales staring at him.

"I thought you guys were dead," the Able Team leader stated.

"So did we," Blancanales replied.

"What happened?"

"We ran into some old friends of ours. It was a nice visit."

"The rumors of our demise were greatly exaggerated," Schwarz added.

Blancanales jerked his head in the direction of the bridge door and asked, "Anybody in there?"

"Not so far as I can tell," Lyons replied.

"Well who's driving this tugboat then?" Schwarz asked disbelievingly.

"Beats me."

"Look, somebody has to be steering the damned thing," the burly Hispanic announced. "I mean, she sure as hell isn't guiding herself."

"I thought I heard the engines shut down earlier," Lyons announced.

"I think you did," Schwarz agreed.

Lyons got an idea. "Schwarz, do you think if we get you inside there you might be able to get some of that equipment up and running?"

"I can sure as hell try," he replied.

"I don't suppose either of you guys happens to have some C-4 or an HE grenade handy, do you?"

"I'm sorry I left all of my pyrotechnics at home for this trip, Mom," Schwarz cracked.

"Let's just get this done," Blancanales said.

"Yeah," Lyons said. "I guess we're just going to have to do this the old-fashioned way."

Before either one of them had the time to ask him what that meant, Lyons aimed the muzzle of his MP-5 K in the direction of the bridge window and opened up on full-auto. The tempered glass was plated and thick, designed to withstand significant pressures of natural forces like typhoons and hurricanes, but it was no match for 9 mm Parabellum bullets. Some of the glass fell in large sheets and others turned into deadly shards propelled across the bridge. If anyone was hiding inside, he would have to be one tough son of a bitch to resist that kind of mayhem.

"All board, Gadgets," Lyons said, smiling triumphantly.

Lyons and Blancanales assisted Schwarz through the window, ensuring that their partner didn't cut himself on the heavy shards of glass that remained in the frame. Once the man was inside, he opened the door for them, so that they could gain access to the bridge. Blancanales and Lyons immediately began to check this surrounding area of the bridge, while Schwarz sat in front of the communications station and began flipping switches.

A quick search of the bridge area confirmed that it was empty.

"Looks like they left in a big hurry," Blancanales noted.

"Yeah," Lyons replied, "but left in a big hurry for where?"

Schwarz didn't bother replying. In fact, Able Team's electronics wizard had a puzzled look on his face. "Everything's dead. There's no power, there's no signal, nada... The place is just a shell."

"Well, they have to be controlling it from somewhere," Lyons remarked.

He looked at Blancanales and asked, "Do you think it's possible that the terrorists have a substation set up somewhere here on the ship?"

Blancanales shrugged. "I suppose it's possible, but I don't have the first idea where it might be."

"Maybe Hearst knows," Schwarz suggested.

"Who?" Lyons asked.

"We ran into one of the Marine guards assigned to provide extra security," Blancanales explained. "A gunnery sergeant named Hearst. I think he's one of the few survivors, at least, one who's armed."

"I don't get this," Lyons said. "If the terrorists planned to take control of the ship, why not just seize the bridge? This ship is top of the line and completely computerized. They would have been able to do anything they want from here. It doesn't make sense."

"Maybe they ran into too much security," Blancanales replied.

Lyons shook his head. "I have a distinct feeling that someone else's running the show. If this is the Ansar al-Islam, I can't believe for a second they would have the resources and personnel in place that were capable of taking over an entire aircraft carrier. We're talking years of planning."

"Well, I hate be the one to break the bad news, but they seem to be doing a good job so far," Schwarz said, standing from the computer console. "And let's not forget that they wouldn't have to take control of the entire ship, only its vital systems. They set up containment in the right area, and they could hold this vessel under their control indefinitely."

"You have any luck with that thing?" Lyons asked, gesturing at the console.

"I have no power," Schwarz told him, "and without juice I don't think that there's any way I could get any communications signal to Stony Man using the equipment here."

"Then we'll just have to find—"

Lyons was interrupted by the sound boots the catwalk, and they were coming closer.

"Sounds like we have company," Blancanales said.

The three men took up positions through the room
and awaited the new arrivals. The difficulty they were
going to have would be identifying enemy from friend.
All of the terrorists that they had encountered so far
were dressed as Marines, and there wasn't going to be
an easy way to tell one from another. They also couldn't
afford to be split up without some form of communicating—it was too risky—which meant they would have
to find a way to get back to their quarters, where they
could procure their communications equipment and additional ammunition for their pistols. The ammo in the
weapons they had taken from the terrorists wasn't going
to last forever.

As the first gunners entered the bridge, there was no
question in the minds of the Able Team warriors that
these were terrorists. Lyons was the first to engage,
raising his MP-5 K and firing at the first man through
the door. He squeezed the trigger briefly, sending a
3-round burst through the terrorist's chest. The man let
out a raspy scream before toppling to the deck.

Schwarz got the second one with a short burst to the
stomach. The 9 mm Parabellum rounds ripped a gaping
hole that was large enough for the intestines to protrude.
The man dropped to his knees, releasing his weapon and
trying to hold what was left of his guts in place. The
electronics wizard let go of a single mercy round that
hit the terrorist in the forehead and blew out the back of
his skull.

The remaining terrorists realized they weren't
dealing with rank amateurs. They took cover outside the

bridge doorway, and as the echoes of Able Team's hand-iwork began to die down, something small, round and metallic bounced through the doorway and settled in the center of the room.

It took the Able Team warriors only a moment to realize they were staring at an M-33 fragmentation grenade. Lyons and Schwarz had the better cover behind the consoles, but Blancanales was still relatively exposed. He looked to his left and noticed the open door of a storage closet; in milliseconds before the grenade exploded, he made it inside. The grenade blast in the enclosure, even given the vastness of the bridge, rattled their teeth and threatened to bring the entire contents of the roof down on top of them. Fortunately, the damage was contained to the center of the room and Able Team managed to avoid being hit by any of the deadly superheated fragments that sliced the air above their heads.

Lyons immediately considered one advantage. If they could take the terrorists down here, it would probably provide them with additional weapons, ammunition and even some explosives. The dust and smoke caused by the grenade was enough to provide him cover, and he risked leaving his place to sprint across the bridge and launch himself through the broken window. Lyons landed outside on the catwalk and found himself less than five yards from the remaining pair. The terrorists were surprised to see that someone had actually survived the effects of the grenade.

It was the last thing that would ever surprise them.

Lyons raised his machine pistol and shot the closer terrorist through the chest, grabbing the man's body before it could fall. He shoved the corpse into the second terrorist, attempting to keep his one remaining opponent off guard. Many years of experience and training had taught Lyons that the secret to success in close-quarters combat was to keep the enemy unbalanced. He was glad that he had listened to his instructors at the police academy.

The terrorist made the fatal mistake of allowing himself to be distracted by Lyons. As he was occupied with trying to disentangle himself from his deceased comrade, the Able Team leader pumped a round through his head at point-blank range. Both bodies hit the catwalk simultaneously.

Blancanales and Schwarz joined him on the catwalk a moment later.

"Jeez, Ironman," Schwarz said, "have you lost your mind or something?"

Lyons didn't bother to answer, instead choosing to frisk the bodies and strip them clean of spare ammunition and six M-33 grenades, which he distributed equally among them. He also checked the bodies for identification, but of course he didn't find any. One of the terrorists had a picture of a beautiful woman in the breast pocket of his fatigues. Lyons looked at the photo briefly but had no reason to take it with him.

"I think we need a place to lay low until we can reload this ammunition into our spare clips," Lyons said.

"Agreed," his teammates replied simultaneously.

"We also need to find a way to get a message back to Stony Man," Schwarz remarked. "What concerns me is that if they are controlling this ship and all of its systems from a remote location, then even if we can get a signal out, it's entirely possible that signal will be monitored."

"It's a risk we're going to have to take," Blancanales said.

Lyons merely nodded.

From a tactical standpoint, the situation wasn't good. They had no communications and no way of knowing whether any signal they did send would reach Stony Man. If the homing devices that had been installed beneath the skin of each man were doing the job properly, then at least Brognola and Aaron Kurtzman's team would be able to home in on their location. Then again, the other possibility was that the terrorists were working with someone smart enough to block any signals coming off of the ship. The other consideration was the status of the X-51. If the terrorists were smart enough to take over the *Stennis,* then they were certainly smart enough to figure out how to use the X-51 against their intended target.

Particularly if they had either gained or coerced support from Jin Shukan.

The threesome did a quick weapons check, then proceeded down the catwalk in the direction of the stairwells. Lyons decided to use the same stairwell that he had used to reach this part of the ship. It was reasonable to assume that with the last of the resistance they had wiped out at the bridge, this area was fairly secure. It was also unlikely that they would encounter further problems simply because of the fact that the terrorists would have limited resources. It was a big ship and there wouldn't be a way to monitor all of it all of the time.

That was probably what bothered Lyons the most. Somehow the terrorists had managed to get an entire army on board a well-guarded aircraft carrier. The security had been extra-tight at the dock the day they boarded the *Stennis* at North Island. That meant, given the ship's complement and the fact that each man would have undergone an identification check prior to boarding, they had considerable resources inside the Navy. Lyons had been informed by Pacheco that everyone on this particular mission had been required to submit to a full background check. Of course, that didn't really mean a thing, since background checks of that kind had to be conducted by the FBI, and Lyons knew firsthand that it sure as hell wasn't an overnight process. It also meant that the terrorists had forged IDs and arranged for a large number of personnel to not show up.

There was no question in Lyons's mind that it had been the job of an insider.

The Able Team warriors pressed on toward their goal. Their quarters were in the stern, just aft of the forecastle, and three decks below the flight deck. It wasn't going to be easy. They had a lot of territory to cover and a very short time in which to cover it, and they didn't exactly have unlimited munitions and equipment. They also didn't have any idea what size of force they were up against. The fact they had faced these kinds of odd before—and they certainly possessed the expertise needed to accomplish their objectives—didn't make the job any easier.

Thus far, they had gained only one ally they could trust, and they didn't even know where he was at the moment. For all they knew, he'd been captured and was breaking under torture right at that moment, giving the enemy Able Team's exact position. Still, Lyons had learned to trust the judgment of his friends. They'd kept him alive more times than he cared to count. If they said this Hearst dude was okay, then that was enough for him.

By the time they reached the flight deck, there were no personnel to be found. It looked as though Hearst was taking advantage of the situation and getting the men remaining above board to safety. Hopefully, they would attempt to get off the boat by whatever means possible. Certainly there were lifeboats, and at one point Lyons had even considered them to evacuate him and his team, but he had just as quickly dismissed the idea as ludicrous. He wasn't about to leave a few poorly armed and poorly equipped Marines to fight an army of well-armed terrorists. That would've been the greatest sacrilege of all. No, Able Team wasn't about to leave this boat under any circumstances. And if they were bound to die in a watery grave, then Lyons would make sure whoever was responsible went with them.

CHAPTER SEVEN

Stony Man Farm, Virginia

The blades of the UH-60 Black Hawk hadn't even finished winding down when David McCarter and Calvin James hit the ground running and headed for the farmhouse. Once inside and clear of the blacksuits who provided security to the entire complex, the two descended to the basement where the rest of the crew sat in the War Room awaiting their arrival. Obviously, Harold Brognola had decided to dispense with any formalities and convene a quick briefing there.

When they were seated, Brognola said, "I'll come right to the point. As you all know, Able Team is missing."

His announcement seemed to add pressure to the already weighty and oppressive silence.

"We don't have a lot of details yet, but I'm going to turn this over to Barb and Aaron." He nodded at Price.

"Time's of the essence here," Price stated, "so I'm going to give you the skinny on this, and you can review the data Aaron printed for you while en route."

"To where?" McCarter interjected.

"North Central Pacific Ocean," Brognola said a bit curtly. "Now listen up, because we don't have a lot of time."

"Three days ago," Price continued quickly, "we assigned Able Team to accompany a Japanese scientist named Jin Shukan on a military operation across the Central Pacific. It was a protective detail we implemented after persons claiming to be members of Ansar al-Islam kidnapped Shukan and demanded a billion-dollar ransom."

"Islamic terrorists ransoming a scientist for money?" Gary Manning said. "That sounds just a bit farfetched."

"Agreed, but we have no other evidence to controvert it, so go with it. The terrorists made random contact with a junior grade Navy lieutenant at North Island, who then passed the information on to his superiors that terrorists took Shukan and were to make known their demands. Naturally, Able Team had been assigned as soon as he was reported missing and, thanks to Aaron, we were able to track down the location where he was being held. Then Able Team did its stuff and returned him safely to the military."

"So what's with this added detail?" T.J. Hawkins asked. "Why not just put U.S. Marshals or FBI on it?"

"This was the Man's call," Brognola said.

"And given that we had to assume that Shukan's kidnapping meant terrorists were operating inside the country, it only made sense to keep Able Team on top of it," Price added. "This way they could monitor the situation while simultaneously gather further intelligence."

"Still sounds like a routine protection job to me," Hawkins remarked.

"That's pretty much what it was," Price replied.

McCarter wasn't exactly sure why, but suddenly he felt a bit irritated. He started to open his mouth and then thought better of it, deciding to instead stew on the information a moment. He wasn't sure if it was Hawkins's sarcasm or Price's explanation of events that had put him in such a foul mood, but he knew that as leader of Phoenix Force he had to demonstrate a level of professional courtesy.

"Well, if it was so bloody well routine, why are three of our people missing?" McCarter asked. "I don't know about the rest of you blokes, but something about this stinks to me. What we need to do is quit sitting around on our arses and start looking for Able Team."

"That's exactly what you're going to do," Brognola said.

"Then why are we still here?" McCarter said, getting to his feet, a signal for the rest of Phoenix Force to join him.

"Yeah, we don't mean to be rude, but we should split," Calvin James added.

Price started to protest, but Brognola stopped her with a gentle squeeze of her shoulder. There was an odd smile in his expression as he said, "The chopper will take you to Andrews Air Force Base."

"Jack's there now," Price said, "and he'll be assisted by an Air Force crew on special detachment from the National Command Authority. You'll be conducting your search in a NEACP."

Hawkins made a cooing sound and a show of fanning himself, and drawled, "Fancy, fancy."

"It's on loan from the Joint Chiefs, so tell Jack I don't want it to end up in the drink," Brognola said as they filed out of the War Room. When all was silent and their voices faded, he mumbled, "Godspeed, men."

HAWKINS HADN'T EXAGGERATED in his description of the National Emergency Airborne Command Post E-4B. Built under congressional approval and joint funding for providing an airborne command center in the event of a thermonuclear war, the NEACP was a Boeing 747 that boasted the most advanced communications array in the world. The government had originally created the NEACP to sustain members from the Joint Chiefs of Staff operations team, as well as support staff from the Air Force and Defense Intelligence Agency, but it had been called upon now and then for special missions. The designated crews for the NEACP handled everything from operations and mission objectives to maintenance and passenger services.

While the crew was lean for this particular operation—by design—the NEACP was no less impressive. Particularly advantageous for Phoenix Force was that the aircraft didn't deviate too much in appearance from a standard Boeing passenger jet, with the exception of a bulge in the flight deck that marked the placement of a radar system, so it wouldn't attract a lot of attention. The plane's nearly 4,500 square-foot interior was divided into six separate mission compartments, each one designed to provide a particular work area for a normal command-and-control element. In addition to sensitive communications and observation equipment capable of communicating with every American-owned nuclear missile site on the planet, the NEACP was also protected from electromagnetic pulses to protect its valuable electronic infrastructure. The craft also possessed a data processing system controlled by a Rolm Mil-Spec Hawk 32 processing system. The Hawk 32 had a 2-gigabyte memory chip and 64-bit processor capable of communicating with remote NetSat linkups developed by DARPA and the NSA. Its inflight refueling ability also permitted it to remain in the air for three days or better if necessary.

But none of that occupied the minds of David McCarter and the other members of Phoenix Force as much as the task at hand. He'd been in such a hurry to get going on their search that he didn't take time to read the fine print until they were airborne and headed for the point in the Pacific where the U.S.S. *Stennis* had simply "ceased communications and was no longer emitting a traceable homing signal." At least, that's what the report from the NSA and Department of Defense said. The other and more disturbing element was what Jack

Grimaldi advised McCarter that he had some news upon their arrival at Andrews AFB, but he was to only divulge the information to McCarter. The very idea set the Briton's teeth on edge; he didn't like keeping secrets from his team.

But that was another matter.

"So in other words, this thing just disappeared," Rafael Encizo said as they were seated around a small, metal conference table aboard the aircraft and reviewing the data uploaded to their electronic handhelds.

"It would seem that way, mate," McCarter replied.

"According to this report," Gary Manning said, navigating through the plain-text pages, "the *Stennis* arrived at its coordinates on time and intact. The X-51 was also launched, but as soon as it left the deck of the carrier, all communications with and from the *Stennis* ceased."

"It also says the X-51 reached radar level and then suddenly lost altitude," James continued. "It's assumed that signal was lost as soon as it hit the ocean. But here's the interesting thing. It had a DK 140 underwater beacon aboard that should have continued transmitting, even if it was submerged. And I'm sure they didn't forget to install it. They're part of any aircraft's minimal essential equipment list."

"Maybe it malfunctioned," Hawkins proposed.

All eyes looked in the direction of Jack Grimaldi for his input.

Grimaldi, who had decided to attend the briefing and leave the initial flight to the Air Force boys, shrugged. "It's possible but unlikely. Those things are rated with a twenty-thousand-foot range in fresh or seawater and a six-year useful life. Even though they're acoustic type, satellites can still locate them quickly. They're even reliable enough that NASA puts them on space shuttles."

"What activates them?" Manning asked.

"They can either be flight-crew activated manually, or designed to trigger as soon as water flooding is detected by an exterior inlet valve sensor," Grimaldi replied.

"Is that instantaneous?"

Grimaldi nodded sharply.

"Well, then, I guess that kills our theories on a malfunction," McCarter said. "Would someone else like to try?"

"We probably won't know what really happened until we get to the site," Manning said. "Anything at this point would be sheer conjecture."

"Maybe so, but I have a theory," Encizo remarked.

"Well, by all means share it," Hawkins said with a chuckle.

Encizo paused for a moment, visibly collecting his thoughts, and then began, "Okay, let's assume that the beacon on the X-51 didn't fail. Let's also assume that there wasn't some type of shipwide power loss or electronics failure on the *Stennis*. That now presupposes that we have some type of sabotage on our hands and that the saboteurs had to be working this from the inside."

"Seems reasonable enough, bloke," McCarter interjected. "Go on."

"So that leaves three questions." Encizo counted them on his fingers as he said, "Who did it, for what reason, and how did they do it?"

Each of the Phoenix Force warriors exchanged glances before James finally said, "It's a place to start."

The rest of the team agreed.

"Okay, so the first question is who," McCarter said. "If we assume it's the Ansar al-Islam then we have some idea of what to expect. We can also theorize that someone inside the project helped them. There's no bloody way in hell I'm going to believe they had the technical know-how to do it on their own."

"But what exactly did they do?" Hawkins asked. "That's what we don't know."

"Jack, you seem to know quite a bit about these underwater beacons," James said. "Assuming no technical malfunction, would there be any other way to disable them?"

"You could shut them down remotely," Grimaldi replied. "But that wouldn't make much sense. Satellites would still be able to identify the aircraft by its transponder number for a while, not to mention a heat signature. And even if it dropped into the Pacific, the reconnaissance aircraft we sent would have picked up something."

"Not to mention that according to our information, the bloody thing's heat signature disappeared, too," McCarter reminded them.

"What about a visual satellite link?" Encizo asked.

James shook his head. "You saw the report. Neither the NSA nor the DOD had a satellite in line of sight for the visual at the moment of signal loss. It took nearly thirty minutes to get one in position."

"And by that time both the *Stennis* and X-51 were long gone," Manning added.

"I also talked to the pilots initially tasked to begin searching for the ship," Grimaldi said. "The U.S.S. *Kitty Hawk* happened to be out on maneuvers at the same time, and they dispatched some planes from Carrier Wing Five to investigate. They didn't find anything."

"This gets more interesting by the minute," Hawkins remarked.

"None of this is getting us closer to answers, men," McCarter finally said. "Even if we assume it *is* Ansar al-Islam, and they did it because they're terrorists and that's what terrorists do, it still doesn't explain how they did it."

"It's probably just like you said," James replied. "The only way for them to pull off something like this is from the inside."

"Okay, that's enough brainstorming for now," McCarter said. "I've got a frigging headache. Let's get standard checks started on our weapons and equipment."

It wasn't a request, and every man took the hint. McCarter didn't want to talk anymore. The men of Phoenix Force filed out, but Grimaldi didn't move. He stood there with one foot propped on a chair—forearm draped across his thigh—and stared at McCarter intently. The fox-faced Briton didn't immediately notice that Grimaldi had remained, having tried to immerse himself in the information Stony Man had provided, but when he did notice, he couldn't repress the sense of dread that suddenly came over him.

"What?"

Grimaldi shook his head. "You still haven't asked me about the little package we brought along."

"That's because I'm not sure I want to know what it is, mate," McCarter replied. "Maybe you should just keep it to yourself."

"No can do, David," Grimaldi said. "There's a lot on the line here. You're the mission commander, not me. And Hal didn't want me to tell you about this until we were airborne."

McCarter sat back in his chair and folded his arms. "So what do I need to know, ace?"

"We're packing a tactical nuke," Grimaldi replied simply.

"What the bloody hell are you talking about?"

"Hal got orders from the Man that if we found the *Stennis* in enemy hands and the crew was dead, we were to destroy it. We're to make it look like it was hijacked and the nuclear reactor went up."

"And Hal didn't want to tell me this himself?"

"I don't know about any of that, or what his reasons were, David," Grimaldi replied with a shake of his head. "I don't think it's all that simple. Maybe he didn't think you would agree to take the mission."

That bothered McCarter, although he knew Grimaldi meant nothing personal by it. He wasn't about to let it show, but he had to admit that the Stony Man chief's lack of trust stung just a bit. He understood that

Brognola hadn't intended to offend him, and he knew Grimaldi wasn't trying to belittle him now, but this wasn't the best time to be hearing that kind of news.

"Listen, mate, I understand this business quite well," McCarter replied. "I know we don't work for a country club here."

"I realize that," Grimaldi replied.

"Hal should have trusted me." McCarter slammed his fist on the table.

Grimaldi remained silent for a long moment before saying, "I don't think that's what's really bothering you. Is it?"

"What are you going to do?" McCarter asked. "You going to psychoanalyze me now, Jack?"

Grimaldi spun one of the chairs around and sat, draped his arms across the top of it, and then pinned McCarter with a hard stare. "Look, David, I'm your friend. Okay? We're all your friends. And it bugs me just as much as it does you that Able Team's missing. But Ironman's one tough son of a bitch, and those guys will take care of each other. We can't go worrying about that now."

"I know, I know!" McCarter sighed. He was irritated, but not really at Grimaldi, albeit the pilot's incessant hounding didn't help. "I *am* worried about Able Team, but not bloody near as much as my people if we actually have to detonate that briefcase boomer."

"Let's just hope it doesn't come to that."

"Yeah, I would prefer a straight and honest fight with whoever's behind this than to find things in a condition that we would have to use a nuke."

"I don't think we'll have to," Grimaldi said. "The former scenario seems more likely. Besides, it wouldn't have done the terrorists much good to simply blow those things into never land. It makes more sense that they would try to hijack the technology than destroy it."

McCarter fired a droll look. "You know as well as I do that terrorists rarely do anything to make sense, mate."

CHAPTER EIGHT

Grid C, Pacific Ocean

David McCarter could feel his stomach rise up to the level of his throat as the NEACP descended from its cruising altitude for their next pass over the Pacific.

They had been searching for any sign of the X-51 or the U.S.S. *Stennis*, and had seen nothing. McCarter had to consciously make an effort not become discouraged and, even more importantly, from showing discouragement to the rest of his team. And it didn't make it any easier when Hawkins would come in every thirty seconds asking if he had found anything new.

"No. Unfortunately my answer's the same bloody one I gave you just a minute ago," McCarter would tell him.

He couldn't blame Hawkins; in fact, he wouldn't have blamed any of them for being concerned for the welfare of Able Team.

"Did you check your equipment, T.J.?" McCarter asked.

"I've checked my equipment three times, boss," Hawkins replied. "You want me to check it again, just in case?"

McCarter eyed him judiciously and said, "Don't get too big for your britches, mate."

"I was being serious," Hawkins said with a grin.

"Yeah, right," McCarter said. "I can always tell when you're being serious, and you weren't being serious there."

"Now I'm hurt," Hawkins said, putting on his best attempt at looking offended.

"Go pound sand," McCarter replied.

Hawkins grinned affably. "So where do you think they might be?"

"Okay we've covered grid D," McCarter said no one particular, "and we're now heading into grid C." He looked up from the map of the Pacific coasts displayed dimly in a tabletop backlight. The map was actually built into the table aboard the NEACP and used 3-D effects to show the topographical hills and valleys beneath the deep waters of the Pacific Ocean.

McCarter directed his attention to one of the Air Force lieutenants Stony Man had sent along to aid in the search. "Lieutenant, highlight the last location of the *Stennis* just prior to loss of signal, and direct it here to this map."

"He can do that?" Hawkins asked, the surprise evident his expression.

"Of course he can do it," McCarter replied. "We've been doing this kind of thing for years. Where have you been?"

"They must've freeze-dried me when I wasn't looking," Hawkins said, "because I sure as hell wasn't doing hard time."

"The information is coming through now, sir," The Air Force lieutenant told McCarter.

The fox-faced Briton gave his full attention to the map and Hawkins sidled up next to him look over his shoulder. A bright red dot flashed at grid Alpha Seven, which was approximately 180 degrees longitude by 60 degrees latitude. After gaining assistance from the Air Force technologists, Phoenix Force established its own set of grid coordinates and decided what areas they would start searching first. They had initially assumed the terrorists, if there were actually terrorists involved, would attempt to get the *Stennis* to some kind of an island base as quickly as possible.

Given that assumption, Phoenix Force knew it had it work cut out. Pacifica was filled with islands, some of which had never been explored. Not only were there vast areas for them to cover, but they had no idea what they would encounter. People who had either visited islands in the Pacific times past, whether intentionally or not, had stumbled onto a wide variety of bizarre things. Scientists had found new kinds of life forms, tourists had simply disappeared, and military personnel had found Japanese soldiers that had been hiding out on the islands—surviving and living off the land—since being abandoned there during World War II.

"It's a big ocean," Hawkins remarked, as if reading McCarter's mind.

"You can say that again," the Briton stated. "The question isn't as much of where do we find them, as much as it may be of where we start looking."

"Well, if I was going to hijack an aircraft carrier, I'd want to get her out of physical sight as quickly as possible."

"It looks like they've already done a snap job of that," McCarter said.

"Maybe not," called a voice from across the room.

McCarter and Hawkins turned to see Calvin James emerge through the doorway leading to a forward compartment. He was waving a sheaf of papers, and the look in his eyes gave the two men some reason to hope that he had good news.

"You know something? You can get lost in this place," James said.

McCarter had no reply for his teammate's attempt at humor. "You have some news?"

James looked to Hawkins. "What's his problem?"

Hawkins shrugged, but then on afterthought he leaned over and said just loud enough for McCarter to hear, "Just ignore him. I don't think he's had any lately, if you know what I mean."

"That's enough clowning for now," McCarter said, putting just enough edge in his voice to let them know he was serious. "What do you have for us?"

"This just came through Aaron's team," James replied.

He tossed papers on the glass-topped map and McCarter and Hawkins leaned over to study them immediately.

A report on top read as follows:

>>>>>START ENC MSG, ENCRYPT-L 5<<<<<

Analysis Team: H. Wethers, C. Delahunt

Subject: Signal patterns, U.S.S. *Stennis*, 1423 hours GMT

Tested: Satellite link pattern from Grid Alpha 7, including signals from SONNET and internal network operations.

Analyses: Signals were truncated and not degraded, suggesting immediate power loss on ship-wide basis. Naval SIGINT Corps suggests this could not be the result of any technical accident, and backup systems should have responded immediately to maintain signals. Signals continued for approx. 8 sec following initial loss detection. Signal loss was patterned, with dampening occurring at several main points across ship deck and expanding outward until completely loss. Intelligence review by NSA suggests this could not have been the result of explosion, since satellite Titan VIS/IR system detected neither debris nor residual heat.

Determination: Inconclusive, but based on patterns and signal loss, this is highly suggestive of some type of cloaking technology.

Action Advised: Team to proceed with caution and be prepared for hostile contact at any point.

>>>>>END ENC MSG, ENCRYPT-L 5<<<<<

David McCarter shrugged. "Okay, I don't get it. It doesn't seem like we know much more than we knew before."

"I have to agree with the boss," Hawkins said.

"You guys don't have any imagination whatsoever, do you?" James said, shaking his head. "Don't you see what this means? It means that Able Team's probably alive, and it also means that the reason we can't find them is because the enemy is using some type of cloaking technology to hide the ship."

"Now wait a minute," McCarter told James, holding up a hand. "This report doesn't prove anything like that. Wethers and Delahunt are making an assumption."

"Yeah, maybe they are. But it's one that just happens to fit the facts. You can't argue with that. Nobody has the ability to just make a ship the size of an aircraft carrier disappear into thin air, David. This seems like the next reasonable explanation, and I'm willing to accept whatever theories Aaron and his team come up with, no matter how crazy they may seem."

"I'm not telling you that we shouldn't investigate every possibility," McCarter said. "I'm telling you that we should be cautious about getting up our hopes."

"Are you telling us to give up hope?" Hawkins asked.

McCarter shook his head emphatically and replied, "I never said that. But I want you to understand that the secret to our success isn't going to be pursuing wild theories and conjecture, it's going to be in collecting facts. We need facts, gents, because I'm not about to waste precious time on some wild-goose chase across half the Pacific Ocean. Our boys deserve better than that."

"I think we should vote on a new tactic," Hawkins said.

The Phoenix Force leader couldn't believe what he had just heard. What Hawkins was suggesting was nothing short of mutiny.

"Calvin, I need you to go get the rest of the guys and bring them back here. Now," McCarter said quietly.

The Phoenix Force veteran didn't argue, instead turning to retrieve his comrades. He knew what was about to go down, and he really was glad that he didn't have to be present for it. This would be one of those times where McCarter was going to have to exert some stern leadership. James had no doubt that McCarter had the metal for it, but he was unsure how Hawkins was going to react. In either case, they needed some privacy and he was happy to give it to them.

McCarter dismissed the two Air Force personnel, as well, that had been working at the computers and providing support. When the compartment was empty of just them, the Briton turned on Hawkins, towering over him and staring him down with green eyes and an expression as hard as chiseled marble.

"T.J., you seem to have some idea that this is a bloody democracy here. We've never had to go through an exercise like this before, but obviously we're going to have to go through it now. I am the leader of this team. I have been since Katz retired, and I will be until I retire, if I live that long. And as long as I'm in charge of this team, you'll take your orders from me without question.

And by the way, we don't put anything to vote here unless I say we do. Is that understood?

"Look, David, I wasn't trying to suggest—"

"We're not going to get into what you were we're trying to do, mate. I'm telling you straight, I'm in charge of this operation as I'm in charge of all the operations. Is that clear?"

"Yes," Hawkins replied quietly, averting his eyes. "I have you."

McCarter realized that he was standing very close to Hawkins, so he stepped away. He was sorry to have to come down on his friend like that, but it had been necessary. They were all professionals, and they should have all become quite used to taking orders by now.

Fortunately, James had returned with Encizo and Manning, so the uncomfortable moment was allowed to pass. Not that it really mattered. McCarter wasn't the kind of man to hold a grudge, and if he knew anything about Hawkins, it was already forgotten. He'd made his point; that was all there was to it.

"You guys saw the report from the Farm?" McCarter asked, nodding at Encizo and Manning.

"Yeah, we saw it," Encizo replied. "You don't honestly think that these terrorists have some kind of cloaking device that would allow them to make an entire ship disappear, do you?"

McCarter shook his head. "I don't know what to think. What I do know is that we don't have much to go on, and if this is the best that they can provide us, then I guess we go with it."

"A cloaking device," Manning said. "It sounds like something out of *Star Trek*."

"Cloaking technology isn't really that new a concept," McCarter replied. "The Navy's been working with the concept for some time now, according to some of the field summaries I've read in Aaron's library."

"Well, we'll find out soon enough," Encizo said. "After we read the report, I contacted Barb and asked her to reach out to her resources at the NSA. They're going to send us everything they have on cloaking technology via secured transmission, including any projects our government's done and who worked on them. We think it contains enough information that the Air Force boys might be able to use it to find the *Stennis*."

McCarter nodded and said, "Good idea, Rafe."

The communications link to the cockpit buzzed for attention. James was closest, so he activated the speaker. "Welcome to Burgerland. May I take your order?"

Grimaldi's voice came through loud and clear over the speaker. "We just passed our first target. During the flyby I wasn't really expecting to see anything, but at the last minute one of our landing sensors picked up infrared heat signatures, and I'm pretty sure they're coming from personnel and underground generators. This might be their base of operations. You guys might think about getting ready to hook up."

The five men exchanged glances. This was the first news they had heard of potentially viable targets. All the previous flybys that he'd done had revealed little more than aquatic life and jungle. McCarter looked back at the map, double checked their position against the grid display and then referenced that back to the map.

"That's this island here," he said, pointing to his map. He referenced a thick book of scientific data that he'd happen to find in the onboard library. He looked up the grid, mapped into the correct index and then referenced it back to data they had on the island. "There aren't supposed to be any inhabitants on that island, native or otherwise, mates. Let's go."

The men of Phoenix Force headed for the forward compartment where they'd stored their gear. The SOP they had decided to adopt was to parachute into any potential hot zone, acting as a forward observation unit while Grimaldi would signal for the assistance of the closest ship in the Pacific fleet. One of the air wing battle groups at Diamond Head was also on full alert, and there was a destroyer group nearby that had an SH-60F Seahawk helicopter ready for deployment at a moment's notice.

Of course, it was possible that this was nothing more than a scientific group, or possibly even a private yachting expedition that had elected to use the land for a makeshift port. It wasn't an unusual scenario, given that there was supposed to be a Pacific storm watch for the entire region. It would be safer for a civilian boat to hold over than to try to return to its home port in hopes of beating Mother Nature to the proverbial punch. In either case, the mysterious islanders were about to have a firsthand encounter with the most secret and advanced antiterrorist unit in the world.

The members of Phoenix Force quickly donned wetsuits over their skintight combat uniforms. They then turned their attention to weapons, packing them in their waterproof bags along with enough rations and equipment to survive a week or better. They wanted to be prepared for anything. Pacific weather was anything but predictable, and it was always likely that some storm or other natural occurrence could hinder immediate extraction.

McCarter could feel the plane dip even lower, and a yellow light flashed above their heads. They had three minutes. He moved down the line of men, double checking each one's gear, and then stood still while Hawkins checked his. Once he received his all-clear sign, McCarter cinched up his waterproof bag, adjusted the goggles until they fit comfortably over his eyes and moved to the jump door. He steeled himself against the sudden rush of wind as he opened the portal. At least they didn't have to jump at night on this one. The deep blue waters of the Pacific rushed past them less than fifteen hundred feet below.

The light turned green, and David McCarter took the first and only step he knew would lead him into an environment that had been the proving ground for the limits of human endurance.

CHAPTER NINE

Rafael Encizo slapped the quick releases of his parachute harness as soon as his boots touched the cold Pacific water. The Cuban warrior sucked air deeply into his lungs to provide himself as much time as possible to get out from under the parachute and surface. The weight of the waterproof bag would take him deep enough, but he would only have approximately fifteen seconds to activate the flotation device built into the bag, otherwise the weight would drag him to the bottom. As soon as he was under water, he cleared his Tanto fighting knife from its sheath, prepared to cut the bag loose if the flotation bells surrounding it failed to expand.

Fortunately, the flotation device performed beautifully and Encizo had plenty of time to clear the parachute before his head broke the surface. Encizo checked his surroundings, insuring that his teammates touched down in one piece. He wanted to have some idea of where they were just in case they ran into trouble before reaching the shoreline. Once he'd counted the other four heads above water, he set off on the eighth-of-a-mile swim to land.

Encizo had been last to leave the plane but the first one to shore. After securing his pack, he withdrew his MP-5 A-3 from the waterproof bag and set up a covering position for the rest of his comrades. Hawkins was the second member to reach the shore. He modeled Encizo and took up his own position to provide a wider range of coverage. The rest of the Phoenix Force warriors reached the shore at the same time a minute later.

McCarter, Manning and James quickly stripped out of their wetsuits and gathered their equipment. McCarter and Manning then relieved Encizo and Hawkins on perimeter guard. Encizo and Hawkins stripped out of their wetsuits while James set up the wireless communications link with Jack Grimaldi.

"Eagle One, this is Red Team. Do you copy?"

"I copy, Red Team," Grimaldi replied to James.

James flashed the team a winning smile before replying. "We're all down in one piece, Eagle One. Over?"

"I copy 'down in one piece,' Red Team. All signs indicate that the target is unaware of your arrival. I have your position marked and locked in, and show the target approximately eight hundred meters due south of you. Over?"

"Roger, Eagle One. Your message is received and acknowledged that target is due south, set at eight hundred meters. Give us an hour before next transmission. Will advise when we're ready for extraction. Red Team out."

After James signed off, McCarter asked, "Where are they?"

James told him.

McCarter nodded, looked around until he'd found a stick and then indicated for them to circle around while he drew in the sand. "We're going to break up into three elements. Rafe has point, Cal is with T.J., and Gary with me. Standard sweep and maneuver formation, fifty meters apart. If they are expecting us, I don't want any surprises. We get bunched up too close together, mates, and they've got grenades or mines, the game is over. Everyone understand?"

The men of Phoenix force nodded.

McCarter tossed away the stick, obliterated the drawing with his boot and said, "Let's move out."

THE PHOENIX FORCE WARRIORS traversed the jungle soundlessly, moving with the expertise of men who had traveled that type of terrain countless times.

They had gone about seven hundred meters when Encizo raised his hand to signal he was stopping. The men immediately obeyed, each of them crouching. Encizo made another gesture indicating for them to remain where they were while he moved ahead to investigate. The Cuban checked his surroundings one more time to make sure that his colleagues were behind cover, and no one was watching, and then proceeded cautiously toward the basso thrumming he heard.

As he got closer, Encizo realized what was making the noise. It was the underground generators that

Grimaldi had told them he believed were being used, based on the infrared signatures. So that confirmed there was an encampment of some kind on this island—one with technology—but also one that conducted operations requiring electricity. Encizo couldn't imagine for a moment that the Pacific natives needed such luxury. No, this was a base camp being run either by scientists, pirates or drug runners.

Encizo quickly returned to the position where he'd stopped the group and activated the communication system.

"Red Point to Red Leader."

"Go, Red Point," McCarter replied.

"Target perimeter is about forty meters ahead. I count noises from two separate generators and there's the smell of expended diesel fuel in the air."

"Do you think we can neutralize them?"

"Roger," Encizo replied. "I don't think they're below ground as originally expected."

"I copy. Break. Red Leader to Red Team Two."

"I copy, Red Leader," James replied.

"Split up and neutralize those targets. Red Point will provide cover. Over."

"Received and acknowledged."

Encizo watched as James and Hawkins left their position and soundlessly moved past him. He knew the job wasn't going to be easy. It was one thing to be able to hear noises from something like a diesel generator, but it was quite another to have to locate them—sounds in the jungle could carry some distance and bounce off solid objects, which created echoes and could even cause some disorientation for the untrained ear.

After waiting for what seemed like forever, Encizo looked at his watch. Actually, less than three minutes had elapsed but for some reason it seemed as if it were taking an eternity. Then again, they couldn't risk rushing the job. If those in the encampment were in fact hostile, it wouldn't do for James and Hawkins to be discovered before they had completed their mission. Encizo thought he knew exactly what McCarter had in mind. They had used this ruse before. They'd shut down the generators, thereby causing a campwide power loss, and one or two people from the camp would be sent to investigate. James and Hawkins would wait close by and, when the time was right they would take them out. The confusion, and what probably amounted to a minor irritation on the part of most of the camp occupants, would provide the advantage Phoenix Force needed to neutralize their potential enemies.

Sure, it was one of the oldest tricks in the book, and yet it still seemed to work on a fairly regular basis. It was particularly effective if the targets had operated the camp for any length of time with impunity. It was only reasonable that if these were the individuals responsible for the disappearance of the *Stennis,* and they had been here operating even for a couple of months undetected, they were probably becoming fairly lax. There was something about the flawed nature of people that allowed even hardened individuals like terrorists to become a bit too comfortable in their surroundings.

Phoenix Force had learned to use those kinds of human weaknesses to their tactical advantage, and to exploit those kinds of common mistakes time and again.

The commando's sixth sense demanded attention as one of the generators suddenly cut out. Only a few seconds elapsed before Encizo could make out some audible curses coming from somewhere within the camp. A moment later the second generator shutdown, but its failure didn't seem to elicit the same response as the cutting of the first. That left him assuming that it wasn't serving to support one of the more vital systems in the camp. Perhaps it was simply serving as a backup for the other, which wasn't the least bit uncommon. Now was the moment that they would see if their plan worked.

Encizo hunched deeper into the foliage and waited patiently.

CALVIN JAMES HATED the jungle. He'd first acquired his hatred for it while serving as a Navy SEAL and medic in Guatemala. Later, he'd found himself fighting another kind of war in another kind of jungle: the mean streets of Chicago. But James would have preferred the concrete and urban jungle over crouching in the damp foliage of a central Pacific island in one of the hottest months of the year for this region. Still, he had a duty to do and he'd damn well do it.

There was a lot riding on this. For every second that elapsed, their chances of finding Able Team—or even finding out what had happened to the *Stennis* for that matter—were greatly lessened. They were already bucking the odds where time was concerned; James knew it and so did each and every man on Phoenix Force. But that didn't matter, because he had no intention of giving up until they had confirmed with a certainty that their friends were actually lost.

James held his breath, standing stock-still behind a wide tree as a man approached the generator. The Phoenix Force commando opted not to do anything to permanently sabotage the equipment. For all he knew the camp could be an innocent operation, such as a group of scientists.

One look at the new arrival was enough to tell him they weren't dealing with a scientific group. Not unless this was some technician who for the sake of protection had decided not to embark on this little Pacific adventure without taking a Type 89 assault rifle along for the ride. The Type 89 was Japanese-made and chambered to fire 5.56 mm NATO rounds. This weapon appeared to be a variant. The standard military-style Type 89 was capable of firing single shots, 3-round bursts and full-auto. This weapon appeared to have only two settings: safe and auto-burn. James was a bit surprised by this, because he wasn't even aware that such a variant existed. It immediately told him that the weapon had been produced on the black market, which made this man a hostile.

As the gunman bent to determine the problem with the generator, James stepped out and clamped a hand around the man's mouth. The Phoenix Force warrior yanked backward and dragged the smaller man with him into the nearby dense foliage, then pinned the man to the ground, the Type 89 slung across his back now trapped beneath him and useless. While keeping a hand pressed against his prey's mouth, James drew his knife and stuck the tip into the soft flesh beneath the man's chin. From the shape of the guy's eyes, James figured he was Asian, although he couldn't really tell what region.

"Make a sound and I'll cut your throat," James told him. "Now this is how it's going to go. I'm going to ask yes or no questions and you're going to blink once if the answer's yes, twice if it's no. Do you understand me?"

The man shook his head vehemently and tried to scream, but it was muffled.

James shook his head and pressed the tip a bit more firmly into the man's chin. "I don't think you understood me. I told you to blink once if yes and twice if no. You nodded, and that's not acceptable because shaking your head makes too much noise."

The man didn't say anything and didn't move his head, but the look in his eyes betrayed his confusion.

James leaned close and said, "Speak English?"

The man shook his head, which was no mean feat considering that James was applying significant pressure to his mouth. The Phoenix Force warrior shook his head with resolute defeatism and then got to his feet before hauling the prisoner to his. It was going to be risky trip back to McCarter and the rest with an unwilling prisoner in tow, but James didn't see that he had much choice. He also weighed the cons of leaving Hawkins on his own, but he didn't think it was wise to knock his prisoner unconscious and risk making enough noise that those inside the camp would send additional personnel to investigate.

James quickly cut through the sling of the Type 89 and secured the weapon, then turned the strap into a makeshift gag. As they traveled, he tried speaking to the man in Korean and Vietnamese—the two languages he spoke fluently—but the prisoner looked as perplexed by that as he did when James had tried English. Okay, so he'd bring him back to McCarter and let the Briton decide what to do.

James quickly found Manning and McCarter waiting in their same position. He could immediately see the concern in McCarter's eyes when he got his first sight of this new turn of events. He couldn't get a read on the fox-faced Briton's position yet, but there was a pretty good chance McCarter would realize James had been short on options.

"What the hell is this, Cal?" McCarter asked.

As he pushed the prisoner to his knees in front of McCarter, James said, "I don't think he speaks any English, and I couldn't just coldcock him."

It was Manning who asked, "And why not?"

"Because we'd already killed the generators and I couldn't risk making the noise."

McCarter's eyebrows rose. "You couldn't just bloody shut him up quietly?"

"If I'd done him up permanently, yeah, but we don't know that these are bad guys yet."

McCarter gestured toward the Type 89 and said, "He was carrying that?"

James nodded as he handed the assault rifle to Manning for inspection. In addition to having undergone formal training in engineering school for demolitions, the big Canadian was also Phoenix Force's resident expert in military small arms. He was a crack rifleman and hunter, and possessed significant knowledge and keen intuition of weapons and ballistics.

"Standard Japanese-made Type 89," he finally said as he extracted the magazine and cleared the chamber, rendering the weapon impotent. He squinted at the first round in the magazine and added, "But this isn't military ammunition. It's civilian-made .223."

"Which means that whoever he got it from wasn't in the market for munitions," McCarter noted.

"You're thinking black market?" Manning asked.

McCarter nodded.

"I noticed something else," James said. "That thing's got two firing modes—safe and automatic."

"Yeah, I was just noticing that," Manning said, having returned his attention to the rifle. "Definitely black market."

"That's what I thought."

"So, what about our friend here?" James said. "I tried speaking Vietnamese and Korean to him, and he doesn't appear to comprehend."

"He looks Japanese to me," Manning observed.

McCarter looked at James and Manning in turn, and said, "Wasn't Shukan Japanese?"

"Yeah, as a matter of fact."

Encizo's voice suddenly broke through their conversation. "Red Point to Red Leader."

McCarter responded immediately. "Red Leader here. Go."

"I don't see either of our boys."

"We've got Chi-town here with us," McCarter replied. "But—"

The air became suddenly and violently alive with reports from automatic weapons somewhere ahead of their position. It wasn't close enough to be coming from Encizo's area of operation, which left only one explanation.

"T.J.'s in trouble!" McCarter snapped.

He ordered James to lash their prisoner to a tree, and the Phoenix Force warrior obeyed while his friends scrambled to assist Hawkins.

So much for doing this quietly, James thought.

CHAPTER TEN

Hawkins had engaged the enemy.

The trouble had started so quickly, he'd barely had time to react. Only his training and experience saved his neck. He'd disabled the generator as McCarter instructed, then waited out of sight for someone to investigate. What Hawkins hadn't counted on was his "someone" actually turning out to be a squad of six heavily armed men. He had heard the communications between Encizo and McCarter, but was unable to respond due to the proximity of the group.

One member of these new arrivals, probably the leader, had instructed another man to investigate the other generator. Hawkins was confident that James would take care of that guy. But what Hawkins hadn't counted on was the leader being in communication with a man. He couldn't understand what the leader had said over the walkie-talkie, it sounded like Japanese, but the man reacted when he didn't get any response. He immediately began to bark orders to his crew and they responded by fanning out.

Hawkins knew it was risky to attempt to communicate the situation to his teammates, assuming the enemy would overhear his transmission. That left him only one option: a direct attack. Hawkins moved the selector switch of his MP-5 A-3 to fire 3-round bursts. He'd have to take as many as he possibly could before they got the drop on him. He wasn't that far ahead of Encizo's position, and it would be less than a minute before reinforcements arrived. The shooting alone would bring his friends running to assist him.

Hawkins broke cover long enough to bring the MP-5 A-3 into target aquisition, and took the first target with a triple burst to the chest. The impacts spun the Asian gunner into a palm tree, his body striking the trunk hard enough that it slammed him onto his back. Hawkins managed to regain cover even as the remaining four gunmen spread out and began to return fire on his position. He considered for a moment that he might have been a bit too rash, but it was too late to second-guess himself now.

The battle had been joined.

The firestorm of hot lead that buzzed past his ears was accompanied by the thunderous reports from the enemy's assault rifles. The firing seemed misdirected and inappropriate, since Hawkins knew they couldn't even see him. Obviously, these were inexperienced men because they were simply blowing off their ammunition in the hopes of hitting something—anything.

Hawkins reached down to his harness and snatched an M-67 fragmentation grenade. Weighing fourteen ounces and packed with Composition B, the M-67 had an effective casualty radius of fifteen meters. He waited for a lull in the firing, then yanked the pin and executed an overhand toss. It was midday but the trees formed a canopy overhead, which made the jungle terrain comparatively dark. His opponents wouldn't likely see it coming. Hawkins could hear shouts of anguish following an explosion close enough to shake the ground. He couldn't tell how many he'd neutralized for certain, but it was at least one, which left the count to three or less.

The Phoenix Force commando detected movement on his right and turned in time to see one of the gunners approaching his position in a dead run. Hawkins tried to bring his weapon to bear but he was too late. The first few rounds pelted the dirt next to his thigh, but the forth winged his shin. He rolled away, trying to find any kind of cover and waited for the inevitable sensation of bits of metal perforating his body.

The autofire came but the bullets didn't.

Hawkins looked in time to see his would-be-assassin dancing backward as rounds peppered his chest and stomach. The Asian gunner did a pirouette and finally collapsed to the soft, moist ground. Encizo approached in a flat run, the stock of an MP-5 40 pressed to his shoulder.

"It's about time you got here," Hawkins said.

More autofire echoed through the jungle air.

"Sounds like the party's just getting started," Hawkins said.

"Yeah, we'd better find the others and see if they can use some help."

The two men set off in the direction of the gunfire. As they moved toward the sounds of the pitched battle, it began to appear that the engagement was increasing in intensity. At one moment, there was a dead silence followed by sustained bursts of assault rifles, and a few moments later an explosion that Hawkins assumed was caused by a grenade. The engagement was quickly going sour.

It had now become a matter of survival.

DAVID MCCARTER AND Gary Manning spotted the enemy before the enemy spotted them. The two Phoenix Force warriors went prone and brought their weapons to bear on a quick count of maybe eight men.

Manning was the first one to engage. The Canadian sharpshooter propped his elbows in the damp earth, sighted down the barrel of his Heckler & Koch G-8 rifle and squeezed the trigger twice. Based on the design of the HK11E, John "Cowboy" Kissinger—the chief weaponsmith of Stony Man—had recently added the G-8 rifle to Stony Man's armory. It was capable of 3-round bursts and had the added advantage of fittings designed to accommodate an electro-optical scope. It was a versatile weapon, fitted with a 50-round drum magazine and boasting a muzzle velocity of 800 meters per second. It had a heavier barrel than most of the weapons Manning was accustomed to, but it was impressive all the same.

The first 7.62 mm round struck the forehead of one gunner and took off the better part of the top of his head before pitching him backward. Manning's second round came close to hitting the first man's partner, but didn't. The big Canadian adjusted and triggered a third round, the high-velocity bullet punching through his opponent's midsection. The man's assault rifle flew from his hand as the impact slammed him into a nearby tree.

McCarter started to sight on his first man, then thought better of it. The Phoenix Force leader reached to his equipment harness and procured an AN-M14 TH3 incendiary grenade. Four of the troops they were fighting had bunched together. It was sloppy under the circumstances, and McCarter planned to use it to his advantage. They didn't have unlimited resources, and if more troops planned to come out of the woodwork they would need to conserve their ammo.

He yanked the pin, let the grenade cook off for two seconds, then lobbed it into the midst of the clustered gunmen, who were still confused and scrambling to find cover. The grenade exploded about waist-high, showering four of the troops with the TH3 mixture. When ignited, the thermate filler burned at more than 4000 degrees Fahrenheit, and because it produced its own oxygen, it could continue burning up to forty seconds with heat capable of penetrating half-inch steel. The enemy troops began screaming as their fatigues combusted and the molten iron grenade fragments cored through their exposed skin.

McCarter turned his attention to the two remaining

hardmen, glancing quickly at Manning to clear his line of fire. He sighted in his Fabrique Nationale FAL battle rifle and squeezed off three rounds. The first two rounds caught one of the remaining pair in the lower torso, shattering the man's right knee and femur. The third round blew out the side of his hip, and the guy went down screaming.

The surviving gunman didn't fall to McCarter or Manning. James sprinted past them, screaming at the top of his lungs and triggering his M-16 A-3/M-203 combo from the hip. The weapon barked 3-round bursts that punched through the target's chest and midsection, driving him back. James didn't stop there, instead turning on a couple of the gunners who were still stumbling through the brush, awash in flames. James ended their anguish with mercy rounds.

A sudden and long silence enveloped them, and for what seemed like an eternity the only sounds in the jungle were that of human bodies burning and the calls of birds. McCarter and Manning slowly got to their feet as James rejoined them. The trio kept a close eye on the perimeter, and less than a minute elapsed before the sound of running footfalls approached him.

"Is it more of them?" James asked.

"Could be," Manning said as he verified the action on his G-8.

"Anyone heard from Encizo or Hawkins?" McCarter asked.

"Well, speak of the devils," James said.

Encizo and Hawkins suddenly appeared through the

brush as if on cue. Neither man looked injured, and McCarter let out a sigh of relief.

"We thought you might need some help," Hawkins said as they joined their teammates.

"You cats are a day late and a dollar short," James replied.

"Yeah, and next time I want you to home by curfew," Manning cracked.

"What happened back there?" McCarter asked Hawkins.

"I took out the generator like you wanted, but that's when it got ugly. Instead of one or two hardmen showing up, I get a whole squad armed to the teeth. They looked Korean, maybe Japanese, and I didn't have any way of getting back to you without risking detection. Seemed like a more sensible thing was to take them there and then, rather than let them butcher me and then ambush the rest of you."

McCarter nodded. "That was good thinking."

"Thanks, boss." He nodded at Encizo and added, "Although it would have backfired on me if this guy hadn't shown up in time. He saved my ass."

"Oh shucks, it was nothing," Encizo replied.

He looked at McCarter and asked, "So what now?"

"Let's go see what there is to see of this little operation. T.J. and Calvin, you come with me. We'll check out the base camp. Gary, you and Rafe check these bodies and see if you can find anything to identify these guys. Then meet up with us at the camp when you're done. And don't forget to bring along that prisoner we took."

"You think it's such a good idea to split up?" Manning asked. He jerked his head in the direction of the camp and added, "There could be a whole army in that camp, just laying in wait for you. If they get you in a cross fire, you'll be sitting ducks, and out here there's little chance we could reach you in time to provide support."

McCarter shook his head. "If we get caught in a cross fire, I doubt there'll be anything left to support. That happens, you get as far away as you can with our prisoner and call Jack for extraction. Besides, I think we've dealt with the real threat. Time is precious, mate, and we need to figure out what's going on as quickly as possible. We have to determine if these blokes had anything to do with the disappearance of Able Team."

Manning nodded, and McCarter turned on his heel and headed for the base camp, James and Hawkins in tow. The threesome moved in a wedge formation with McCarter on point.

Something bothered McCarter about this situation, and it was the battle they had just fought. Obviously the men they had gone up against weren't professionals. They had been disorganized, inefficient and taken by surprise at the arrival of Phoenix Force. It *was* possible they were some kind of a special military team, perhaps a special-ops group like Phoenix Force. They were heavily armed and seemed quite willing to fight to the death.

That meant they had something to fight for.

Something else was involved here, and McCarter intended to find out just what it was. He only hoped that the group they had just encountered wasn't in fact a special operations training team. He'd been instructed by Stony Man to proceed with caution not impunity, and it wouldn't look good to have created an international incident over a simple misunderstanding. Brognola had enough problems without adding *that* to his list of things that surely the President of the United States would insist be explained in full detail.

McCarter stopped as they reached the perimeter of the camp. While he was certain they had neutralized the opposition, he wasn't about to go rushing into anything like some madman. They'd come this far without getting killed, and he didn't intend to see his life or the lives of his men ended because he'd been rash. The Phoenix Force leader studied the camp for a couple of minutes. He didn't detect any movement or sound, and the entire camp was comprised of only five tents. Four of the tents were set up in pairs facing each other, creating a natural walkway between them that led to the entrance of the fifth tent. The walkway was made of plain dirt, compacted from high foot traffic and indicating that the camp had obviously been there for some time. The tents were constructed of special material designed to withstand the inclement weather of the Pacific. These tents were definitely commercial-made, which ruled out any chance that they had been used by an official military unit of some kind.

McCarter signaled for James and Hawkins to move

ahead of him and enter the camp. The two men breached the perimeter quickly and quietly, and the Briton watched from cover as they checked the first tent. Hawkins and James slowly moved inside and a tense minute passed as McCarter waited for them to clear it. Moments later they emerged from the tent and Hawkins tossed him a thumbs-up.

McCarter left the cover of the surrounding jungle as his teammates checked the other tents. When they were ready to check the tent at the head of the pack, McCarter took the lead. He slowly moved aside the front flap with the muzzle of his FN-FAL battle rifle and stepped through the small opening. What he saw was the last thing he expected to see—two young Asian women in the corner, hugging each other. McCarter's eyes locked on to those of the apparent older of the two, and suddenly the woman leaped into action. She charged him screaming and waving a large, wicked-looking blade.

McCarter stepped aside and easily deflected the attack. He jarred the knife from the woman's hand with a palm strike to her wrist, then delivered a rock-solid punch to the side of her head. The blow sent the woman reeling into a nearby table, and she and the contents of the table—some cookware—crashed to the ground.

The Briton had turned and looked at the second woman to insure that she wasn't planning a similarly foolish move as Hawkins and James suddenly burst into the tent, their weapons leveled and ready for action. McCarter held up his hand to indicate the situation was under control.

"Don't blow anyone away just yet," McCarter said.

James took a close look at each woman in turn, then shook his head with mock disgust. "That's just like you, homey. We're here risking our hides, and you're busy entertaining the ladies."

"Well, doesn't this beat all?" Hawkins said. "I was expecting we might find something of interest, but a pair of the female of the species certainly isn't what I had in mind."

McCarter examined the two women with a practiced eye before replying, "These two look terrible. It looks like they were here as entertainment for the men. They probably had them on hand to do the cooking and cleaning too."

James nodded, unable to hide the disgust in his voice. "I'm sure you're right. None of those guys we ran into back there looks underfed."

"So what the hell was really going on here?" Hawkins asked.

"Let's see if we can find out," McCarter said.

He moved over to the woman who attacked him and gently assisted her to her feet. He then righted one of the overturned chairs and sat her in it. He then ordered Hawkins and James to get the second one up and moving.

"Split them up," McCarter said. "I don't know if they'll be able to provide us with any useful information, but if one of them speaks English they may be able to interpret for us."

He looked at the older woman. "Do you speak English?"

The woman nodded, and replied, "I speak little."

McCarter looked at the younger girl. "What about you?"

"I speak English," she said in a squeaky, almost timid tone.

McCarter nodded at Hawkins and James, then inclined his head toward the entrance to the tent. The two men wordlessly escorted the woman outside. The Briton returned his attention to the woman in this chair, who was now studying him with what bordered on un-adulterated hatred in her eyes.

"What you do with her?" she asked.

McCarter shook his head. "They're not going to hurt her, and I'm not going to hurt you. We just want some information."

"I no know nothing," she replied quickly.

"Really," McCarter said. The Briton took a knee and scratched his chin as he studied her. "You seem pretty certain about that. I haven't even asked you a question yet."

"I have nothing with this." She encompassed the air around her with a sweeping gesture.

"With what?" McCarter asked.

For the longest time the woman simply stared at him. He knew he was getting through to her, and he also knew that by the very fact she had protested that she didn't know something meant that she probably did. There was something in the woman's mannerisms—something in the way she held her head and the glint in her eyes—that betrayed she knew more than she was letting on. It didn't take long for him to understand the situation. She had honestly played a willing part in supporting these men, but they had obviously abused that privilege by taking liberties with the other woman.

"Who is she?" McCarter gestured toward the entrance to the tent. "Is she your daughter?"

"She my sister," the woman said.

"Did those men hurt her?"

The woman didn't appear to want to answer at first, and McCarter chose not to press the issue. He figured it was better to deal with this slowly. What was the old Yank saying? Oh, yeah, you could catch more flies with honey. He needed to find a way to appeal to the woman's baser nature, exploit her protective instincts. Gaining her trust would make it easier to obtain information from her and her sister.

"Everything's going to be okay," McCarter said with a gentle nod. He keyed up his transceiver.

"Red Leader to Eagle One, do you copy?"

The response was immediate. "Eagle One here. Go."

"We're clear and ready for extraction," McCarter replied. "We'll be five plus three."

"I'm on my way," Jack Grimaldi replied.

CHAPTER ELEVEN

True to his word, Jack Grimaldi extracted Phoenix Force and its prisoner from its jungle hell in the SH-60F that had been standing by.

"Where's the NEACP?" McCarter asked as they lifted off.

"We landed it at a makeshift field at Midway."

The two men had to shout to hear each other over the whine of the powerful General Electric T700-G-401 turboshaft engines and the incessant beating of its four titanium-core blades. The Seahawk was part of the U.S. Navy's ship-based LAMPS III program, designed to provide tactical surveillance and targeting superiority for American amphibious forces. Its standard observation equipment included a Teledyne Rying Doppler radar, a Texas Instruments 360 degree search radar, and an AN/UYS-1(V) Proteus Acoustic Processor developed by IBM. Its standard armament included two Mk-46 torpedoes.

Grimaldi gestured to the helmet hanging by a hook, indicating McCarter should put it on so they wouldn't have to yell at each other. The Briton complied and Grimaldi switched over to another frequency—one commonly used and was licensed specifically to the DOJ as a cover for Stony Man—so that Grimaldi's Navy copilot couldn't overhear the conversation.

After verifying the connection, McCarter said, "I thought Midway Island had been closed?"

"It is closed, officially," Grimaldi said. "It was made into a tourist attraction after the Navy abandoned it as a Pacific station, and even that was shut down due to a lack of visitors. Mostly it's under protection by the government as a natural landmark, but we still use it now and again in the event of an emergency."

"Very nice," McCarter replied.

"So what happened?" Grimaldi asked. "And why the company?"

"They're all that's left," McCarter replied. "It was a small base camp of about fifteen or sixteen Asians. We're thinking maybe mercenaries, but we haven't been able to communicate with the surviving male, and the females aren't much for chatting. I don't suppose you speak Japanese."

It wasn't really a question. Grimaldi just grinned and replied, "Sorry, pal. I've flown there plenty of times but never learned to speak the language. I'm going to have to see if I can convince Hal to pick up the tab for linguistics school."

McCarter snorted. "Good luck."

Through the forward view port of the chopper, McCarter saw the outline of their destination on the horizon, its flag flying high in the Pacific breeze. Based on information he'd gleaned prior to their jump, it was the U.S.S. *Fletcher,* a Spruance-class destroyer. The ship was a modern feat of engineering and was a testament to American sea power. Four General Electric LM 2500 gas turbines powered the ship, which had in excess of an eight thousand ton displacement and could travel in excess of thirty knots. In addition to carrying two SH-60F Seahawk LAMPS III helicopters, the *Fletcher* sported a missile defense that included eight Harpoons, eight Tomahawks, six Mk-46 torpedoes and a full compliment SM-2 Block IV Extended Range and Sea Sparrow missiles. The *Fletcher* also had two five-inch Mk 45 guns and a pair of 20 mm Phalanx Close-In Weapons System—CIWS—that were capable of expending up to three thousand rounds per minute.

McCarter noticed that an entire crew of sailors was on the deck and awaiting their arrival. It appeared that an officer accompanied the crew. The Briton wasn't sure why the big reception. After all, they were a special ops unit, not the President; such pomp and circumstance would definitely attract attention.

"This isn't really the kind of publicity I'd planned on," McCarter told Grimaldi.

"The Farm pulled some strings upstairs somehow," Grimaldi said. "Once I'd left instructions with the AF crew that took charge of the NEACP, I bailed out and they already had a boat waiting to retrieve me. I'm telling you, these guys were nothing but spit-and-polish around me. They got me a clean flight suit and some hot chow, and then briefed me during the preflight check on this baby. Whatever I needed, they were cooperative."

"That sounds like we've got the weight of the Man."

"Could be," Grimaldi replied. "What I *do* know is that the captain was ordered to give us whatever we needed, no questions asked, and to cooperate with us. He told me while I was doing the preflight on the chopper that anything we needed we got, and that included his ship and crew, if necessary."

McCarter whistled. "What the bloody hell did Hal do? Take the Oval Office hostage?"

Grimaldi didn't answer, instead turning his attention to the landing ahead. The aft section of the ship held parallel helicopter bays for the twin SH-60 Seahawks assigned to most Spruance-class destroyers. Grimaldi touched down on the landing pad just to the rear of the bays. As soon as he gave a thumbs-up to McCarter, the Phoenix Force leader turned and gestured for the rest of his team to escort the prisoners off the bird. James and Hawkins handled the females while Manning and Encizo took charge of the man.

McCarter was last off the chopper, ducking beneath the rotor wash even as the engines wound down. The Briton was surprised to find a Navy officer saluting him as he stepped off the landing platform, since he was wearing neither a military uniform nor rank insignia. McCarter returned the salute smartly rather than bothering to advise the officer he wasn't a military man.

The guy then offered his hand. "Sir, I'm Lieutenant Pederson, deck officer for the dayshift. Welcome aboard the *Fletcher*."

"Thanks, Lieutenant, although I don't think we'll be here long," McCarter replied.

Pederson did nothing to hide his review of the three prisoners surrounded by the heavily armed men of Phoenix Force. "Your pilot advised us that you would be arriving momentarily, but he, er, well, sir, he didn't mention anything about…civilians."

"He didn't know about it until we called for extraction," McCarter explained. "And until further notice, these three individuals are under our supervision, and considered under arrest by the U.S. government."

"You're saying they're prisoners, sir," Pederson said.

"If that's how you prefer to think of them."

"What are the charges?"

McCarter shook his head and lent Pederson a warning smile. "We can't decide charges until they've been interrogated."

"Will they need counsel, sir? Because frankly we don't have anyone on this ship that can—"

"They're not U.S. citizens or POWs and therefore they're not qualified for legal representation," McCarter said.

"Begging your pardon, sir, but—"

"Don't 'but' me, Lieutenant," McCarter cut in. "I'm not in the mood. They'll be treated humanely and that's all you need to know. Now if you don't mind, we need a place to temporarily stash them so my men can get changed into fresh gear, and I need to speak to your captain."

"Actually, that would be Commander Streator and he's on the bridge, sir. My men can assist your people while you follow me to the CO."

McCarter nodded, turned to his team and ordered them to work with Pederson's team, and the two men marched to the bridge. Streator was a tall, good-looking man in his early forties with short blond hair and intense gray eyes bordered by wrinkles. His skin glowed with a tan that could only have come from a good deal of time spent outdoors under the Pacific sun.

Pederson addressed him following a salute. "Sir, may I present, eh—"

McCarter offered a hand to Streator and using one of his many aliases said, "The name's Brown."

Streator only nodded as he accepted McCarter's hand. "You're the CO on this ship?"

Streator nodded, then turned to Pederson and said, "You're dismissed, Lieutenant. Thank you."

"Aye-aye, sir," Pederson said, saluting and sparing one last glance at McCarter before he left.

Streator gestured for McCarter to follow him into a small room off the bridge area. The guy at least had some feel for the sensitivity of the operation, which told McCarter that Streator obviously had more information than was to be expected. Streator closed the door behind him, then turned to face McCarter with his arms folded.

"I'll get right to the point, Brown. I've been

ordered to cooperate with you and your people, and those orders come right from the top, so for now, you have the exclusive resources of my ship. However, I won't permit any shenanigans that might compromise the *Fletcher,* orders be damned. My first responsibility is to the safety of this ship and crew. Are you clear on that?"

McCarter nodded.

"Good. You're going to find out something very quickly about me, and that's I'm a no-shit, tight-assed son of a bitch who won't play games. So let's get down to business and skip formalities. I've told you what I expect from you, now you do the same."

McCarter would have preferred not to spend time enduring Streator's little spiel, because he really didn't have time for games. Still, the *Fletcher* was Streator's command, and the men of Phoenix Force were the intruders. He'd have to play his cards right, but something told him, despite the speech, that Streator was in fact a mean SOB who would go the extra mile, and that was something McCarter admired.

The Briton cleared his throat. "Look, Commander, my friends and I aren't interested in running your ship or stepping on any political toes. But we have three prisoners with us, and I believe they have information that can tell us where the *Stennis* made off to, and I'm going to find out everything I can about it. Now if we can agree on that, any support you can lend me is appreciated. Bottom line, it's your ship and your show, and frankly I'm all for keeping things just as they are."

"Wait a minute," Streator said. "You're looking for the *Stennis*?"

McCarter nodded and something on the destroyer commander's face changed.

"Well why in the hell didn't someone tell *me* that?" he asked. "Listen, Brown, whatever you need, I'll try to provide if it's in my power. Harry Pacheco is a close friend. I'm certain you're aware he was on the *Stennis* when it stopped transmitting."

"So were three of our friends," McCarter replied, "and we're not giving up the search until we've determined exactly what happened. Is that good enough?"

Streator delivered a curt nod and said, "You'll have my full support. Now…tell me how I can help you."

WITH MCCARTER INDISPOSED by his meeting with the *Fletcher*'s commanding officer, Encizo elected Calvin James to take charge of the interrogation. James had the most experience with questioning prisoners, since he had utilized questioning techniques in times past using truth serum. James had some with him—he always brought a special concoction in his medical bag—but McCarter had instructed him earlier that he wasn't to use it. James didn't mind, since use of truth serums— even with the advancements in modern chemistry—still occasionally resulted in undesired side effects.

Instead, James used the influence of Phoenix Force to get the two women food and water, and a Navy corpsman to attend to the cuts and bruises that had resulted from the abuse suffered by the younger sister.

His attendance to their needs and guarantee that they would be treated humanely went a long way, and it wasn't long before James had the older woman, whose name he learned was Shokyo, translating for him as he questioned their prisoner. They were seated in a cubicle off the main brig, which consisted of a small room with a metal table bolted to the floor and some folding chairs with rubber padding that were secured to the walls with heavy-gauge wire.

"Who are you?" James asked the male prisoner.

"His name is Ichiro Usheba," Shokyo translated.

"Why were you encamped on that island?"

Shokyo spoke to the man, but he simply grunted something and shook his head. Shokyo told James, "He not say."

"Do *you* know why they were there?"

She shook her head. "I no know. But I know who put us to be there."

"Who?"

"He name Jin Shukan," she replied brokenly. "He not a very good man. But he powerful and he have money."

James turned to exchange a glance with Encizo, who stood behind him with his back against the wall and arms folded. James knew immediately from the expression on the Cuban's face that he recognized the name. James inclined his head toward the door, a way of telling Encizo that McCarter would probably want to hear this. Encizo took the hint and departed the room.

James returned his attention to Usheba. "What about the camp? Why were you there?"

Again Shokyo translated James's question for Usheba, and again the man refused to reply with anything other than a mumble and a shake of his head. James didn't hold back with a harder, frostier expression for a minute or so, keeping his eyes fixed on Usheba with no other purpose than to make the man uncomfortable. He then showed Shokyo a similar look and spoke slowly and deliberately.

"You tell this dude for me that if he doesn't start cooperating with us and answer questions, I'm going to toss him overboard to the sharks." James returned his gaze to the prisoner, and with a wan smile added, "I assume he can swim."

Shokyo appeared uncertain, almost afraid to translate, but one look from James got her talking. It was a perfect ruse. Of course, James had no intention of actually tossing the prisoner overboard, but he wasn't past taking the guy up to the deck and holding him over the edge just to make it look like he'd make good on the threat. Fortunately, the implicitness wasn't lost in the translation, and the guy's eyes widened toward the end of Shokyo's little speech.

The man immediately began to stutter, his eyes going wide, then he started speaking in what sounded like full and complete sentences, barely bothering to stop as Shokyo began translating.

"He say that Shukan is leader of group, and that he just follow orders. He no know why they told to wait there. He just know that Shukan say to wait for them. He say Shukan say he will send us signal when ready."

"What kind of signal?"

The man shook his head and replied, which Shokyo translated, "He no know what kind. He say you kill the leader."

"Is that true?" James asked, directing the question to Shokyo. "Did we *really* kill the guy in charge?"

Shokyo nodded slowly. "He speak truth."

James nodded and then said, "Ask him what Shukan is leader of. I need to know who he's with."

James listened as the two spoke for nearly a full minute, taking turns at what sounded like verbal lashing toward the other. Their voices increased in speed, frequency and intensity, and it quickly became clear that they were involved in some kind of argument. James thought about stepping in—the shrieking playing havoc on his ears—but he decided to let them go at each other. It seemed like Shokyo was trying to convince Usheba to cooperate, which was good because it would go a whole lot easier on the guy if he told them the truth.

"He say if he talk they kill him," Shokyo finally told James with a deep sigh.

James frowned. "If he doesn't tell me who he's working for, *I'm* going to kill him. Maybe you need to remind him about those sharks."

"I do tell him about sharks, but he still refuse."

"Okay, tell him to stand up."

James started to rise but the guy began to rock back and forth in his chair, trying to escape the bonds. Hawkins, who had taken up station right outside the door following treatment of his leg by a Navy corpsman, had secured the man to the chair with a pair of plastic riot cuffs. He might upset the chair, but James knew there was little chance the guy could break the thick cuffs; more likely he would break his wrists before the heavy plastic.

The man finally ceased struggling and lowered his head. He began to say something, unintelligible as much due to volume as due to the man's seeming unwillingness to speak. Shokyo waved off James with a hand, gesturing for him to take his seat. Usheba had obviously experienced either a change of heart or a dose of common sense arising from self-preservation.

What he said obviously had an effect even on Shokyo. Her eyes grew wide as he continued speaking slowly and steadily. James couldn't understand a thing being said, except for maybe a word here or a conjunction there, but he could have sworn that Shokyo's expression turned from one of surprise to horror. She started to speak but McCarter suddenly came in with Encizo and Manning.

"Rafe said you wanted me down here," McCarter said. "What's up, mate?"

"Just hold on," James said, a little agitated. "You're busting up the party. We were just getting to the good part. Go ahead, lady."

"He say he part of Aum Shinrikyo," she said slowly. "I no know that he part of them. He is filthy!"

Abruptly, she turned and began pounding on the man with her fists and spitting in his face. James grabbed her and hauled her out of the room as McCarter and Encizo moved to protect their prisoner. James quickly turned her over to Hawkins, instructing him to take the woman back to her cell with her sister, and then rejoined his friends and the prisoner.

For a long moment James studied the man with resolute skepticism. He wasn't sure what had set the woman off. Hell, he wasn't even sure he knew what the hell she'd meant. What had she said he was a part of? He directed the question to McCarter and Manning. McCarter shook his head, not sure he'd heard it correctly, either, but Manning seemed almost dreading as he answered James.

"It sounded like she said Aum Shinrikyo," Manning replied. "I just hope to hell she didn't."

"Wait a minute," James said, snapping his fingers. "They're a terrorist group, right?"

"Some might say that's an understatement. We'll have to get more information from Hal, but if memory serves, they're a group of Japanese religious fanatics, although I think they recently changed their name to Aleph."

"Now *them* I've definitely heard of," McCarter said.

"But what does it mean?" James asked. He furrowed his eyebrows, rubbed his head and put his left hand on his hip. "Is it possible this is something masterminded by Shukan, and Ansar al-Islam has nothing to do with it?"

"There's only one way I know of answering that question," McCarter said.

"What's that?" Manning asked.

"Find the bloody ship," the Briton replied.

CHAPTER TWELVE

Stony Man Farm, Virginia

Barbara Price had found a reason to become hopeful
when McCarter's first report arrived. He had uploaded
the information to Stony Man's dedicated satellite
linkup, and Carmen Delahunt had immediately latched
on to it and sent it over to Kurtzman after decoding and
recording. Kurtzman had wheeled his wrestlerlike body
into Price's office and set the information on her desk,
barely giving her time to peruse it as he chatted inces-
santly with excitement.

Price and Kurtzman had an intimate and yet entirely
platonic relationship. Through the years Barbara Price
had grown quite accustomed to the big man in the
wheelchair with the low, booming voice and keen intellect. Yet she knew another Aaron "The Bear" Kurtzman.
Beneath those rugged features and that sensational mind
was a sensitive and compassionate man. Kurtzman was

intelligent, well-read and a vital asset to the operations at Stony Man. In fact, there were moments when Price wondered what they would do without him. There was very little that Price wouldn't tell him, given the often long and stressful hours they spent together.

Price looked up from the report. "The Aum Shinrikyo?"

Kurtzman nodded.

Price could hardly believe it. Of course she knew of them—as she did most terrorist groups—from information gleaned during her days with the National Security Agency. A man named Asahara Shoko, aka Chizo Matsumoto, had originally founded the group and obtained recognition for it as a religious movement in 1989. Roughly translated, its name meant "teaching the supreme truth about universal destruction and creation powers," but their philosophy proved quite deadly for the Japanese government.

In the middle to late 1990s, the Aum Shinrikyo decided to practice what Shoko had been preaching by boarding five separate subway trains in Tokyo, and at a set time exposing thousands of people to sarin gas. But the violence was only beginning. Later attacks included assassination attempts on high-ranking Japanese diplomats, additional sarin gas exposures that maimed or killed innocent bystanders, and at times even the kidnapping of their own members. There were no hard facts on their strength, but Price recalled that it was somewhere around seven or eight hundred dedicated members.

Those allegiants who actually *believed* in the tenants

of Aum Shinrikyo practiced their religion based on a cross of Tibetan Buddhism and Hinduism. Additionally, the religion taught its people that a good part of their strength and enlightenment came from yogic techniques and other ascetic practices. Unfortunately, Shoko preached more about apocalyptic ways of "enlightening" others, and as often happens in the birthing of terrorist groups, enough people believed him and decided to do something about it. Their attacks had become increasingly violent and sadly effective since that time.

The most unique aspect of the Aum Shinrikyo was its propensity for finding creative ways to deliver its message. Its members were known for striking fast and hard at their targets, almost always without warning, and their success rate was practically trademark in terrorist circles. Their membership also comprised some of the wealthiest and influential people in Japan, and it didn't surprise Barbara Price to learn that Jin Shukan was possibly a leader in the organization.

"You know, this is starting to make some sense," Price said. "Where's Hal?"

"I sent him home. He was turning into an old grouch," Kurtzman said with a half-smile. "I think the poor guy was so tired that he was even starting to get on *my* nerves. I told him to get some rest."

"What about you?" Price asked with genuine concern. "You look pretty tired yourself, Aaron."

Kurtzman waved away her concern. "I'll be okay. I'm thinking about maybe going upstairs for a nap, now that we have some information." He nodded at the report. "You think this disappearance of the *Stennis* and the X-51 and these Japanese terrorists dug into some Pacific island in the middle of nowhere are related?"

"Well, if we can believe this intelligence from the prisoners taken by Phoenix Force, there's absolutely no doubt. What I can't understand is how we missed it. The Navy watched Jin Shukan practically day and night."

"Except when he went to Japan on vacation," Kurtzman reminded her.

"You're right," she said with a nod. "I hadn't thought of that. So when Shukan was selected to oversee the X-51's construction, he obviously realized there was an opportunity to strike a major blow for Aum Shinrikyo."

"Okay, that all sounds well and good, but what about Ansar al-Islam? Where do they fit into all of this?"

"That's a good question," Price replied. "Unfortunately, I don't have an answer for it. I would say that maybe the Ansar al-Islam's kidnapping of Shukan was mere coincidence. Perhaps they didn't know anything about his terrorist affiliations."

"Do you honestly believe that?" Kurtzman asked.

Price shrugged, hearing the hesitation in her own voice. "Not really, but it only seems logical. I can't believe that the Aum Shinrikyo would ally themselves willingly with Ansar al-Islam."

"Unless Shukan did it on his own," Kurtzman said.

"But for what reason? Even if Shukan was highly placed within the organization, he would never have gotten the support of his peers by bringing Islamic extremists into the deal. And the aims of the Aum Shinrikyo have always focused on self-preservation and overthrow of the Japanese government. To my knowledge, they've never really touted a view toward America, pro or con."

"I beg to differ, but I can clearly recall some incidents involving the Aum Shinrikyo and American citizens in Japan," he interjected.

Price smiled and nodded. "I'm sure you could with that steal-trap mind of yours. But those were probably isolated incidents whereby Americans just happened to be interspersed with Japanese citizens when attacks were made. There's certainly no shortage of Americans either working or studying in Tokyo and Osaka. In fact, those sarin gas attacks on the subways involved Americans as well as Japanese."

"So what do we do now?" Kurtzman asked.

"Well, the first thing I need to do is touch base with my contacts at the NSA. I also want Akira to start working on collating any information we have on the Aum Shinrikyo."

"I can handle that."

Price shook her head. "No, the first thing I want you to handle is a few hours of shut-eye."

Kurtzman looked at first like he was going to protest, but then said, "Yes, Mommy."

"Now beat it. I have work to do."

PRICE HAD BEEN HARD at work for nearly six hours straight when Harold Brognola arrived. The Stony Man chief didn't look much better than he had when she'd last seen him, and it still appeared as if he could have used several more hours of sleep. In fact, he looked rather unkempt. If Price had been asked to describe his appearance in one word, it would have been disheveled.

"You didn't rest very well," she said. She stood upright from where she'd been bent over stacks of files scattered across the large conference table. "And it looks like you slept in that suit."

Brognola only grunted at first. "Coffee on?"

Price rubbed her lower back as she nodded in the direction of the coffeepot. "I just made fresh."

Of course, that didn't make much difference. The coffeepot they were using was older than sin, and whether it was fresh or twelve hours old, it tasted exactly the same way: bad. Still, a majority of the Stony Man crew seemed to live off the stuff, and it did help them get through these occasional marathon shifts. Price was beginning to feel the physical effects. She knew it was only a matter of time before she'd have to take a break. She tended to think of herself as immune to operational exhaustion, but eventually her intellect would take over and she'd come to her senses. A tired mission controller was an ineffectual mission controller, and for the sake of the Stony Man field teams—as well as her own—Price would eventually allow herself to rest.

"You don't look like you've slept at all," Brognola remarked, as if he'd been reading her thoughts.

"I haven't. And before you lecture me on it, I'll hit the rack after I've talked with you. For the moment, I need to bring you up to speed."

She gestured for him to sit as she went to the coffee-pot and poured him a cup. He took it and sipped gingerly. The look on his face betrayed his lack of enthusiasm, but Price didn't take it personally. Nearly all of them complained about the coffee and still they all drank it as if it might be their last cup.

"So what's to report?" Brognola asked.

Price sat next to him, slipped off her shoes and began to rub her feet as she talked. "Phoenix Force sent some information on their present status. They're aboard the U.S.S. *Fletcher,* a destroyer assigned to Pearl Harbor, but I understand they've probably left it by now and are headed back to their plane."

Brognola nodded with satisfaction. "Sounds like the Man kept his word about availing every possible resource to assist."

"Agreed," Price replied. "Apparently, they hit an uncharted island in Grid C, which isn't too far from the area where the *Stennis* disappeared. They found a group of terrorists dug in there."

"Ansar al-Islam?"

"No, and you're not going to believe this when I tell you, but they were from the Aum Shinrikyo."

"The religious group in Japan?" Brognola frowned. "What the devils is that about?"

Price reached for one of the nearby folders and set it in front of Brognola. "Well, according to the prisoners Phoenix Force took at this island, the group was waiting on Jin Shukan."

"Waiting for what?"

"I don't know, but McCarter thinks that perhaps they were waiting for him to bring the *Stennis* to them."

"That's an interesting theory, but what do *you* think?"

"I don't know what to think," Price said. "I wasn't there, Hal, and I'm not about to second-guess McCarter. Aaron and I discussed this at some length this afternoon, though, and we decided to put Akira to work in finding everything he possibly could on Aum Shinrikyo's activities for the past few years."

"I can tell you that off the top of my head," Brognola said. "They've been too damn quiet, and it's been making the Japanese government as nervous as hell."

"Are you aware of any anti-American sentiments on their part?"

"Are you kidding?" Brognola asked. "The past few years have seen a drastic increase in the numbers of their members who dislike America almost as much as their own government. They consider the Japanese political leadership to be little more than puppets of the United States."

"I wasn't aware of that," Price said, shaking her head.

"So what does the Aum Shinrikyo have to do with our missing ship?"

"We believe that they meant to hijack the *Stennis,* with Shukan at the helm."

Brognola expressed puzzlement. "For what purpose?"

"That's the part I don't know…at least, not yet. But here's what we do know. That little student demonstration that Shukan participated in turned out to be a little more than just a student demonstration. Some individuals were apparently hurt during the demonstration, which, by the way, lasted over twenty-four hours, and Osaka law enforcement primarily blamed members of the Aum Shinrikyo for stirring things up."

"It's odd that we missed that during Shukan's background investigation."

"It wouldn't have mattered," Price said. "The incident was fairly minor enough, just a couple of people hospitalized, that it didn't even make international news. And what did apparently get into the papers and radio spots prompted little reaction."

Brognola sighed. "I suppose that doesn't surprise me. Background investigators tend to overlook those kinds of things, simply because they are only allowed to deal with the facts on hand. Most of them aren't permitted to question any seeming improprieties that extend more than ten years back, or to draw correlations from what might be related incidents."

"Not to mention that this would have been the kind of incident the Japanese policing community would have preferred to keep as quiet as possible."

"As well as the elected officials overseeing them," Brognola reminded her.

"It always comes back to politics," Price replied, shaking her head.

Brognola chuckled and said, "Ain't it the truth. The guys are always complaining about that."

"Well, you can hardly blame them. It makes their jobs that much tougher."

"Yes, but through it all they manage to get results."

"Agreed."

"So what about the Ansar al-Islam? Have we completely dropped the idea that their involved in this somehow?"

"Not entirely," Price replied. "Bear presented the possibility that they're working with Aum Shinrikyo."

"A Japanese religious cult teamed up with an Iraqi-based terrorist organization?" Brognola asked, his voice dripping with incredulity. "I'd have a lot of trouble swallowing that one."

"I would, too," Price said, "except for that kidnapping and ransom demand, which I think is entirely out of character for the al-Islam."

"I would definitely agree with you on that point."

"Then maybe you'll agree on this one. Let's suppose for just a moment that Shukan has betrayed the United States and is a high-ranking member of the Aum Shinrikyo. In order for him to be effective, he's going to need to find help from outside sources. He's got the technical knowledge, sure, but I doubt either he or a good majority of his people are up to the task of seizing an entire aircraft carrier. Besides the fact, he needs someone to execute the operation because he's on board the *Stennis* and completely incapable of facilitating such a fantastic coup on his own. So he reaches out to a group that has experience in attacking American military targets, and makes them some kind of offer they can't refuse. And I believe that group was Ansar al-Islam."

"That's just it, though," Brognola interjected. "If we agree that your theory has merit, and I'm certainly willing to concede the point for now, then we have to figure out what Shukan could have offered the Ansar al-Islam that would have made them agree to such a coalition."

"It could be something as simple as hatred of a common enemy."

"Maybe. And just maybe it's something with higher stakes."

Brognola stood and began to pace the room, his hands clasped behind him. Price could see the concentration in his expression now. The Stony Man chief was thinking on his feet, literally, and focusing all of his thought processes on her theory. That was really all it amounted to, though: a theory. She didn't have a thing to serve as proof-positive that Shukan had made a deal with Ansar al-Islam. In fact, she didn't even know with a certainty that Shukan was behind the disappearance of the *Stennis* or the JUCAS plane. All they had was the word of a prisoner, who barely spoke English, that Shukan was a member of Aum Shinrikyo, and that he'd told a group of its members to wait for him at some small, dinky island in the middle of the Pacific.

The evidence was damning but it certainly wouldn't have been enough to grab a conviction in either a legit federal U.S. court or, worse yet, the court of world opinion. The evidence was circumstantial, at best, and she knew that Stony Man would have to do better than that if they were to have enough quantifiable data upon which to act. And as soon as she did have some solid leads, she knew Brognola *would* act.

The big Fed suddenly stopped pacing and looked at Price. His expression was one of revelation.

"Did you just have an epiphany of some kind?"

"You might call it that," Brognola replied. "Shukan has spent the past—what?—four or five years helping us with the X-51?"

Price nodded and said, "That sounds about right."

"There's no question that he's grown attached to the craft."

"Naturally."

"So there's also a pretty good chance that he sees the X-51 as really belonging to him, and not so much to the United States."

"It's not really a part of his psychological profile, but I suppose what you're saying has some merit."

Brognola smiled. "The main problem with the Aum Shinrikyo, the fact that it hasn't flourished or been able to achieve many of its aims, has been money. The al Qaeda terrorist network certainly isn't short on funds. Suppose Shukan offered to sell the X-51 to Ansar al-Islam."

"That would certainly be a tempting offer for them."

"And very lucrative for the Aum Shinrikyo."

"Okay," Price said, "let's assume you're right. Why take over an entire aircraft carrier? Wouldn't it have been just as easy for Shukan to program the plane to fly wherever he wanted it to go?"

"Not at all," Brognola replied. "You have to remember something about the X-51. As long as the thing is airborne, it can be tracked, whether by satellite, communications signals or infrared heat signature from its engines."

"All of the reports say that the X-51 reached radar level before suddenly disappearing. If Shukan purposely crashed it into the Pacific, and mind you we still haven't found any evidence of that, then I would think recovering the plane would involve a major operation. That's not something Ansar al-Islam could pull off unnoticed, Hal."

"Have you considered the possibility that the X-51 never left the *Stennis*?" Brognola asked, raising his eyebrows expectantly.

"What are you saying now? Are you trying to tell me that they faked the X-51 launch?"

"Why not?" Brognola countered, shrugging. He returned to his seat and continued. "There were only perhaps a half dozen personnel who knew the private transponder codes of that plane, and Shukan was one "of them. He could have easily duplicated them from a remote site. And it would have been *easy* for just about anyone to falsify a radar blip for a couple of seconds. It might have even been done remotely at the base in Guam where they were monitoring the X-51's progress."

"Well if you're right, then we should have Phoenix Force get under way for the Marianas."

Brognola nodded. "I also want you to start looking into the black market activities for all al Qaeda groups in the past two years. See if you can find any record of unusual purchases."

"And by 'unusual' you mean in what context?"

"Marine parts, specifically scrap or otherwise used on submarines."

"You think they took the *Stennis* using a submarine?"

"How else would they have gotten enough men aboard to hold the crew at bay? There are a lot of servicemen on an aircraft carrier, around five thousand, if memory serves me correctly. They would have needed a significant force to take over that ship, assuming it wasn't destroyed, and the only vessel close enough to monitor the waters immediately surrounding the *Stennis* was the ship itself."

"Which means that in order for them to get close enough undetected, someone would have had to sabotage those detectors," Price concluded.

"Exactly, and that means someone who had access to the bridge or other sensitive communications equipment."

Price stood. "I'll start having our people get to work on it right away."

"And then you're off duty for at least eight hours," Brognola said.

"I still have work."

"It's not a request, Barb."

She nodded and then headed for the doorway that led into the adjoining command and control center. On afterthought, she turned and said, "You know, this is becoming more convoluted by the moment, Hal."

"I can't imagine what it's become for Able Team," Brognola replied quietly.

CHAPTER THIRTEEN

Pacific Ocean

The next two hours turned out to be a nightmare as Able Team struggled to get to their quarters. The fierce trio knew there were only a certain number of routes from the bridge, and it seemed every one of those was cut off. The way was either blocked by locked steel doors designed to isolate flooding, or guarded by heavily armed crewmen dressed like Marine security troops. Able Team had decided in favor of moving with stealth; it made sense to avoid confrontation, if at all possible, given their limited ammunition. They had already barely escaped two run-ins with roving patrols.

They were now sequestered in an antechamber that led to who knew where and quietly discussing their options.

"We've tried three different routes to our quarters and no luck," Lyons said. "This place is crawling with terrorists."

Blancanales shook his head. "It's beginning to make me wonder just how the hell they did this."

"Yeah," Schwarz concurred. "And where the hell is the crew? We left that Hearst character in charge of creating a diversion, and he hasn't done squat."

"Maybe they got to him," Lyons proposed.

The sound of movement outside the antechamber demanded their attention and they broke off the conversation and split. Schwarz moved into the room that led down a set of metal steps and Blancanales and Lyons covered either side of the door, their backs pressed to the hard, cold steel walls. The new arrival entered the antechamber, pushing aside the door that Able Team had closed so there was only a hairbreadth crack between it and the frame. The first thing through the door was the muzzle of an assault rifle. A familiar figure emerged a moment later.

The light was poor in the antechamber, but Blancanales's eyes adjusted enough that he immediately recognized Mason Hearst. The Able Team commando raised his weapon and pointed it at Hearst's head. The guy reacted with a start, but then a smile flashed across his face when he recognized Blancanales. It disappeared just as quickly when he suddenly felt the muzzle of Carl Lyons's pistol pressed roughly behind his ear.

"It's not silenced, but I'm sure your skull will muffle the sound," the blond warrior said.

"Listen, friend, you got the wrong brother. I'm on your side... I think."

"It's okay, Ironman," Schwarz said, coming forward from his hiding place. "It's Hearst."

Lyons lowered his pistol, but his expression immediately told the other pair that he didn't like this at all. His reticence made perfect sense, though. Twice now they had managed to contact Hearst, but they hadn't run into any other crewman, and that didn't look too good on the young marine. In fact, it was pretty suspicious and Schwarz decided to mention this fact.

"They're sick," Hearst replied.

"Come again?" Lyons asked.

Hearst turned to face the Able Team leader. "I said they're sick. No bullshit, either, my man. I was on deck with that group your pals here saved, including yours truly, and they started collapsing. Some complained of stomach cramps and others were throwing up. I'm telling you, it was like an epidemic."

"That's probably because it was," Lyons said, turning to face his teammate with a grim, knowing look. They all knew it could only mean one thing.

"Poison," Blancanales said, echoing the thoughts of the other two.

"Say what?" Hearst said.

"They were poisoned," Lyons said.

"By whom?"

"Probably by whoever's behind this whole little invasion here," Lyons said with a slightly irritated tone. "I'd bet if you think about it for a while, you'd probably be able to draw a relatively similar conclusion."

"Hey, go easy on the guy," Blancanales said. "He's been through some hell, too."

"You know what bothers me about that theory of

poisoning?" Lyons asked. "The fact that *he's* not sick. Doesn't that seem a bit odd to either of you guys?"

Schwarz shrugged. "Well, he either managed to avoid exposure so far, or he's got some type of immunity."

"Then what about us?" Lyons asked. "How come we're not sick? You can't tell me we're under some kind of lucky charm."

There was a long silence as they thought about it. Of course, poisoning made perfect sense. The terrorists had used some kind of bioweapon, perhaps an airborne particulate, to cripple the vast majority of the crew and limit the chance of potential resistance. If they were correct, then there existed a potential that they could be exposed to it—meaning they would have to find a way to protect themselves—and consider the possibility that the majority of the crew had been disabled. That meant they couldn't expect much help.

"The food," Blancanales finally said.

"What?" Schwarz asked.

"Somehow they managed to poison the food. Remember, none of us chose to eat in the mess hall last night or this morning. We chose to eat the rations we'd brought along so we could stick together and keep an eye on Shukan and the other activities."

"That's right," Schwarz replied, snapping his fingers. "And we kept offering to get Shukan something and he kept saying he wasn't hungry."

"What about you?" Blancanales asked Hearst. "Did you eat breakfast this morning?"

"No, I had to pull a double shift so I was exhausted," Hearst said. "I went right to bed last night and slept through as late as I could because I had another double shift today."

"It's so hard to find good help anymore," Schwarz cracked.

"Sergeant Hearst here may be all the extra help we can expect," Lyons replied dryly.

"Listen, do you guys have any better of a grasp on what's going on here than last time we spoke?" Hearst asked Blancanales.

The Able Team commando nodded. "We know that the scientist who was in charge of this whole thing has probably gone rogue, for whatever reason."

"Dr. Shukan?" Hearst asked.

"Yeah," Lyons interjected. "What do you know about him?"

"Are you kidding? Everybody knows who Shukan is. The guy was practically a legend back on North Island."

"Do tell," Blancanales replied.

"Sure. The guy knew everybody and everybody knew him. He used to hang out regularly at the EM club. The officers would regularly invite him to functions at their own place, but for some reason he liked to hang out with the enlisted men. He was actually pretty popular with everyone."

"Let me guess," Blancanales said. "He'd come around, ask some questions about what enlisted life was like, what you did during duties. In fact, I'm guessing he got to know a better part of the crew aboard this ship."

"Well, I don't know about that," Hearst said. "This ship's present complement is 4,789, including you three. What you have here is a floating city, gentlemen. Jeez, we've got a PX and barber shop on board this ship. And I'm sure you noticed the running track that runs around the entire carrier. No, I don't think Shukan got acquainted with everyone assigned to this float, but he knew enough."

Blancanales looked at his two friends and said, "He probably got chummy with the key personnel. This isn't good, boys."

"Agreed," Lyons said.

He looked at Hearst. "We need to find a way to our quarters, Marine. You know this ship well enough that you might be able to get us there?"

"That depends," Hearst said. "Seems like our visitors have cut off or locked down a good part of the ship. Where are your quarters located?"

Lyons told him.

"That's the stern part of the ship. We're talking at least an eighth of a mile through a couple hundred separate compartments. We could easily get pinned down or caught in a trap, and then the ball game's over, fellas."

"Well, unless you know of a place where we can contact our people so we can let them know our position, and then procure enough weapons to hold off a whole band of well-armed fanatics until they arrive, we'll just have to take our chances," Lyons said with a cold grin. "So lead the way."

THEY WEREN'T LONG into their journey when Able Team and their new ally encountered the first wave of trouble. It came in the form of a half dozen terrorists dressed as Marine guards standing in a circular room designed for boiler maintenance. They weren't spotted at first, and the terrorists seemed pretty lax in their behavior. Obviously, they weren't expecting serious resistance and so Lyons knew his group had the element of surprise. He whispered orders for the other three to engage, then lifted his machine pistol.

The noise of shifting feet alerted the terrorists to the danger, but they were a moment too late in their reaction. Lyons's MP-5 K vibrated in his steady grip as he delivered the first volley. The reports were deafening inside the cavernous room, making his ears ring as the first terrorist fell under the assault. The 9 mm Parabellum rounds struck the terrorist with a velocity exceeding 350 meters per second. His head exploded under the impact, showering the immediate area with blood and brain matter, and he toppled to the ground.

Blancanales got a pair with well-placed shots from his Spectre M-4. The submachine gun rattled with fury as his first shots caught one of the terrorist gunners in the leg, neatly cutting his sole means of support and dumping him flat on his back. The man began to scream even as he watched his partner produce a grotesque dance of death under the onslaught. The bullets ripped through the terrorist's chest and stomach, blowing blood and hunks of wet flesh in every direction. The dead man collapsed on top of his still writhing, screaming comrade.

Schwarz missed on his first attempt and grabbed cover just in time to avoid a return burst of lead missiles. Schwarz had faced more furious and deadly foes than this crew, but he'd never quite experienced such tenacity. When these guys set out to kill someone, they had no qualms about unloading the kitchen sink, and it was taking all of his skills now to keep from being ventilated from the steady stream of autofire being poured on his position. Bullet ricocheted in every direction or tore jagged furrows in the metal walls, the gouges leaving razor-sharp protrusions.

He took up a new position on the overhead catwalk that lined the circular room and reacquired his target. The terrorist noticed him just before Schwarz squeezed the trigger. The man never had time to react. The 9 mm Parabellum rounds ripped through tender flesh, punching exit holes in the man's back the size of tennis balls. The impact drove him to his knees, his body jerking spasmodically as his weapon left numb fingers. Schwarz was already sighting for another target before the terrorist's body hit the ground.

Lyons noticed that Hearst didn't seem to be having much luck. The young Marine was prone on the catwalk, carefully aiming his Spectre M-4 and firing one shot at a time. He may have been trained with firearms, but it appeared the poor guy had never been engaged in a live firefight with the enemy in his life. Lyons returned his attention to the floor below and noticed one of the terrorists had gone for the shadows and was sighting his assault rifle on Hearst's position.

Lyons snap-aimed the MP-5 K over the railing and triggered a sustained burst. The first few rounds punched harmlessly into the floor next to the man, but those following landed on target. The terrorist responded with jerky motions and a half dozen Parabellum rounds drilled through his spine and kidneys. Hearst apparently noticed that Lyons had just spared him from being ventilated, because he flashed the blond warrior a grateful wave.

As the echoes of gunfire died down, Lyons heard footfalls in the boiler room. He could see that one of the terrorists was escaping. He would have let him go under normal circumstances, but he didn't know how many others they would have to contend with. If that man got word back to his superiors, it was possible he could bring the whole group down on Able Team, or the terrorists would begin to sense the resistance and start executing unarmed serviceman, or worse, destroy the *Stennis*.

Lyons couldn't allow that man to get back to his people alive.

"Pol, I'm going after him!" Lyons yelled even as he headed down one of the two stairwells that led from the catwalk to the lower floor. "You guys keep going! I'll catch up!"

"We shouldn't split up, Ironman!" Schwarz protested, but Lyons pretended not to hear.

It wouldn't have been his first choice—splitting up

his team—but this was too important to let pass. He had no idea how long it would take them to get to their quarters where they could communicate with Stony Man as well as draw upon reserve weapons and equipment, but he planned to buy them all the time he could. And letting this guy report back to others wouldn't help that situation. As long Shukan and whoever was helping him couldn't pinpoint their exact location, they stood a chance of making it. Of course, it was possible that men awaited them at their quarters, but Lyons knew they couldn't afford to post too many there if they wanted to maintain some type of security aboard the ship. And a few men was hardly enough to take out Able Team. They'd have to do much better than that.

As Lyons approached the doorway through which the terrorist had gone, he slowed and readied the MP-5 K. The door opened onto a large corridor that led to another door about twenty-five yards ahead. Lyons quickly rushed through the corridor, moving low and fast even though he knew that ambushers had no doors or windows from which to launch an attack. As he stepped through the doorway at the end of the hall, something heavy landed on his shoulders and drove him to the ground. Lyons realized that his quarry had been waiting in the girders above that comprised the ceiling in this area of the ship.

Lyons felt the MP-5 K leave his grasp and heard it skitter across the floor. His face was suddenly slammed roughly against the hardened floor, so hard in fact that the impact split open his cheek and sent stars dancing in his vision. This just wasn't going to work. The Able Team warrior wasn't about to let it all end here.

Lyons reached behind his head and managed to grab some part of his attacker's clothing, perhaps a shirt-sleeve or collar. In any case, it proved effective as Lyons slammed his head backward while yanking on the clothing. There was a loud, sick cracking sound followed by yelp of pain. The pressure on his neck eased and the Able Team leader turned and bucked his hips. The maneuver threw off the man who had pinned Lyons to the floor with his bodyweight.

The man got to his feet, holding his nose as blood poured freely from it. Lyons started to move forward, but the terrorist took his mind off the pain and obviously got it on murder as he yanked a knife from a belt sheath and flicked the blade into play. Lyons searched the immediate area for anything he could use as a makeshift weapon, but he saw nothing—at least nothing in reach.

Going unarmed against an opponent with a knife wasn't the most ideal of situations, even if the knife-wielder was unaccustomed to using a bladed weapon. Lyons had the scars on his body to testify to that fact, as did every single one of his fellow Stony Man warriors. Still, Lyons wasn't afraid because he knew fear was the biggest killer. He stepped back and started to reach for his Glock 26 but the terrorist came at him with a blood-curdling scream.

Lyons barely sidestepped the attack in time. He sized up his opponent as the terrorist turned and came again. He quickly realized he was larger and likely much stronger than the terrorist. That thought didn't make it easier when the terrorist leaped forward with the knife aimed at Lyons's chest, and this time made contact. The sharp knife ripped a jagged laceration in the meaty rib area, as Lyons barely avoided an attack meant for his heart. The terrorist lunged a third time, this time missing a slash intended for his opponent's wrist.

The two circled each other, Lyons's eyes flicking momentarily in the direction of his machine pistol. He could have risked another attempt for his pistol, but he knew that would tie up his hands long enough for the terrorist to succeed in his murderous intentions. No, he'd have to do this the good old-fashioned way with brawn and brains.

The terrorist tried to skewer him in the belly, but Lyons was ready for him. The Able Team warrior spun just in time to avoid the blade that whistled past his gut, and latched on to the terrorist's wrist with a viselike grip. He shoved downward hard and then twisted the wrist back in the direction of its owner. The joint-locking technique doubled as a way of quickly disarming and overcoming a knife-wielding opponent with little force. The force of the attacker's own momentum became the primary tool involved in success or failure. For Carl Lyons, it was success.

The knife flew from the man's numbed fingers as he landed hard on his back. Lyons yanked upward on the terrorist's forearm with all the force he could muster, which was enough to hyperextend the elbow tendons and dislocate the shoulder. Lyons finished the move by driving a knee into the man's elbow and then following up with a stomp to the throat. Tender cartilage and bone turned to mush under the heel of his boot, and the terrorist gurgled his last few utterances before lapsing into death.

Winded, Lyons turned and quickly retrieved his MP-5 K. While he was bent over, the air above him was suddenly filled with a new firestorm of hot lead. Lyons dropped to the deck, scooped up his MP-5 K and triggered a burst in the direction of the fire. None of the rounds contacted the dozen or so terrorists that had assembled outside the compartment and were taking up various firing positions.

Lyons knew to stand and fight them off without the support of his comrades was tantamount to suicide, so he instead yanked one of the precious M-33 fragmentation grenades from his pocket, snatched the pin and lobbed the bomb in the direction of his enemy before turning and running like hell. There were shouts of confusion mixed with surprise that were followed a moment later by an explosion that echoed through confines of the ship. That would keep them busy for a while.

Lyons set off to find the rest of his team, feeling somewhat hopeless about the entire situation. If someone from the military or Stony Man didn't find them soon, all would be lost. For all he knew, they had a ship full of sick sailors and a nuclear-powered aircraft carrier toting a highly advanced airplane had fallen into the hands of fanatics who were most likely hell-bent on accomplishing whatever it was they had set out to do.

And all he and his fellow warriors could do was buy

Stony Man as much time as possible to find them. He didn't doubt for a moment that Brognola would send Phoenix Force to find them. He trusted that his friends would come to their aid as quickly as they could—they wouldn't consider Able Team lost until they saw their cold, dead bodies firsthand.

And Carl Lyons intended to make sure that *never* happened.

CHAPTER FOURTEEN

Jin Shukan couldn't remember a time he felt more pleased than he did right now. His plan had worked perfectly, and there wasn't a single person in the room at this moment who could have or would have dared disagree. Of course, it would take some time for the U.S. government to figure out what had happened to their precious ship, but by that time the *Stennis* would be berthed at their secret base of operations and he would oversee its dismantling. Personally.

However, his first order of business was to get rid of his cohort. He'd agreed to this silly alliance forced upon him at the urging of ranking members within the Aleph—formerly called the Aum Shinrikyo—but he had never really liked it. For one thing, he didn't trust Hamid Adil or his men. The man was entirely too smug and confident, in addition to being boisterous and rash. Shukan could tell that Adil wasn't very keen about the relationship either. But they both had others to answer to, so he would keep their agreement. But the operation was soon coming to a close, and before long Adil and his men would depart in their submarine after they had delivered the X-51 to its new home.

But that wouldn't be for nearly another three hours. The engines were finally started again and they were under way, but they had to move slowly. Shukan had devised what he considered to be some very clever methods for covering their noise and electronic signals. From his position here in the bowels of the ship, he could steer and navigate the *Stennis* as he chose, but there was one thing no amount of technological trickery could hide—the telltale wake left by a ship on the water. To keep the U.S. government's long-range satellites fooled, they had to travel very slowly. In one of the many "friendly" conversations he'd had with the ship's master chief, the CVN-74 weighed more than ninety-seven thousand tons; there was no way to easily hide such displacement, so very slow travel was the answer.

The rest of it had been veritable child's play. While the American scientists continued to *talk* about cloaking technology, Shukan had spent his every waking moment working on it while utilizing the resources so generously donated by monies from DARPA and the USAF. The tarps that now covered the ship's communications arrays were made of a very lightweight material similar to that of Tyvek. The difference was that within the material were lined wires designed to act as interceptors for any incoming or outgoing signals, which effectively acted as a dampening field over anything it covered.

The huge canopies served a dual role. Their exteriors were covered with a material capable of reflecting sunlight and using this heat to generate a literal mirage across the ship. The technology was actually simple in design. Just as a desert mirage was capable of visually obscuring objects, the reflective material on the canopies performed much the same way. Working in conjunction with the sensitive wiring set into the tarps, capable of sending specific heat signatures, the ship could move through the water and take on the appearance of a large whale or other deep-ocean creature. When viewed very closely—within twenty or thirty meters—it was ineffective. But in this case it was the perfect camouflage against satellite cameras and low-level flybys.

As to implementing the plan, it had been quite simple. He'd arranged for the X-51's sensors to start transmitting bizarre readings to the bridge. He knew that would cause them to summon him there, which got him away from the protection detail, and particularly the rude blond. Once he was free of his security men, Shukan had proceeded toward the bowels of the ship where he had his system set up instead of to the bridge. Once there, he'd triggered the complete power shutdown and rerouted systems to the portable computer system he'd set up.

Within moments he'd had total system and navigational control of the *Stennis*. As soon as the power had been cut and he confirmed control of the ship, four of the men he'd managed to infiltrate into the Marine guard over the past two years set up and fired the launchers containing the cloaking tarps. The air currents did the rest of the work, expanding the tarps and then creating a pocket of air as they fell into place. It had been a work of short order then for Adil's men to secure the tarps in place so they would perform the function for which Shukan had created them.

Once the cloaking tarps had been set up, the remainder of Adil's men had boarded the *Stennis* from a submarine and secured the most vital areas of the ship. Any stragglers who hadn't been brought down by the ricin poisoning of the water and food supplies couldn't send communications of any kind from the bridge, but it would still be possible to sabotage some of the mechanical sections of the boat, and that required protection of those areas.

Yes, his plan had been executed without a single problem, and Shukan wasn't remiss to congratulate himself on that fact. There were others who possessed an equal intellect to his own, but none of them were on the *Stennis,* and he thought of Adil as a mere barbarian and soldier who was barely respectable enough to share his company in the same room. The Middle Easterner should have considered himself honored that Shukan would even bother to speak to him.

"You've done well," Adil told him. "You should be proud of this accomplishment."

"What is confidence you mistake for pride, Adil," Shukan replied modestly. "I am happy that my plan succeeded, and that we will both achieve our respective goals. And I'm confident that we can complete our mission despite our religious squabbles."

"And I am," Adil began, not without venom, "equally confident that we should not underestimate our enemy. The United States government is powerful and resourceful. They will not stop until they have determined the disposition of this ship, and that means every moment that the *Stennis* is on the water makes our end of the bargain a bit more risky. I have a good mind to sink this ship here and now."

"Be careful," Shukan said. "I would choose my words a bit more carefully in present company, Adil. I am a patient man and tolerant, but I will not subject myself to insulting and uninformed rhetoric."

"You call me uninformed?" Adil replied, his face turning a shade darker. "Such a statement would result in death in my country."

"But we are not in your country, are we?" the Japanese scientist shot back. "Neither are we in mine. This is neutral territory, and it is upon these facts that we've agreed to this very temporary partnership. And I did not call you uninformed, because to do so would be calling you uneducated and I have not the first inkling of your educational background. What I said I would not tolerate is 'uninformed rhetoric' and I am certain that you're intelligent enough to not require me to define this terminology or the difference between the two."

The two men stared at each other for a long moment, and Shukan couldn't decide if Adil was thinking about what he'd said or considering how best to murder him.

That was one of the main difficulties he had with this man. He was a fairly good reader of people, and also strongly adept at influencing others. It was one of the reasons the Aleph leadership had chosen him for this assignment.

Adil finally replied, "I will accept this as an apology."

"Accept it as whatever you like."

Before either man could utter another word, a sweating and rather beleaguered looking soldier of Ansar al-Islam stepped through the doorway into the makeshift operations center. His appearance immediately led Shukan to conclude that wherever he'd come from he had covered the entire distance in a flat run.

"What is it?" Adil asked.

"We have met with resistance," the man replied, wheezing. "Heavy resistance in three different sections now."

"What? What are you talking about?" Adil demanded, stepping forward and grabbing a handful of the soldier's shirt. "We were supposed to have neutralized all of the potential resistance."

"They've t-tried, sir," the soldier stammered, "but they somehow managed to get some weapons and—"

"What do you mean by 'they'?" Adil asked, incensed at what he was hearing. "Who are you talking about?"

"There are three or four of them, one of them is a Marine guard. The other three we cannot tell because they are dressed as civilians."

Adil and Shukan exchanged worried glances. Reports had come in that a vast majority of the crew was already starting to show the first signs of the ricin exposure. Shukan had expected that a few pockets, maybe five to ten men, would put up a fight, but as they were unarmed he had figured it wouldn't prove much of a challenge for Adil's men. However, armed combatants was another story entirely. That wasn't something for which Shukan had accounted, and now he wasn't sure how to proceed.

"You said this would be...I believe the word you used was 'simple.'" Adil said to Shukan scornfully. "What happened?"

"This sounds like the security detail that was guarding me. They are armed with pistols, and no more."

"Not true," the al-Islam gunner interjected. "They are using automatic weapons taken from those of us they have killed, and it is also believed they might have some explosives, perhaps grenades or plastique."

Shukan produced a mocking laugh. "They are FBI agents, nothing more and nothing less, and should be easy to deal with. Still, I think I should leave this to the expertise of you and your men, Adil."

"How gracious of you," Adil said. "But I think that you should know, FBI agents or otherwise, it has been my experience that four armed men can do quite a bit of damage."

Shukan showed him a cool smile. "Then I guess you should go and find them quickly, shouldn't you?"

Adil looked as if he were going to return a stinging retort, but instead he appeared to think better of it, turned on his heel and exited the room.

Finally, Shukan had peace and quiet.

SHUKAN WAS A COWARD, Hamid Adil thought.

And then the Ansar al-Islam leader had wondered why he'd ever agreed to such an unholy alliance. There wasn't a thing about Shukan or the Japanese that he could respect, but he couldn't say that. Well, he *could* have said it. He could have done just about anything he wanted. After all, he was the head of one of most powerful terrorist organizations left in the Islamic order, and one of the largest within the al Qaeda network, but it would have defeated his higher goals.

The destruction of his enemy, the United States of America, and everything she represented was the ultimate objective. The X-51 would simply help him to accomplish that mission, or so that's what Shukan kept promising him. Frankly, Adil wasn't sure if he could trust the Asian bastard or not. Adil had no particular dislike for the Japanese or any of the Asian cultures for that matter; ethnic ideologies and cynical prejudices weren't his style—unless the subjects were Americans. He had never believed the mandates of this jihad extended to ethnic cleansing, and he probably wouldn't have bothered to pursue such a goal even if they were.

No, this was a war of attrition and the only ones who would suffer would be the American people. Right at that very moment they slept under some false blanket of security, thinking that they were invincible to attack. Of course, their attitudes had changed some with the victories in New York and Washington, D.C., but some years had passed since then and now they had easily lapsed into their old ways. Adil wanted to send them a reminder, and he planned to start with the infidels that had shot up his men and dared oppose him.

Adil eventually found his second in command on the deck, bent over the bodies of four of their men and studying them intently. Rasam Budai had been a fellow student with Adil at the training camps in Afghanistan, and immediately they had become friends. Adil had moved through the camps at an accelerated pace, and Budai stayed on his neck. Adil was impressed with the young man's tenacity and thoroughness, and when Adil left the camps he told Budai to come to Iraq if he ever needed work. Budai showed up less than two months later.

Since that time, they had fought side by side against the Kurdish warmongers, and eventually—either through attrition or loss in battle—Adil found himself in charge of the group and in desperate need of a lieutenant that would be true to the cause and maintain personal loyalties to Adil. Rasam was the ideal candidate, and he'd served in his capacity with all of the honor and respect Adil had expected.

"What is going on?" Adil demanded of Budai.

Budai rose and held up a hand with the blood of one of their men on it. "This is what's going on. Some of those American Marines killed our men, and they have now managed to escape."

"Escape to where?" Adil snorted. "Come now, you don't believe that they actually left the ship."

Budai looked at first as if he were going to respond n the positive, but instead just shook his head.

"Then that means they're still on this ship, and I want them found."

"Yes, Hamid, we will certainly find them. I will lead the search team myself."

"No!" Adil let out a furious stream of curses. "I need you to maintain a visible position near me. In fact, I want you at my side. I don't trust this Shukan and I want you to be prepared for my signal if he needs dealing with. Send whoever you think is best to find these men, but you're to remain with me."

"It shall be as you wish, Hamid," Budai replied.

The terrorist fighter turned and appeared to consider each and every man with him. Finally he picked four that seemed to satisfy him and gave them quick orders before sending them on their way.

That satisfied Adil for the moment, but he still wasn't feeling good about the situation. He felt his spirits sink further into a desolate pit when another soldier approached them on their way back to Shukan's center belowdecks.

"What is it now?" Budai demanded, not giving Adil the time to ask the exact same question.

"We have found more of our men above, sir," the terrorist replied. "They are dead."

"How many?"

"So far we count nine."

"This is insanity!" Adil spit. He turned and glared at Budai. "We cannot afford these kinds of losses. This mysterious force is decimating our people. We must stop them. We must stop them now!"

"It will be done," Budai promised.

Sure, it would be done. As he whirled and continued back to where he could keep an eye on Shukan, he thought about how many times he'd heard that before. More than a dozen of their men had already been lost to this band of cutthroat agents. These men probably didn't have the slightest sense of what they were going up against. There were more than two hundred of his men on this boat, less the deceased, and an additional force of one hundred awaited their arrival in Saipan along with one of Shukan's contacts.

That was, of course, assuming they could trust Shukan's men to adequately guard the place where they'd planned to store the X-51—a small island between the Marshall and Wake Islands—until it could be safely smuggled back to Afghanistan. Adil had wanted to leave some of his men with the group, but Shukan had refused, citing high chances that they could be discovered before their arrival. Again, Adil had chosen to let Shukan call the shots, since he didn't know this region at all. He'd considered just simply asking Shukan to program the X-51 to fly at top speed to a predetermined set of coordinates in Afghanistan where his people could more easily deal with it.

"If we attempt such a tactic, the Americans will surely shoot it down," Shukan had told him. "And then where will your prize be?"

Everything had seemed to go okay, but now it seemed as if the situation were becoming a bit unstable. Adil wasn't about to admit that he was out of his league.

While he certainly had experience and education in these areas, he wasn't an overly technical person, and that was rapidly proving to be his undoing. He wished his request for a technical person or two had been honored by his superiors, but they were in high demand and couldn't be spared. In some ways, this incensed Adil. What could have been more important than stealing a plane capable of flying at great speeds and launching quick strikes against their enemies?

It didn't help Adil's mood when he returned to find Shukan seated on a couch, drinking sake and enjoying a cigarette.

"I see you feel there's time to relax," Adil observed, raising one eyebrow.

"One should always make time in one's day to relax," Shukan announced in a defensive tone.

Good, that was what Adil had been hoping for. He didn't like Shukan; he didn't like him at all. If he'd had a choice, he would have shot him point-blank between the eyes in that moment, but he dissuaded himself from taking such a rash action. For now, he needed the ego-maniacal scientist. But when he didn't need him anymore, and if the opportunity arose, Adil swore he'd kill Shukan.

"What of these resistors your men spoke about?" Shukan asked. He looked in Budai's direction, obviously taking note that Adil had decided to return with his second in command and occasional bodyguard.

It was Budai who noted the look and decided to answer. "They're being dealt with now."

"So, you've executed them?"

Adil didn't want to answer but he knew he had to. "No."

"Then might I inquire as to what fashion you have dealt with them?" Shukan asked with mock surprise.

"We will deal with them soon enough," Adil snapped. "These few FBI agents that you claim were protecting you would seem to be a bit more skilled than you anticipate."

"Really," Shukan interjected.

"Yes. They have killed more than a dozen of our men, and it would appear that they've now managed to get belowdecks. This means that we will have to start searching the ship for them, and that won't prove to be easy. This is a very large craft. Some help from your men would be nice."

"Security is your domain, not mine," Shukan said, taking a sip from his glass. He then rose and said, "However, I will be happy to ask my men to assist in the search. Where should they meet with your crew?"

Budai told him where his team would begin the search.

Shukan nodded and said, "I shall dispatch my people to meet yours. I can assure you that they're quite competent. They'll find these agents causing you all of this trouble. And then they shall wipe them from existence."

CHAPTER FIFTEEN

It took some time, but Carl Lyons eventually caught up with his friends. Unfortunately, it was right in the middle of a firefight. He found the threesome alive but pinned down by a handful of terrorists at the other end of the corridor.

"Damn!" Lyons said as he took up cover next to Schwarz. "And here I was expecting a warm welcome."

"Sorry, but we ran short on the roses and kisses," Schwarz replied.

"What's the situation?"

"FUBAR," was all Schwarz replied before sighting on a terrorist who had foolishly exposed himself to try gaining a forward position. The Able Team commando triggered a burst from the weapon and took the terrorist down. The enemy gunner's body convulsed as he collapsed with a loud thump.

"How's our man Hearst holding up?" Lyons asked.

"He was the first one to spot these characters," Schwarz said. "Saved our collective asses."

"Well, put him in for a medal when we get back," Lyons said.

"You mean *if* we get back?" Schwarz snapped.

"No backchat or I'll ground you."

Lyons got an idea; he wasn't sure it would work but at this point he saw they didn't have a damn thing to lose. Keeping his belly to the floor, he crawled over to Blancanales's position and asked him for one of his grenades. His teammate couldn't help but toss Lyons a helpless look.

"You can't actually expect you'll be able to get it off before they put you down," he said.

Lyons shook his head. "There's no time to argue, now give me one of your grenades."

Blancanales shook his head as he reached into his pocket and withdrew one of his pair of M-33s. He obviously didn't like the situation, but Lyons didn't have time to worry about that now. He knew that whatever happened, his men would trust him. The trio had come to rely on one another for their very lives, and not a single one of them had let the others down in that regard. This was just one of those times when they would have to trust him.

"Get ready to charge them," Lyons said.

"What?" Pol and Gadgets responded simultaneously.

"You heard me," Lyons snapped. "All of you get ready to charge. When I give the signal, you advance with weapons on full burn. Ready?"

The Able Team leader didn't give them a chance to respond. Instead he jumped to his feet, yanked the first pin and tossed the grenade. He then grabbed the second grenade, the one and only he had, and did the exact same thing. One of the terrorist's managed to get off a round that zinged past Lyons's arm and ripped a gash in his bicep.

The Able Team warrior went down and through clenched teeth shouted, "Now!"

His teammates immediately got to their feet and headed in the direction of the terrorists who had climbed to their feet and were running away. The pair opened up with the Spectre M-4s, taking the terrorists in the back as they retreated. One of the terrorists stopped and turned when he saw the men around him fall, and it only took him a moment to realize he and his deceased comrades had been duped. He raised his weapon to fire, but Hearst got him with a short burst to the chest that slammed him against a bulkhead.

Lyons climbed to his feet, sweat ringing his shirt and forehead. He nodded at his two friends, then turned on Hearst as the Marine sergeant got to his feet. He couldn't believe that the guy had lagged behind.

"Listen up, Hearst," Lyons began, jabbing a finger into Hearst's chest. "I don't give a shit if you stay with us or strike out on your own, but if you decide to hang out, you follow my orders to the letter. No questions asked. Is that clear?"

Hearst seemed taken aback at first, but something in the man's expression told Lyons that perhaps he'd over-stepped his bounds.

"Is that right?" Hearst shot back. "And just who are you to be giving me orders? You're not military, you're civilian federal agents. Right? So explain to me why the fuck you've got jurisdiction here. I'm a noncommissioned officer and Marine guard on this ship, so come to think of it, I should be giving *you* orders."

Before Lyons could reply, Blancanales stepped in and put a hand on Hearst's shoulder. "Look here, Sarge, you're most likely barking up the wrong tree. Now we can't tell you who we work for, but I can assure you that we're more than just FBI agents. Take my word for it."

Hearst looked at Blancanales, unsure if he believed him, and then traded glances with Lyons. His breaths were growing shorter and quicker, and his body had started to shake a bit. The adrenaline high was finally kicking in. Lyons knew it on sight—it was a obvious sign in greener troops. He'd seen it plenty of times when training the blacksuits at the Farm, and he had experienced it quite a bit himself when he was younger.

"Yeah," Lyons said, putting one hand on the Marine's shoulder and squeezing it firmly. "Take his word for it. Now, if you want to offer your help, then we could use it. But I call the shots here. Is that okay with you?"

Hearst gave Blancanales another look, and he nodded and winked at him. He returned his gaze to Lyons and nodded slowly.

With that out of the way, they turned their attention to the business at hand. Schwarz had retrieved the two grenades and returned them their respective owners. He couldn't repress a smile, and Lyons returned the grin as Schwarz shook his head with disbelief.

"I can't believe you pulled that stunt."

"I can't believe they fell for it," Lyons replied. "Oldest trick in the book."

"Well, it's obvious we're not dealing with the brightest crowd here, Ironman," Blancanales said as he secured his M-33.

Lyons turned his attention to Hearst. "How much farther do we have to go?"

"Well, if we're talking distance, I'd say at least another thirty compartments. Timewise it would be hard to tell without knowing how much more resistance we're going to run into." Hearst shook his head. "I still don't understand what you're risking your hides for. What's so important about getting to your quarters anyway?"

"We've got equipment there that we can use to contact our people," Lyons replied.

"Not to mention plenty of additional ammunition," Schwarz added.

"I don't know how much luck you're going to have reaching anybody," Hearst said.

"What do you mean?" Lyons asked.

"I already got to one of the SEAL magna-phones we carry on board just for this kind of thing. I wasn't able to get any transmission out. They've covered this entire ship with some kind of cloaking material."

Well, that explained a few things to Lyons, such as the sudden darkness and the fact that they hadn't been located yet. Each of the Stony Man field members had agreed to having a microtransmitter inserted beneath their skin. The thing was inert unless activated by a signal sent out from Stony Man's central computer system. They had consented to the tags in the event one of them was taken hostage. It had saved the lives of some of them on more than one occasion, but if what Hearst said was correct, it was possible that Stony Man had been unable to activate the microtransmitters and thereby unable to locate their position.

"It sounds like even if we get to our communications gear, we may not be able to reach anyone," Blancanales told Lyons. "Do you still think it's worth the risk?"

"It's better than sitting here and doing nothing," Lyons countered. "As long as we keep moving, it will be more difficult for them to pin us down."

"We also need to see if we can locate some of the other crewmembers to help us," Hearst said. "We're going to have a tough time making it all the way to your quarters if we're the only ones who can fight back."

"You think there are still some on board who haven't been exposed?"

"It's a strong possibility," Hearst said. "If the four of us didn't ingest whatever they laced the food and water with, it's pretty likely there are more who didn't get exposed."

Schwarz looked at his teammates. "Hearst has a point. We can't do this on our own. We need to find some others who can keep the terrorists busy and act as a diversion until we can get to our quarters."

Lyons considered it for a long time and then nodded. "Okay, it sounds like plan. But we give it no more than an hour. We don't find any takers by then, we continue toward our quarters. Agreed?"

The men nodded.

"All right there, Hearst. You've got point, so lead the way."

IT TOOK TIME BUT they eventually found what they were looking for. Hearst had elected to go to the infirmary, which made complete sense when he explained his reasoning to Able Team. The place was a veritable floating hospital, and rightfully so as it had to be able to cater to five thousand sailors, the population of a small town. Hearst also reasoned that for the terrorists to maintain control of the ship, they would put their heaviest security on the mechanical areas like boiler rooms, the engine room and local communication centers. And of course they would have plenty of roving guards near the planes.

Lyons had to admit he'd grown more impressed with Hearst by the hour. The guy was pretty sharp, and seemed dedicated enough to duty. He would seriously consider recommending the guy for a medal after all. He just hoped they didn't have to award the thing posthumously.

The arrived at the infirmary door and Hearst wrapped on it in Morse code, repeating the SOS signal of three dots-three dashes-three dots. Eventually, a man in a doctor's lab coat opened the door a crack and stared at the foursome.

"What's the password of the day?"

"Give me the challenge," Hearst said, gripping his weapon tightly.

"Lightning," the man said.

"Cumulus," Hearst replied.

The man quickly admitted them and closed the heavy flood door behind them, sealing and locking it. What they saw in that next minute disturbed Lyons so greatly that thoughts of medals and life or death suddenly vacated his thoughts. Hundreds of men lay on beds or mattresses on the floor, or were huddled up on blankets. The room stunk of sweat, urine, feces and vomit. Some looked worse than others and still more looked just plain dead.

"Who are you?" the man asked them once he'd secured the door.

"I'm Mason Hearst, Sergeant, U.S. Marine Corps. These gentlemen are, ah…"

"Federal agents who were assigned to a security detail," Blancanales said.

"Randy Johnstone, Petty Officer Second Class."

"Who's in charge here?" Lyons asked.

"Well, medically speaking Lieutenant Commander Danner is the physician on duty, and apparently the only one who can still stand on his own two feet."

"The other doctors have taken ill?"

"Yes, sir, it's a regular epidemic. Damnedest thing I've ever seen, short of the fact we can't seem to communicate with anybody above deck, let alone the outside world."

"Join the club," Schwarz said.

"What about military personnel with some combat experience," Lyons said. "You got anyone taking charge of the troops who seem okay?"

"That would be Master Chief Carrico," Johnstone replied, and he pointed the man out after searching the room for a moment.

Lyons nodded and headed in Carrico's direction. He'd first met the guy when coming aboard the *Stennis*. Carrico was a gruff, old mule with plenty of kick left in him. While Lyons didn't know his military experiences, he did remember seeing several campaign medals from both Gulf wars, as well as other less-remembered combat operations, which meant Carrico had enough grease to have attained the highest enlisted rate possible in the Navy. And he obviously knew his stuff or he wouldn't have been placed in charge of maintaining order among so many enlisted men aboard one of the most powerful aircraft carriers in the Pacific Fleet.

"Master Chief Carrico?"

Carrico looked up from where he was seated next to a soldier and dabbing the guy's face with a wet washcloth. He turned and squinted at Lyons, which reminded the Able Team warrior that the older man had worn glasses and was probably blind as a bat without them.

"Who's that? Oh, wait a minute… Irons, with the FBI, right?"

"That's right, Master Chief."

"Although I'd guessed you weren't really with the FBI." He let out a laugh followed by a cough. "Ain't that right?"

"Let's just say I'm a specialist in certain areas outside of routine law enforcement."

"I knew it!" Corraco said, slapping his knee. "Damned black ops guys are always hanging around, and usually at the worst times."

Lyons looked around to see if anyone had overheard, and then said, "Listen, Master Chief, I'd prefer if we not discuss that just right now. We've got a plan to start dishing out what we've been taking up to this point, but I'm going to need your help."

Carrico seemed surprised at the very suggestion. "My help? What do you think I can do against a band of heavily armed terrorists?"

"I'm not suggesting that you can do a whole lot against them," Lyons said. "But you can pull what men and resources you have together to keep them occupied long enough for us to find a way to get word back to our people and let them know where we are."

"You're kidding me, right? Take a look around here, Irons. You got any idea what you're asking for? Can't you see what we're up against?"

Lyons sighed deeply, doing his best to keep his temper in check. "I see exactly what you're up against, which is why I'm trying to help. One of the Marine guards who's been helping us said that the only way he can get us to our communications equipment is by creating a diversion. And you know what? It makes absolute sense."

"What makes sense?"

Lyons crouched so he was eye level with Carrico

before continuing. "Look, the terrorists numbers are limited. They've got maybe a hundred, maybe less, on board and we've got four thousand or better. Those aren't good odds for the terrorists. We're trying to find our way to those pockets throughout the ship where others may be hiding. The more men we can pick up, the better our chances of getting out of this alive."

"You some kind of crackpot or what?" Carrico asked, beginning to laugh. "Look at all of these sick boys. We go committing what little forces we have to fighting the terrorists, there will be nobody left to take care of our sick."

"I understand your dilemma, Master Chief," Lyons said. "But if we don't get some help here there won't be anybody left to take care of these men period. Look, somehow the terrorists have contaminated the food and water supplies with some kind of toxic agent. We're not going to be able to save these men's lives unless we neutralize the enemy that caused it first. And the only way we can do that is by finding a way to give American forces our position."

Carrico appeared to think about it for a long moment. Lyons could have just gone around him, but he knew it would have been a lot more difficult for three strangers to solicit cooperation than if the orders came from the top salt on the ship. Not a single sailor on board the *Stennis* would refuse an order from Carrico. Enlisted men in the Navy had as much devotion to the ship's master chief as Army grunts had to their first sergeants.

"All right, all right," Carrico said finally. "You make

a pretty good argument there for yourself, Irons. Johnstone, front and center!"

Johnstone practically appeared at Lyons's side. "Yes, Master Chief."

"You go through this whole compartment and gather every man you can for detail. Only those who look strong, Johnstone. We don't want anybody crapping out in the heat of battle. You hear me, Petty Officer Second Class?"

"Aye-aye, Master Chief."

"Move out."

Johnstone turned and left to carry out his orders. Lyons nodded grateful acknowledgment to Carrico and then began moving through the infirmary to get a better look at the disabled seamen. Most of them only looked slightly debilitated, but it was obvious they were severely ill all the same. Lyons couldn't understand it. He was able to buy the theory that the terrorist's had somehow contaminated the mess, but he couldn't figure out how.

Lyons walked the length of the infirmary, then turned to find his teammates when he was caught up short by a young, sweaty man in a lab coat. Lyons's eyes flicked to the guy's nametag. It read "LCDR Danner, MD."

"You're the physician in charge here?"

Danner nodded. "That's right. And I just learned from Master Chief Carrico that you're about to take what little help I have with you."

"That's right," Lyons said.

"I can't let you do that, sir," Danner said, although

there was nothing but exhaustion in his voice. He lacked any real conviction to actually stop Lyons.

"Unfortunately, you don't have much choice, Doc," Lyons replied.

"I understand that," Danner said, "but these men can't survive without constant attention."

"Have you figured out what's wrong with them?"

"Not yet, but I'm working on it. I've run every known test I can think of, and nothing seems to be working. It doesn't appear to be contagious, so whatever it is happens at the systemic level."

"We think the food and water supplies were contaminated by the terrorists. It's not the best theory, but I'd focus on it anyway. Check for anything that is colorless and odorless and has this kind of effect."

"I would like to," Danner said, "but all of the computer systems are down."

"You can't research the information manually?"

"I'd like to, but all of the books were transferred to the aid stations on either end of the ship when we put the new computer terminals in here. Which brings me to ask a favor. I need someone to get to one of those stations and bring those books back to us."

"You've got be kidding. Look, Doc—"

Danner's reaction surprised Lyons so much he wasn't ready for it. The man reached out with both hands and grabbed the collar of Lyons's black fatigues. "Damn it, listen to me, man! If I can't find out soon what's happening to these boys they're going to die! Don't you understand that? Now if I'm cooperating with your little recruitment effort here, the least you can goddamn do is help me help our sick men!"

Lyons grabbed the doctor's wrists and squeezed hard enough to make the man release his grip. He then put his hands on Danner's shoulders and looked him straight in the eye. "Okay, Doc, you win. One of us will bring your manuals back."

"Really? You'll do that?"

"You have my word," Lyons replied.

CHAPTER SIXTEEN

Lyons had just completed briefing his friends and Hearst while overlooking a blueprint of the ship. Carrico had fortunately possessed enough foresight to retrieve this information—along with the carrier's security codes for unlocking weapons and arming missiles—from the safe in captain's quarters once he realized the *Stennis* was being hijacked. What Lyons couldn't understand is how the terrorists had cleared the bridge so fast, and yet Carrico had managed to escape without being captured. Certainly the terrorists would have been thorough enough to grab up the senior enlisted man on the boat.

Well, it didn't really matter at this point. It was just lucky for Able Team that they had someone who knew this ship that well, and that if the terrorists had any thought of using the *Stennis* against any rescue ships or planes, they would have a much more difficult time without the access to unlock the heavy weaponry. Not that they would have. Lyons suspected there was another

game afoot here—one that involved much more insid-
ious and nefarious motives.

"You're kidding, right?" Schwarz asked disbelievingly.

"No," Lyons replied. "We'll split what we have into
two groups. Three will come with me and you, and
Blancanales and Hearst will take the other three."

Schwarz appeared to give it some additional thought,
chewing on his lower lip. Lyons knew that Gadgets
wanted to argue it further, but they didn't have time for
that now. Blancanales and Hearst would take their group
and head for the medical bay in the stern. They had
three mission objectives: get the communications
equipment from Able Team's quarters, retrieve the
research manuals for Danner and get back to the infirmary alive.

Lyons and Schwarz would take the remainder of the
enlisted men and head for the aft area where the engines
were. They were going to create a diversion and make
it look as though they were trying to sabotage the engine
room. This would most likely cause the terrorists to
throw additional personnel into that area, and hopefully—if all went as planned—that would clear a path
for Blancanales and his team.

Blancanales walked up next to the pair as he checked
the action on his Glock 26. They had turned over their
Glock 26 pistols to various members on their teams.
They kept the Spectre M-4s, since they were the best
trained in how to use the subguns, but Lyons was still
concerned about putting firearms, even semiautomatic
pistols, in untried hands. Still, they couldn't very well ask

these men to accompany them against a group of terrorists and not provide a way for them to defend themselves.

With the three Glock 26 pistols plus Hearst's standard Beretta 92-SBF side arm, that left only one man on each team unarmed. It was agreed that these men would stay in the middle until they had a chance to acquire additional weapons from any terrorists they took out of action.

"We could go back to that boiler room and pick up the additional weapons," Hearst suggested.

Lyons shook his head emphatically. "No, there isn't time for that. We're pushing the enveloped as it is. You'll have to just scoop additional guns and ammo as you go."

"Did I happen to mention how much I hate this idea, boss?" Blancanales said.

"You did," Lyons said. "And I can't say I blame you, but we don't have time to put it to a vote. If we don't get a signal out soon, well—"

"I know, you don't have to tell me that. I was in that infirmary, too."

Lyons then turned his attention to the entire group. "Listen up, men. You all know the stakes here, so I'll save the patriotic speeches. Now, Agent Rose here will be in constant contact with us via these walkie-talkies one of you beautiful people managed to scrounge up. Per Master Chief Carrico, he's in charge, which means if he tells you to jump you ask him how high. Got it?"

The men nodded, some of them murmuring, and whether it amounted to agreement or dissension Lyons couldn't really tell. Not that it mattered to him. He continued, "We don't need any heroes or cowboys out there. Now I don't know exactly what you'll come up against, or what the numbers are, but I'm not guessing they're real high. We've already knocked out somewhere between twenty and thirty, which leaves me guessing maybe a hundred and maybe less.

"The plan's simple. My team will try to buy you some time while you're going for some badly needed equipment and supplies. In the event Rose buys it, pick a leader among whoever's still alive and keep moving. Your ultimate objective is to get back here with the equipment as noted, and preferably with your collective asses in one piece. That's your mission and it takes precedence over everything else."

One of the sailors raised his hand and Lyons recognized him.

"Stouffel, sir, gunner's mate. Does that objective include forgetting about our other guys out there?"

Lyons saw no reason to lie about it. "You're damn right it does."

"Well, begging your pardon, sir, but there are probably a lot more sick sailors hiding somewhere on this ship. Shouldn't we be looking for them and rendering aid instead of going after equipment?"

The other men nodded in agreement and additional mumbling began to ripple through the group.

"All right, pipe down," Lyons said.

When he'd regained their attention, he looked Stouffel straight in the eye and said, "Whatever the terrorists have done to most of this crew can't be undone without additional help, and we can't get that help if we can't communicate beyond the confines of this ship. The enemy learned something a long time ago about American military personnel. For every soldier they injured, they knew it would take at least two more to get that man out of the battle zone. It's simple numbers, gentlemen, and right at the moment the terrorists have more able bodies than we do.

"Now, I'm not saying you don't help out a fellow crew member. You find someone along the way that you think is salvageable, then you do what you can. But I'm telling you now, don't waste a lot of time and keep moving. You might all live a bit longer that way. And whatever you do, don't refuse help wherever you can find it. Just make sure they're on our side before you get chummy. Understood?"

The men nodded their affirmation and agreement one last time, then Lyons dismissed them. For the moment, he'd decided to send his team first. They would need a little extra time to get to the aft compartments on the lower decks, and it wouldn't do any good to send them without having redirected the terrorist forces in another direction. Ultimately, Lyons intended to make sure that they started meeting the terrorists in places and under conditions of his own choosing, and not at the choosing of the terrorist leaders.

As the men geared up, Lyons leaned close to Blancanales's ear and said, "Give us thirty minutes and then move out."

"Will that be enough time?"

Lyons flashed him cocksure smile and said, "Well I guess it'll just have to be. Won't it?"

"Good luck, *hermano,*" Blancanales said, extending a hand.

Lyons shook and replied, "To all of us."

He hoped it wasn't the last thing he'd ever say to his friend.

CARL LYONS WATCHED and listened with care, or as much as was possible. With the exception of a few deck lights, the area was dark. He'd sent Schwarz across the deck first, not willing to risk the lives of their charges. Lyons knew he couldn't baby-sit these men, but he also thought it was foolish to send them to a needless death. Still, each of them had volunteered after they were informed of the risks. They were a ballsy bunch, Benson, Sizemore and Ericsson, and Lyons had nothing but the deepest respect for every last one of them.

Once Schwarz was across, he flashed his penlight twice and Lyons instructed the first man to move in likewise fashion. Seaman Apprentice Lloyd Benson didn't hesitate, climbing to his feet and sprinting quickly and quietly to Schwarz's position. Next in line came Petty Officer Third Class Ed Sizemore, a small and lanky career man from Alabama; Chef's Assistant Charlie Ericsson was the final man on their crew. Once Lyons had joined them, he signaled for them to fall on him.

"All right, now listen to me," Lyons whispered. "We're about to go belowdecks. I don't know what we can expect, but whatever it is won't be good. So stay sharp and don't get eager." He looked at Benson and Sizemore and continued, "And for those of you who are carrying pistols, make sure of your target before you start shooting. The last thing I need is a bullet in the ass. Understand?"

They nodded and Lyons indicated for Schwarz to take point and lead them in. Lyons had elected to take the top deck to the engine room since it didn't seem heavily defended and would be much faster to move across than through the narrow compartments below. The ship certainly wasn't as cramped as a submarine, but it was hell in a firefight. Everything was metal, which meant bullets had the ricochet potential of rubber balls, as well as the difficulties with maintaining some sense of direction and distance. Plus, they were able to use the objects above deck, like the aircraft and other equipment, as cover.

For just a moment as they headed to the first lower deck by a maintenance stairwell, Lyons wondered how they had ever ended up in this situation. The job should have been simple: guard Shukan and make sure nothing happened to him or the X-51. He was convinced that they were dealing with Ansar al-Islam, though. The terrorists he encountered so far all seemed to be of Middle Eastern descent, which meant that they were probably from the Iraqi terrorist group.

Lyons also figured that Shukan was in on this deal. He couldn't figure out what the motive was, but he hadn't liked the guy from the beginning and he believed that Shukan was responsible, at least partly, for what had happened to the *Stennis*. Nobody else aboard possessed the expertise on the X-51, and nobody else aboard had the kind of unlimited access he had. Add to that, Lyons had heard the ship screws start up again and, while he couldn't really get a sense of movement due to the massive enclosure, he knew someone had to be controlling it from somewhere aboard, and remote access was Shukan's specialty.

When I catch up with that traitorous leech I'm going to kill him, Lyons thought.

The Able Team warrior's attention returned to the present. The five men had reached the lower deck safely, and after an all-clear signal from Schwarz they proceeded down a main corridor that would take them to the aft compartments. The air in the corridor suddenly came alive with autofire.

Lyons pushed Ericsson to the floor and followed him there. A trio of terrorists, probably assigned to stand guard on the corridor, had opened up on them with submachine guns. One of the men carried an M-4 Spectre, but the other two were brandishing AKSUs. A shortened version of the AK-74 assault rifle, the AKSU was a veritable bullet hose and capable of expending in excess of 800 rounds per minute. It fired the 5.45 mm Soviet cartridge, but it wouldn't have been Lyons's weapon of choice as its short barrel made it difficult to control when firing even short bursts. That small detail proved to be what saved their lives.

Schwarz got off the first response to the ambush, sighting on the closest target and taking him with a double-tap to the midsection. Both rounds scored and punched through the soft flesh of the terrorist's gut like an air pellet through paper. The man screamed and twisted oddly before dropping his AKSU and sprawling across a compartment doorway.

Lyons got the other terrorist with the AKSU, keeping the Spectre low and aiming by pure instinct. A single 9 mm Parabellum slug punched through the terrorist's lip, cracking his lower jaw and continuing through to his neck. The terrorist's head bobbed before he landed on his back, dead before he hit the ground.

Neither of the Able Team pair could tell if their shots at the remaining terrorist had struck because Benson and Sizemore triggered round after round from their pistols. Each shot caused the terrorist to jump, and sparks marked where at least half the shots missed entirely. Still, they managed to bring him down, and it looked as if Schwarz had managed to get an extra shot in before the terrorist fell.

"Take it easy with that ammunition, men," Lyons said as they slowly got to their feet.

Benson and Sizemore started to advance with them, but Schwarz shook his head. "No, you guys stay here. Ironman, I'm going to go ahead and make sure it's secure."

Lyons nodded. He didn't like it, but he sure as hell wasn't going to argue with his friend. Schwarz was an experienced combatant, in fact a battle-hardened veteran, and Lyons trusted the older man's judgment.

Once the electronics wizard had given the all-clear,

Lyons and the three sailors joined them. Schwarz quickly and expertly stripped their enemies of ammunition and divvied it up evenly. He then snagged both AKSUs, keeping one for himself and giving the other to Lyons. The Spectre M-4 he handed over to Ericsson.

"You know how to use this thing?" Schwarz asked the young kitchen hand.

"My pop taught me how to hunt," Ericsson drawled with a Tennessee twang. "And I fired a rifle in boot camp."

Schwarz nodded and handed the weapon to him. He traded a glance with Lyons and both men silently agreed that Ericsson looked pretty unnatural holding the thing. Schwarz pushed the muzzle down when Ericsson started waving the weapon a little irresponsibly.

"Take it easy with that thing, sport. You ever seen one of those before?"

Ericsson shook his head. "No, sir, I've never fired nothing like this."

"Well, there's a first time for everything, so listen up. That subgun is called a Spectre M-4. It fires 9 mm ammunition and it doesn't have a safety to speak of. So when you aim and pull the trigger, make sure you're ready. Keep the thing held low, like this, and when you're ready to fire, squeeze the trigger a few times. You got that?"

Ericsson nodded again.

"It's going to ride up on you the first few times," Lyons added helpfully, clapping a firm hand on the much younger man's shoulder. "But you'll get used to it."

He motioned for Schwarz to move them out and

the five continued onward, moving deeper into the bowels of the ship. Lyons figured they would encounter at least two more roving or stationary patrols before they even got close to the engine room, and he figured a significant force would be guarding that part of the *Stennis*. There was something bothering Lyons more than he wanted to admit; however, he had elected to keep it to himself. This ship contained two very powerful nuclear reactors, and Lyons didn't wonder if the Ansar al-Islam had some disastrous plan to overload them. Certainly, an entire aircraft carrier was too valuable a prize to simply use as a nuclear bomb, but Lyons knew that trying to second-guess the logic of a bunch of fanatics was a futile effort.

They reached the end of one of the corridors and Schwarz called for them to halt. The group immediately got down, keeping to one side of the corridor. He peered around the corner of the hallway and immediately ducked his head back. He then gestured for Lyons, pointing first to his eyes, then holding up two fingers and then extending his palm with fingers closed.

Lyons nodded, knowing immediately what it meant: Gadgets had spotted two guards on a closed door. The only reason terrorists would spare guards on a closed door was if something important happened to be on the other side. Lyons intended to find out just what that "something" was. He turned his attention to the three sailors.

"You guys stay here," he ordered. He focused on

Sizemore and said, "You're highest ranking, so you're in charge. We're going to take care of this little problem. We run into trouble, you turn and hightail it back to the infirmary."

"What about the diversion?" Benson asked.

"Yeah, that's right," Sizemore said. "I thought we needed to accomplish this mission no matter what."

Lyons considered it for a moment, exchanged looks with the three eager faces, then nodded. "All right, if something bad goes down and you can find another way to the engine room, then go for it. Otherwise, don't waste your lives. You understand me?"

Once each man indicated they understood, Lyons joined Schwarz at the corridor junction.

"How do you want to do this?" Schwarz asked.

"As quietly as possible," Lyons said. "You got a knife on you?"

Schwarz shook his head with an expression of disgust. "No, it's in our quarters with every other damn thing."

"All right then, we'll have to just nut-up and take them by hand. Did you get a look at their weapons?"

"The usual fare…machine pistols and knives. But they had them slung so we've got a chance to reach them before they react."

"Let's hope so," Lyons replied.

He gave a silent count, then they started to move. Lyons felt himself suddenly yanked backward and saw the same thing happen to Schwarz as he heard Benson screaming for them to get their asses down. As Lyons landed on his backside he noticed a crew of terrorists charging their position from the opposite corridor.

And then all hell broke loose.

CHAPTER SEVENTEEN

Blancanales checked his watch: eight minutes to showtime. Lyons had instructed him to wait thirty minutes, and every single one of them had ticked by at an agonizingly slow pace. In a lifetime thirty minutes was nothing, but Blancanales had to admit that he couldn't remember a thirty-minute time frame as long as this one.

"Are you nervous, man?" Master Chief Carrico asked him.

Blancanales was taken aback by the question, but he quickly recovered with a smile. "No, just a bit anxious I guess."

"About what?" Carrico asked as he reached into his pocket and withdrew a case of chewing tobacco. The old sailor helped himself to a hefty dip, then offered some to Blancanales who politely refused.

Carrico shrugged indifferently and replaced the case, then repeated his question. "What you so anxious about?"

"I guess I'm a bit concerned for my partners," Blancanales replied, not even sure why he had decided to confide in the older guy.

He wondered for a moment if it had something to do with age group. Carrico had been around the block a few times—that was as plainly obvious as the years of torment and pain blasted into his face. The eyes made it especially obvious; there was pain behind those eyes, and he could recall having seen it on the faces of others like him.

"They left you behind, eh? The big blond one... Irons, is it? I guess he's in charge."

Blancanales was impressed with Carrico's insight. "Yeah, he's top dog. But he's never treated us as anything but equals. We're a team and we're most effective staying that way. I wasn't keen on him splitting us up."

"I wondered if that was the problem," Carrico replied with a nod. "I saw you guys arguing about something there right before his little briefing. I can't say as I blame you. Breaking up a group isn't the swiftest of moves."

"Being a leader isn't easy," Blancanales said, immediately coming to Lyons's defense, although he wasn't sure that he really had to.

"You don't have to tell me that, son. I've been a leader most of my life."

Blancanales didn't know whether to chastise the old-timer or break out laughing for the "son" moniker, but he finally settled on just letting it roll off his back. He didn't sense any actual intent on Carrico's part to be condescending.

"Well, at any rate, he made a decision and I'm going to stick by it."

"So what's your plan?"

Blancanales was immediately suspicious at first, but he quickly dismissed it as natural paranoia. Carrico didn't pose any real threat to the operation, such as it was, and he sure as hell wasn't one of the bad guys. He'd demonstrated that simply by the sincerity with which he tried to help Danner comfort the infirmary full of sick American boys.

"The first team will attempt to create a diversion for us by sabotaging the engine room. We're hoping this causes the terrorists to throw all their forces toward the back end of the ship. That will clear the way for us to then get to an armory and aid station in the forward compartments."

"And hopefully you'll be able to pick up some reinforcements along the way, eh?" Carrico said, jabbing an elbow lightly in Blancanales's side.

"Exactly right."

"Well, you just take yourself and our boys out there."

"Aye-aye, Master Chief," Blancanales said, rendering a smart salute.

The Able Team warrior looked at his watch again: 2210 hours and time to move out. Blancanales signaled for his team to get themselves together and form on him, then led them to the bay door. The locked, steel door had proved their only defense against an enemy bent on their destruction. For a small time, he had relished in reprieve, but now it was time to move forward. Thirty minutes meant thirty minutes, and even if this meant his funeral, Blancanales didn't want to be late for it.

"Let's do it," he told the men.

Blancanales elected to take point while Hearst brought up the rear. The young Marine had proved himself enough that the Able Team warrior knew he could trust Hearst to watch their backs and cover their asses if it came right down to it. The men were accompanied by Seamen Jerry Norris and Stephan Gornich, as well as PO2 Johnstone, the man who had originally admitted Able Team and Hearst to the infirmary.

Blancanales moved in the opposite direction they had come, intent on retracing their steps. Since he'd decided not to let Hearst lead the pack, he had to navigate from rote memory. Their two days on the ship had certainly provided Blancanales with enough opportunity to get the lay of the land, as it were, but most of his travel had been between his quarters and the showers or the bridge. Although they were detailed to protect Shukan, there had still been parts of the ship that were restricted even to federal law enforcement.

As they approached a stairwell that led to the upper decks, Blancanales considered their situation. They had originally tried to make the forward part of the ship before moving across the upper deck and then descending through a main entry at the ship's stern, figuring they could backtrack. However, the terrorists had that part of the *Stennis* well guarded and Blancanales wasn't sure he wanted to try it again. Chances were they had moved with the news of the diversion Lyons's team was supposed to create, but he couldn't rely on that alone. Anything could have gone wrong, and if there were no diversion then he knew they'd have to revert to a more direct method.

Blancanales could only hope that the first team did its part. He pushed that thought from his mind. He would just have to trust, his friends. One way or another he knew they would pull through. There was no doubt about it.

CARL LYONS REACTED with the speed and agility for which he'd become well-known within his most intimate circles. Lyons snap aimed his AKSU and squeezed the trigger, sending a heavy volley of autofire in the direction of the charging terrorists. The terrorists suddenly found themselves bunched up, the first couple stopping short and causing those behind to run into them and knock them to the ground.

Lyons could even see the panic on the faces of the closest pair as they scrambled to find some kind of cover in the narrow confines. They had obviously not been told to expect a group with small arms that possessed skill and a burning desire to use them. Lyons taught those first two terrorists a final lesson as the 5.45 mm Soviet shells that spit from his weapon found their marks. The first terrorist got stitched from crotch to sternum, the high-velocity shells drilling through vital organs. The second took three rounds to the head that hit with such impact it split his skull apart like a melon. The now practically headless corpse staggered around for a moment before falling.

The next terrorist fell with a sustained burst from Ericsson's Spectre. The young sailor had apparently not heeded Schwarz's advice on how to fire the submachine gun. Lyons cringed as Ericsson exhausted nearly half his clip on a single terrorist.

"Short bursts!" Lyons shouted as he sighted in another terrorist and blew him away.

Before the shooting had started, Schwarz had actually been in motion and the sudden change in plans caused him a bit of heartache. Not to mention a bullet fragment in the cheek, the result of a ricochet from the machine pistol of one of the pair of door guards. Schwarz rolled in time to avoid being cut in two by a swathing line of autofire, triggering his AKSU as he did. The weapon performed just as designed, spitting rounds in a irregular pattern and finding both marks. One man died immediately under the assault, the slugs from the AKSU striking him in the chest and groin.

The second terrorist avoided death by twisting away in time to suffer a graze in the lower part of the back from a bullet meant for his midsection. Schwarz completed his roll and put his foot against the wall as leverage to twist himself into a kneeling position. The terrorist was still trying to reacquire his target, and Schwarz didn't wait for an engraved invitation. He triggered a short burst that slammed his opponent into the door. The terrorist slid to the ground, leaving a gory mess in the wake of his descent, and the electronics expert opted to put one more round in his head for good measure.

He spun on his knee and yelled, "Ironman, the door!"

Lyons nodded, continuing to fire to keep heads down more than for effect.

Schwarz jumped to his feet and went to the door. He turned the handle left, but it didn't budget. He then tried right and the wheellike handle began to move smoothly. He opened it quickly, then whistled for his companions to join him. Lyons ordered Ericsson to go first. The man got to his feet but made the critical mistake of turning and running. Lyons screamed a warning at him, but it was a moment too late. Ericsson was fully upright and moving away from the terrorists in a straight line, making himself the perfect target. The terrorist gunman didn't hesitate to risk exposure for a sure thing, and they cut Ericsson down instantly.

Lyons could hear the shouts of pain and surprise coming from the young man—even though he didn't dare turn to see the carnage—even over the din caused by the gunshots. A brief pang of regret ran through Lyons, but he didn't dare let it consume him. He turned it into a vengeful fury, going from his sitting position to one knee and using the wall for cover, he began to pour on the heat.

"Go!" he told Benson and Sizemore. "And keep your asses down!"

The pair didn't have to be told twice, having now witnessed firsthand what could happen to the human body under the present circumstances. They kept their heads low as they ran in a jagged pattern toward Schwarz who was waiting on the other side of the door but still laying down covering fire with Lyons. Once the two were clear, Schwarz continued firing and yelled for Lyons to join them. The Able Team leader delivered a few more bursts for good measure, then made good his escape while his partner covered him.

As soon as he got through, the electronics wizard closed the door behind them. He started to lock it but Lyons shook his head, restraining the man's hand as he flashed him a wicked grin. Lyons held out his hand with an expectant gaze and Schwarz knew in an instant what he wanted.

"No way, man," Schwarz said, shaking his head. "I'm not giving up one of my frags."

"Come on, Schwarz," Lyons protested. "I'm down to only one, and you've still got two."

"That's because you decided to waste one of yours."

"Waste?" Lyons said. "I've never wasted a grenade in my life, and I take offense at the very suggestion. Now are you going to give me a grenade or not."

"Well…"

"Listen, pal, maybe I'll wait for you to make a decision but they sure won't."

"All right." Schwarz reached into his pocket and retrieved a grenade.

As Lyon's wedged the grenade against the wheeled handle and gently detached the pin, Schwarz turned to see the two younger men staring incredulously at them.

They had actually thought the argument was serious, not realizing that there were moments that the men of Able Team couldn't resist just a little comic relief to add to the rush of combat. It was a natural response, but one that men as green as those two were couldn't possibly understand.

Lyons turned and joined Schwarz, noticing their look.

"What's wrong with them?"

Schwarz shook his head as if at a loss for words. "I don't know, but if they keep standing there like that with their eyes wide, their faces will freeze in that position."

"Nice," Lyons said with a wicked grin. "Come on, let's blow this pop stand."

The foursome proceeded at full speed down the hallway and rounded the first corner they came to. Lyons urged them to keep moving, then waited back to make sure his handiwork paid off. Sure enough, he heard the movement of the door come before the heavy sound of it opening. Lyons was counting on the fact that the terrorists would proceed cautiously through the doorway in anticipation of an ambush, and they didn't disappoint.

The M-33 exploded at just the right time, separating appendages from a couple of the terrorists and sending superheated metal fragments into the others that escaped the full brunt of the blast. As the smoke from flaming clothes dissipated, Lyons quickly verified that nobody had survived before running to catch up with his friends.

Now it was time to find the engine room.

WHEN ONE OF HIS MEN arrived to report the status of their search, Hamid Adil cut him short and insisted he go outside. He didn't want Shukan to overhear the conversation, particularly if it was bad news. Shukan had made it quite clear that security was a matter for Adil and his fighters, and so the Ansar al-Islam commander would make sure that Shukan wasn't involved at all if he could help it.

"What do you have to report?" Adil demanded.

Budai stood behind him with folded arms and an expectant expression.

"We found some more of our men, sir," the young terrorist said, swallowing hard and barely able to get the words out.

"What do you mean, you found more of our men?" Adil said. "Found them where, idiot?"

"Th-they are…that is, they were dead. They were found on deck three in one of the boiler rooms in the midsection."

"Dead," he whispered.

"There was nothing we could do, Master Adil. Our team arrived well after—"

"Did I say there was anything you could do?" Adil roared, barely able to control the rage welling within him. "Get out of my sight!"

The terrorist turned and hastily left the outer room connected to Shukan's makeshift operations center. The room was wide, with papers and other valuable material dealing with the time schedules and operational objectives of Ansar al-Islam's plans for the X-51. Buried beneath the material and Adil's scrawled notes was an entire layout of the ship, a massive blueprint that identified every last crevice and nook on the *Stennis*.

Adil marched over to the table and swept the papers aside, causing them to scatter in every direction. One of the terrorist guards assigned to the quarters stepped in to collect them, but Adil ordered him out and Budai followed him to the door, slamming it closed once the guard was through the doorway. Budai then returned to his master's side.

"If that simpleton is correct," Adil began, referring to bearer of bad news, "then we have identified a pattern. The first two areas we found our men killed were here on the deck and also at the bridge. That's more toward the aft section. Now, we find some more of brothers massacred at this point, which is about the midsection of the ship."

"They are moving forward," Budai concluded.

"Exactly, which means they are trying to reach the stern."

"They might have already accomplished their objective had you not brilliantly ordered us to post a heavy guard at the main entrance and patrols for the access points."

"True," Adil, accepting the compliment as if he was deserving of all adoration. "However, what escapes me is understanding what they could possibly want. If their intent was to sabotage this ship, they would try for the engines."

"Could they be planning to access one of the other communication rooms?"

Adil shook his head and replied, "If they are, then a very nasty surprise awaits them. I insured that the men used incendiary devices on all of the equipment, except for the bridge, since Shukan had shut it down entirely."

"Well, there is a significant armory in that part of the ship, but we have wired it for explosives per your orders. If they try to access it, they shall be instantly destroyed."

"Excellent," Adil said with a satisfied nod. "And what of the crew members? Do we know how many were actually infected?"

"We do not know the exact number, but we are certain that it was a very large majority. At the most, there might be one hundred that were unaffected, but that number will likely decrease if any of them drink the water."

"Good," Adil said. "I remember arguing contamination of the water with you, thinking that infecting the food supplies would be enough. It was foolish of me."

"It is nothing, Hamid. We have been friends too long for me to allow a trifling disagreement like that to come between us."

Adil turned and put his hand on his trusted commander's shoulder. "You are my *only* friend here, Rasam. I do not trust Shukan. I cannot trust him. If he attempts to betray us, I want you to kill him. Do you understand?"

Budai nodded. "You may consider it my pleasure."

"Good." Satisfied that he had sufficiently erased his troubles with the Japanese infidel, Budai turned and studied the blueprints for a bit longer. Finally he said, "I have it in mind that our friends are attempting to woo us into believing that they're heading toward the stern, when in fact they *are* planning to sabotage the engines."

"It is a possibility I considered, as well," Budai said.

Adil turned and smiled. "Perhaps the old saying about great minds is true. Still, I think it would be wise that we divert most of our forces toward the rear compartments."

"But, Hamid, you're talking about reducing our forces in critical parts of the ship."

"What critical parts?" Adil replied with a derisive laugh. "As you've already said, the armory is wired with explosives. We have eliminated their ability to communicate, and there are not enough well crew members on this ship to create any sort of insurmountable problem. They have very little resources or chances left, and I believe that they will attempt to overpower our people near the engine rooms."

"Then what are your orders?"

"I want you to deploy all of our troops to the rear compartments. Leave one roving patrol of twelve men at the front of the ship, and send the rest to approach the engine room from every possible access point. Slowly yet surely, we will choke off the resistors' escape and expose their bluff." Something almost demonic came over Adil's expression as he slammed his fist on the blueprint and added, "We will then crush them with a single and decisive stroke!"

CHAPTER EIGHTEEN

Marianas U.S. Naval Station, Guam

It was an old saying among American sailors at the Marianas Naval Station: "Guam is where America's day begins." It was also turning out to be where Phoenix Force's night would begin. Calvin James was as tired as his colleagues, but he didn't have any choice. The minutes continued to tick by and the Air Force technicians aboard the NEACP-4B still hadn't found a trace of the *John C. Stennis* or the X-51, even with the information provided by DARPA. Now Price had asked Phoenix Force to take time away from their search to investigate the possibility that someone might have tāmpered with the monitoring equipment at the station's communications and control center.

Someone, James thought, and it made him want to vomit. Under his breath he said, "This is a waste of time."

He believed that Stony Man could have used the NIS

to conduct this investigation while Phoenix Force continued its search of the Pacific around the ship's last-known position. Instead, they had to start poking around where their noses didn't belong to begin with, hoping that maybe something about this mysterious someone might fall into their lap. That was assuming, of course, that the whole thing wasn't bogus to begin with.

This wasn't Phoenix Force's first visit to the Marianas. The island had been released to American possession as a part of the Treaty of Paris following the Spanish–American War of 1898, and in the control the United States ever since. It had come under brief rule of the Japanese following surrender of U.S. naval personnel in December 1941, but it was Charles Nimitz who wrested it back a short three years later. There were more than two thousand islands of this kind scattered between the Philippines and Hawaii, and Guam was the largest of them. Nearly one-tenth of the island population consisted of military personnel and families.

McCarter had elected James to ride from the airfield to the command center alone, since he was former Navy and accustomed to the environment. James hadn't minded in the least, because it left the others time to continue working additional angles. Even Jack Grimaldi had decided to get in on the act, reaching out to his contacts on the nearby islands, guys with whom he'd flown in Vietnam and now were making their livings island-hopping. Phoenix Force hadn't been able to hold back a fit of laughter when Grimaldi went on about how pilots

knew things and heard a lot of things. Still, McCarter had
chosen to give him leave to pursue the information.

At this point in the game, the Briton wasn't turning
down anything.

Price had advised that according Stony Man's information, a man named Commander Matthias Rico was
in charge of the naval station's entire communications
and command monitoring facility, and it was Rico who
met James personally on his arrival.

The first thing James noticed when he emerged from
the government sedan was how surprisingly young Rico
was. He appeared in fairly good shape, with dark hair
and eyes that could have easily allowed him to pass as
a Chamorro, the local natives of the island.

"Colonel Smith," Rico greeted him, stepping forward
and saluting the Briton.

James felt a bit out of step playing the role of a
military officer, particularly a superior, but he knew
from Rico's salutation that Stony Man had obviously set
up his cover to get him a bit more clout and personal attention. It was just as well, because James didn't plan
on staying that long anyway.

He took Rico's hand. "That's right. And no offense,
Commander, but you seem a bit young to be in charge
of all this."

"Yes, sir," Rico said with a grin, accepting the back-
handed compliment as if he heard the same thing every
day, "but I guess that comes with good living and
knowing just the right people."

"Such as?" James pressed.

"My father was in service with the Diplomatic Corps in Argentina. That got me into Annapolis and the rest is history. I also posses a master's degree in Defense Technical Sciences, so I know my way around these kinds of systems pretty good." He jerked his thumb over his shoulder, gesturing in the direction of the CCC building spread out widely behind him.

"Shall we proceed inside?"

"Is there air-conditioning?" James cracked.

"You bet, sir. If you'll follow me…"

James had to take long strides to keep pace with the studious, almost nerdy Rico. The guy was short but as quick as a hare, his stride smaller than James's but about times three on the speed factor. Rico began to chatter aimlessly about the CCC and all the things it was capable of, but James tuned most of it out. He was here to get some information and make a determination, and he'd already known what that determination would be. They didn't have time to go digging into the backgrounds of the umpteen individuals with access to the CCC.

Once inside, James had to admit he was impressed. Mostly it was because the place was that impressive. A set of computer servers lined one wall, nested in a three-tier rack nearly sixty yards wide that held more computers than James could ever remember seeing in one room. Against another wall were rows upon rows of data storage tapes and other media. The main operations center was sunken into the middle of the oval-shaped room. A massive screen with a full geographic map of the world took up one wall, and it glowed with an almost mesmerizing effect. A score of technicians, controllers and monitors surrounded that screen from all sides, and James realized that Kurtzman had nothing on the United States Navy.

"Impressive, isn't it, sir?" Rico asked.

"I have to admit that I've never seen anything quite like it before," James replied truthfully.

James noted something else, however, and that was the number of SPs posted throughout the room. They had also been required to issue James a temporary security pass that noted him as a visitor, and required that he surrender his side arm. James hadn't been real keen on the idea but he agreed, realizing that Stony Man's influence could only reach so far. With an entire aircraft carrier and its crew missing, the U.S. Navy wasn't about to breach security protocols, and James wouldn't have asked them to. Phoenix Force already had enough work ahead of it without adding potential security problems at the station to the mix.

"I understand you're with a military cell of the NCIS," Rico said.

James was suspicious at first, but the tone and inflection in Rico's voice seemed conversational enough. James decided to play along for the moment and make nice-nice with the boy with the influential daddy.

"That's right."

"Strange," Rico replied as he led James across the room. "I could have sworn that NCIS had gone strictly civilian. Sounds like they decided to hold on to a few military boys, is that right?"

"What sounds right to me, Commander," James said with a smile, "is that you don't ask too many questions."

"You'll have to forgive me, sir," Rico replied. "But aside from natural curiosity, we were part of the X-51 training ops, and my people were monitoring all signals. In fact, we were probably the last station to actually have any kind of contact to the *Stennis*."

"And that's why I'm here," James replied.

"And that's why I'm nervous." Rico shrugged when James threw a hard look at him. "Sir, I don't intend any disrespect, but at the risk of seeming insubordinate, I think I should tell you that this is my command, and I'm very protective of my men."

James could relate to that. Rico seemed like a pretty decent officer and, according to their intelligence, he had an impeccable service record. The same couldn't be said for a number of officers that came up like Rico, handed everything in life and never having to earn their own way. Sure, Rico may have been born with a silver spoon in his mouth, but it seemed in spite of that fact that Rico's father had been somewhat heavy-handed with Rico.

James put a hand on the officer's shoulder and flashed Rico his best smile. "And I wouldn't expect anything less, Commander. Look, you have nothing from me to worry about. I won't be here long. I'm going to interview those staff members who were on duty, and that's it. You set me up in a room with them where we can be comfortable, I'll ask my questions, and when I'm done I'll leave. You can even be present during questioning."

Rico seemed a bit incensed. "I didn't realize this was to be some sort of interrogation, sir."

"It's not an interrogation," James said. "So why don't you just relax, Commander?"

Of course, James knew that's exactly what it amounted to. He just couldn't see any reason for them to continue wasting their time with this. Still, he had already considered there might be something to Stony Man's theory, and so he'd pursue it as far as he could. The best thing he could hope for was that either Grimaldi or his fellow warriors would come up with something before that.

In one sense, James didn't agree with McCarter. They weren't running out of time; in his opinion, they were already out of time. James, just like all of his team members, realized that the lives of everyone on that ship might very well hang in the balance. What Phoenix Force did wouldn't make a lick of difference until they had some solid answers.

And Calvin James intended to do everything he could to get them.

JACK GRIMALDI HAD DECIDED to go after a few answers of his own. He couldn't understand why his suggestion that he might know some people that could provide intelligent information had brought such guffaws from the members of Phoenix Force, but he wasn't going to get hurt over it. Grimaldi had always considered himself the kind of guy to go after something he wanted, especially when others told him he couldn't have it. That only worked to strengthen his fierce mettle and resolve.

Grimaldi started his quest by using the secured satellite phone on the NEACP-4B to contact a friend he knew was working as a contract pilot to American businessmen out of Tokyo. Grimaldi was going on the hunch that the Aum Shinrikyo theory McCarter had mentioned was as good a place as any to start, and given the number of friends—guys as well as girls—that Grimaldi had in even the most remote ports of call around the world, he figured someone could tell him something he wanted to hear.

"What's the buzz?" Grimaldi asked Gerald "Crow" Vassar when the man answered his cell phone.

"Jack?" His voice sounded pleasantly surprised and Grimaldi relaxed some.

Grimaldi had served with Vassar in the same unit in Vietnam. Grimaldi was piloting Hueys at the time and Vassar had been performing forward recons in a fixed-wing Mohawk. The two had become friends and remained in touch, even with semi-regular visits, following the war. After Vassar's bitter divorce and loss of his only child to drugs, he decided to move to Tokyo and take a job with a startup company. His dreams were short-lived as the company folded within a year, but Vassar had never been one to let life get him down. The man bounced back quickly and was now making good money working for himself.

"How are things in the big T?" Grimaldi asked.

"Never been better," Vassar said. He added, "Hey, please tell me you're calling to say you're coming into town."

Grimaldi smiled into the phone. "Sorry, Ger, but I'm

actually here on business. I'm at layover on Marianas Naval Station."

"Yeah, I remember you were flying for some super-secret gig, like the Company or something like that," Vassar replied.

Grimaldi winced at first, not sure he liked that his friend had opted to discuss something that sensitive over an open line, but then he quickly dismissed his paranoia. They were on a secure line, after all, and he also knew that Vassar was a long time out of the game. Well, as long as the man didn't use his last name, Grimaldi knew he didn't have much to worry about.

"So to what do I owe the pleasure of this call?"

"I need some information and I need it quick," Grimaldi said.

"What, no flowers or serenading me first?" Vassar cracked.

"I'm sorry." Grimaldi chuckled, then turned serious again. "But it's important and I don't have a lot of time. Listen, some people, some friends of mine…they're in trouble."

Vassar's tone instantly became one of intensity coupled with concern. "What kind of trouble? Do you need some help, Jack? You know that any time you need anything you can call on me. I'll be there—"

"I know that, Ger, but that's not my issue right now," Grimaldi cut in. "I just need some information for now and I know you're probably the best guy to provide it."

"Okay, I'm all ears. Shoot."

"What do you know about the operations of the Aum Shinrikyo there in Tokyo?"

"The religious cult?" Vassar asked in a surprised tone. "Hell's bells, I don't know."

"Oh, come on, Gerald," Grimaldi replied. "I know you well enough to know that you're a savvy businessman. You fly people to and fro and you don't ask questions, and that can get you a long way in a city like Tokyo. And I happen to know that not every single job you've ever taken comes with the condition that there be no illegal goings-on. A pilot who keeps his mouth shut and minds his own business is a valuable commodity in a city like that. You probably get a couple of job offers now and then to come on privately."

It was Vassar's turn to laugh. "Two or three a week most of the time, but it's for that reason I can't do a lot of talking. You want me to get a bad rep?"

"Listen, I don't care about your rep. I care about the lives of my friends."

"Jack, we've been friends a long time. You know I wouldn't betray your confidences any more than I would betray those of one of my clients. And you definitely know that has nothing to do with our friendship. It's a business arrangement, you see? I fly them from point A to point B, they do their business, I fly them back to point A and they give me a check."

"Most of them deal in cash, and you know it," Grimaldi said. "And don't pretend you're all hurt by my very suggestion, Ger, because I know you much better than that."

Vassar sighed over the phone and Grimaldi knew he was slowly wearing the guy down. He hadn't wanted to call and insult his friend, and he certainly didn't want to lose him, but Grimaldi was quite aware that Vassar dealt with some pretty shady characters. And the fact that Vassar, an American and decorated war hero, was flying them, made it all the better for keeping up appearances. The laws in Japan had been written by the paranoid, as far as Grimaldi was concerned, and for Vassar to operate with the impunity he did and still maintain his reputation meant that more than few political and legal palms had been greased along the way. That took money, lots of it, and Grimaldi knew it wasn't coming from entirely legit business interests.

"I'm not trying to step on your tail," Grimaldi finally said. "You *know* I'm not, but I need your help and I'm asking you for information."

"Okay, what specifically do you want to know?"

"The Aum Shinrikyo," Grimaldi replied. "What's their story? Have you seen or heard anything unusual about their movements, or are you aware of any recent incidents involving them?"

"Like what?"

"Well, for example, have they been increasingly active?"

"Not really."

"What about unusual reports of gas attacks or press articles about them?"

"Nothing that I can recall off the top of my head," Vassar said.

"Come on, Gerald!" Grimaldi exclaimed.

"Oh, you come on, Jack," Vassar said. "What do you want me to say, huh? You want me to go blabbing their business to you? I've already told you I can't… Wait a minute."

"What?"

"You know, there *is* something, now that you mention it, that maybe can help you. And this was in one of the local papers."

"What is it?"

"There was a story about the police on Saipan."

"What kind of story?"

"Well, apparently they captured some local there who was apparently in communications with the Aum Shinrikyo," he said. "Possibly something to do with some kind of suspected arms smuggling."

A warning bell went off for Grimaldi. "That's perfect, Ger! That's exactly what I was looking for."

"You need help with some contacts there?"

"I'm not sure, yet," Grimaldi said. "But if I do, I'll be sure to get back to you."

And with that, he ended the call.

CHAPTER NINETEEN

Jack Grimaldi was enthused to receive the report from Stony Man, completely detailing the arrest of the suspected Aum Shinrikyo sympathizer on Saipan.

"According to Kurtzman's report," Grimaldi told McCarter, "the suspect's name is Mafnas Ogo."

"What the hell kind of name is that?" Hawkins drawled, obviously unable to resist the temptation of poking some fun.

A sour look from McCarter shut him up. The Briton returned his full attention to Grimaldi and asked, "What's the story with this guy?"

"Yeah," Manning added. "And what makes you think he's got anything to do with Able Team?"

"It makes perfect sense," Grimaldi replied, "if you think about it. And you have to admit that the timing's just too perfect to be mere coincidence." He noted the four blank looks and said, "Oh, come on, guys! What more do you need? Use your imaginations! Look, the

Stennis up and disappears without a trace along with forty-five hundred or so of its crew. Then we just happen upon an island swarming with armed Japanese terrorists, and *they* claim they're Aum Shinrikyo ordered to wait there by Jin Shukan. Now the police have a man in custody accused of potential smuggling for the Aum Shinrikyo. You have to admit that the timing's very odd."

"I don't have any doubt that this bloke is tied to the Aum Shinrikyo," McCarter said. "I'm just not sure how he can help us."

"I agree with David," Manning added. "You can't honestly think it's a good idea to waste time on a possible lead like this, can you? We're much better off continuing our search by air. We shouldn't even be here wasting our time. We should continue looking for Able."

McCarter noticed that Encizo was now sitting contemplatively and not saying a word. The Cuban was usually more involved in things like this, and enjoyed staying that way, and this sudden moment of silence or introspection or whatever it was disconcerted the Phoenix Force leader.

"What is it, Rafe?" Manning asked, noticing McCarter's stare.

Encizo looked at his friends and shook his head slowly. "I'm afraid I'd have to disagree with both of you on this one."

"Disagree?" McCarter said, scowling and apparently oblivious to the fact that he was openly showing he'd taken offense to the mere suggestion. "What do you mean?"

"I mean just that. I'm with Jack on this one."

Grimaldi smiled triumphantly.

Encizo leaned forward, placed the elbows of his crossed arms on the table and said, "First, I think he's right about this being no coincidence. Now either this Ogo is the real deal, and he was responsible for supplying materials and other stuff to those Aum Shinrikyo terrorists we found on the island, or the entire thing's an elaborate setup."

"And if it *is* a setup, then who masterminded the damn thing?" Hawkins interjected. "I mean, that had to be someone really thinking ahead."

"How so, mate?" McCarter asked.

"Well, they'd have to know we were going to hit that island, they'd have to know that at least one of the people there would talk, and they would've had to rig this whole arrest thing in order to draw our attention."

"And that's assuming that whoever was looking for the *Stennis* would have to know we'd take the bait," Encizo said. "It doesn't seem plausible to me, and it doesn't sound like it does to T.J., either."

Hawkins nodded in confirmation of Encizo's observation.

Encizo continued, "Plus, there's something else we haven't considered here. If the authorities on Saipan decide to question this Ogo, and he's got information on the *Stennis,* they could damn well kill him before he has a chance to talk. They're not known for being real kind to terrorists, and while a terrorist trained to resist torture doesn't say a whole lot, a dead terrorist says nothing at all."

Manning nodded. "That's a good point?"

"So what are you suggesting?" McCarter said. "Are you telling me we should go to Saipan and just whisk their bloody prisoner right out from under them? We wouldn't get within a hundred meters of him before they started blowing holes in us."

Grimaldi and everyone else at the table knew he was right. Saipan was a part of the Commonwealth of Northern Mariana Islands, which also included Tinian and Rota. While Saipan was part of a U.S. Commonwealth, they were still self-governed by their own legislature. They did not have the same rights as official states, but their voice was significant and, due to the money brought in from tourism, they had a fairly large pocketbook.

"Okay, so we ask them politely," Manning said.

"And if that doesn't work?" Hawkins inquired.

"Then we bloody well take him," McCarter said.

"So, where do we go from here?" Enciso asked.

McCarter turned to Grimaldi. "What do you know about law enforcement on the island?"

"As I recall, there are two main law-enforcement agencies, the Department of Public Safety and the Ports Authority. As I understand it, Ogo was caught by the Authority but they ended up turning him over to DPS. He's going to be taken back to the Japanese mainland at some point."

"When?" Enciso asked.

Grimaldi shrugged. "Nobody seems to know when...or even how for that matter."

"I wonder how easy it would be for Bear to get the information," McCarter said.

"I think that would depend on how badly we need it," Manning said.

"Why don't we just get the Oval Office to make a formal request for extradition to the U.S.?"

Manning shook his head and replied, "Hal wouldn't go for that, and neither would the Man."

"Why not?" Hawkins pressed.

It was Encizo who answered. "Because it would raise too much suspicion. Listen, if the local authorities there had so much as an inkling that the government wanted him extradited to the United States, they would immediately start asking a lot of uncomfortable questions that we wouldn't want to try to have to answer without a very thorough response prepared."

Hawkins nodding, realizing the wisdom of the older man's words.

"But we can at least all agree that this seems a bit too much for coincidence and that Ogo might actually have some useful information on the whereabouts of the *Stennis*," McCarter said. "Agreed?"

The rest of the group nodded.

"Then I guess we go to Saipan," McCarter said.

"Okay, but then what do we do once we get there?" Grimaldi asked.

"Yeah, and what about Cal?" Hawkins asked.

"Call him and tell him we're going to check out a lead and we'll be back for him." McCarter turned to Grimaldi and said, "And as far as what we do when we get there? Well, mate, we'll just have to make it up as we go along. I'm just bloody glad you made that call after all. Sorry we doubted you."

"No worries," Grimaldi said, waving it away and rising. "I'm going to go start preflight checks."

The pilot made his way to the cockpit where he found the copilot fast asleep in his chair. Grimaldi thought about waking the guy up, but at the last minute he changed his mind. What would it hurt to let him catch a few winks before takeoff? He could do the preflight himself—he'd done it a thousand times before and this was no different. The pilot climbed into his own seat and began the rundown.

He was pleased that McCarter had acknowledged his efforts. He'd put his best foot forward and it had paid off. Now all he had to do was ensure that his best foot forward didn't also mean his ass hung out in the breeze to get shot off. Only time would tell. And Grimaldi wondered for the very first time in his life if he hadn't bitten off a bit more than he could chew.

And if he could trust Gerald Vassar to keep quiet.

San Jose, Saipan

THE HOT, HUMID BREEZES were starting to pick up when Phoenix Force arrived at Saipan, and the morning sky had darkened with the threat of torrential rains. The weather in Saipan was like this most of the year. While it wasn't quite as hot as the neighboring Guam, there were definitely similarities in the weather, although it tended to be a bit less damp on the northern islands.

The four Phoenix Force members decided to take public transportation to the Criminal Justice Center in uptown San Jose rather than risk attracting attention. They boarded a shuttle bus from the airport that would take them to within a block of the CJC, having traded their black commando outfits for slacks and silk shirts that Grimaldi found for them inside the airport shops. They were wearing only pistols in holsters at the smalls of their backs.

Encizo and Manning were carrying their trusted Glock 26s, and Hawkins had a Beretta 93-R. McCarter had elected to bring a pistol he'd long been comfortable with, the Belgium-made Browning Power. Browning had originally designed the pistol in 1916 but it wasn't until just prior to World War II that it first saw service. It had gone through a number of improvements during that time, and been a popular side arm for British special forces. McCarter had a special attraction to the pistol and he never went anywhere without it.

"Okay, so what's the plan?" Encizo asked McCarter once they were off the bus and within walking distance of the CJC.

"Well, we have one of two options," the Briton replied. "We can either see if they'll let us talk to him voluntarily or we figure out the most opportune time to snatch him."

"Yeah, but you already said that they're not just going to let us walk out of here with him," Hawkins reminded McCarter.

The Briton appeared to consider that, then said, "Maybe we don't need to take him. Maybe we just need him to give us the information we're looking for."

"Well then, I suppose time's wasting," Manning said.

The foursome continued to the justice center and when they were within view of the door, Encizo stopped the group. "You know, it's going to look just a little suspicious all four of us walking in there. Maybe two of us should wait out here."

The rest of the group nodded their agreement, but before anyone could say a word McCarter said, "All right, Gary and T.J. will go, and Rafe and I will have your back."

"And just what exactly would you like me to tell them?" Manning asked.

"Use your imagination, mate." McCarter grinned, patting his friend's arm and saying, "You'll think of something."

Manning gestured for Hawkins to follow and the two men waited for a break in traffic before crossing the street. It was still early, so the automobile traffic was light and there wasn't a single pedestrian visible anywhere. Manning checked his watch and noted it was just a few minutes shy of eight o'clock. He started to ascend the stairs and then thought better of it, turning and motioning to McCarter and Encizo that they were okay.

Encizo shook his head. "Uh-oh."

"What in the bloody hell is he up to now?" McCarter added.

The only thing the two men could do is stand there and watch, which suddenly started to become more of an effort as the first droplets of rain began to fall. The sky was continuing to darken, and both men knew that if it started pouring, they were going to have a very long wait. They watched with interest as Manning and Hawkins entered a leather shop a few doors down from the CJC.

A minute later the men emerged from the shop, each of them carrying a briefcase.

"What are they trying to look like, businessman?" Encizo asked.

"They look more like tourists with briefcases to me," McCarter replied. But then he suddenly understood and a smile came to his face.

THE TWO CASUALLY DRESSED men pushed through the front door of the CJC carrying briefcases.

Sergeant Raul Ducamp had been on duty all night, and he never usually saw types like this during the graveyard shift. Whoever they were, they had arrived at an hour much earlier than that to which Ducamp was accustomed. In fact, the only contact he had with the public involved his officers and any lawbreakers brought in for processing during the night.

There wasn't usually that much trouble in Saipan. The two biggest problems were the tourists and the alcoholism, which ran rampant. Of course, Ducamp wouldn't have been surprised by anything less; at least not for Saipan. Ducamp had been born and raised on the island, and he knew the area like the back of his hand. His father and mother, French-Polish immigrants from the war, had decided to move to the islands and make their fortune in opening a restaurant dedicated to tourism. Neither of them had lived long enough to see their dream come to fruition.

But Ducamp had decided to stay rather than attempt to emigrate to the United States. After all, he'd been born here and he intended to die here, and unlike most men at twenty-six, he already held a responsible position in a job he loved.

"Can I help you?" he asked the men.

The taller man, who appeared to be the leader of the pair, had dark blond hair. He looked like he was in pretty good shape considering that the briefcase betrayed he was some kind of stuffed white shirt who obviously thought he was better than everyone else. He flashed an identification badge, barely giving Ducamp time to look at it.

"We're here to represent Mr. Ogo."

"Yes, and we'd like to see him right away," the younger man added. This one was maybe an inch shorter.

"I see," Ducamp said, dutifully reaching for a paper roster tacked to a clipboard. He handed it over to them, indicating they had to sign in. "Are you counsel?"

The taller man nodded as he immediately scrawled his signature on the paper and then directed for his partner to do the same. He then replied, "Yes, Sergeant. We understand that our client has been here for some time now and has been denied his right to lawful representation."

"He needs two attorneys just for smuggling charge?" Ducamp asked.

"That's none of your concern," the taller man answered as the other man signed. "But if you must know, *I* am Mister Ogo's counsel, and this is my para-legal who will be assisting me in preparing the case."

The second man smiled, his looks almost boyish as he said, "I'm studying for my degree. I've been with this firm for many years now. This is my first big case before I graduate."

Ducamp nodded, trying to pretend as if he were in-terested, even though he couldn't have cared less about that. He gave the printed names and signatures only a cursory glance, then handed each of them a visitor's pass. Once they had affixed the tags to their jackets, Ducamp led them down a hallway off the main recep-tion area.

"Oh, I forgot to ask you guys if you have the order from the magistrate's office assigning you as counsel. You're going to need it if you plan on accompanying him to Tokyo."

"Tokyo?" the attorney echoed. "Nobody said anything about him going to Tokyo. When did this come about?"

Ducamp had to laugh at that one. Bureaucrats: they were capable of screwing up a one-car funeral. Here they had dragged this poor lout from bed at what had probably amounted to some ungodly hour, and didn't even bother to tell him that they would be moving the prisoner to Tokyo in a few hours. Ducamp couldn't help but look at the attorney with amusement.

"You mean, you didn't know anything about him being moved to Tokyo?"

"No," the attorney replied. "I'm not licensed to practice in Japan."

"Oh, you won't have to worry about that," Ducamp replied. "He'll be tried here for smuggling. But he's going to spend a week in Tokyo under interrogation by the Japanese authorities. I guess he's tied up some how with that band of religious fanatics called the Aum Shinrikyo."

"Goodness gracious," the paralegal said. "Why, aren't they like…terrorists?"

"Depends on who you ask," Ducamp said, making eye contact with the paralegal as they turned a corner that led them to a series of rooms just off the main cell wing. "We've never had any trouble with them before on the island."

"Do tell," the attorney said, nodding with interest.

"Well, that's why the Japanese authorities are so interested in talking with him. They thought it was pretty interesting that he would be participating in smuggling."

"I wonder why that's so interesting to them," the attorney replied.

"We wondered, too, until they told us that their intelligence leads say they've been operating with increasing frequency in Tokyo and Osaka, and there's been a lot of traffic through the rumor channels. Not to mention the fact that they've allegedly stepped up operations throughout Micronesia, although this is the first real evidence we've had to substantiate such claims."

"So you're saying he's only going to Tokyo on loan?"

Ducamp laughed. "Of course. He was caught smuggling off the island of Saipan and he'll be tried here on Saipan. We take care of ourselves."

"Actually, I just moved my practice here less than a year ago," the attorney replied.

"Where you from originally?"

"Well, I, um…I was practicing law on the Mariana Naval Station down in Guam."

"You're ex-military?" Ducamp asked, impressed by the attorney's revelation.

"Well, not exactly. I mean, yes, I am a veteran, but I wasn't military counsel, I was attached as a civilian consultant to the Navy's Civilian Contracts and Legal Affairs Office."

"Hmm…so it's been awhile since you've seen the inside of a courtroom then."

Manning smiled sheepishly and said, "It's been some time on a case of this kind, yes."

Ducamp snorted and said, "Then you've got your work cut out for you. And I'll just bet you're wondering right now how you got so lucky. Right?"

"The thought had crossed my mind."

Ducamp nodded knowingly, although he didn't *really* know. Well, the attorneys had turned out to be friendly enough, but he still didn't much care for their kind. There was just something about most lawyers that was too squeamish. Ducamp even entertained a brief notion that the attorney and his paralegal shared a bit more than just a professional relationship, but he decided to keep such a suggestion to himself. What they did on their own time was their business, just as long as they didn't expect him to get involved.

They arrived at the containment area right off the

main cell block where they provided chairs for visits and a few rooms for legal consultations.

"You'll need to let Officer Wong here search your persons with a wand. I'll go get Ogo for you.'"

He started to turn but stopped when he saw the attorney cling to the briefcase that Wong tried to take off of him.

"I'm sorry, sir, but you are going to have to let me search that," Wong said.

"No, I'm the one who's sorry. Attorney-client privilege."

"Look, Counselor," Ducamp began, stepping forward, "if you want to meet with Ogo, then your person and belongings are subject to search."

"What if we leave our briefcases out here in your custody and let you wand us down?" the paralegal asked. "Does that seem like a reasonable compromise?"

Ducamp looked at Wong, who was probing him with pleading eyes, messaging that he didn't want any trouble. Ducamp finally nodded his approval, then turned and headed for the cell block.

Bureaucrats, Ducamp thought.

CHAPTER TWENTY

Mafnas Ogo certainly wasn't what Gary Manning had expected.

The Aum Shinrikyo smuggler was short and stocky, with long dark hair and a pudgy face. He also had a massive sweating problem, something that both the Phoenix Force warriors noticed immediately once he was brought in.

The thing that brought the most relief to Manning was that the police had not argued the point of going through their briefcases. Only Hawkins's quick thinking had prevented a potential disaster. If the police had opened those briefcases—or even if they decided to jimmy the locks now—they would find their pistols and that would bring the curtain down on the show. So far, they seemed to be okay.

For nearly a minute Manning and Hawkins simply studied Ogo. He was a definite a case for the history books, and the kind of man that could puzzle scientists for aeons. By any standards, he was a rather disgusting creature. As they watched him, he huffed and puffed—obviously out of shape and possibly even from some as yet unknown ailment like emphysema—and felt it wasn't the least bit inappropriate to belch or break wind whenever it suited him.

Manning determined immediately that they were going to have to make this quick.

"So, I hear you lawyer for me," Ogo said in broken English.

Ogo's voice was low and hoarse and difficult to understand since the man seemed incapable of enunciating his words.

"Not really," Manning said. "That's just the story we told to get inside so we could talk to you."

Surprise flashed across Ogo's face and for a moment he started to open his mouth to scream but as he did, Hawkins wrapped a muscular forearm around his throat and used a free elbow to push Ogo's head forward. The scream died out to a choking sound, and Hawkins eased off just enough pressure to keep the guy from passing out.

Manning placed both hands on the table and bent over directly across from Ogo so his eyes and the smuggler's eyes were level. "Now listen to me carefully. You're going to answer our questions, and you're not going to cry out. If you refuse to answer our questions, my friend here will deal out a little more of that. If you lie to me, more of the same. And if you attempt to raise any sort of warning, I'll kill you myself before anyone can get here to help you. Understand?"

The man tried to nod, but Hawkins still held him tightly enough that the guy couldn't shake his head. He simply gasped and gaped at Manning, and that was enough to tell the Canadian that Ogo wouldn't cause any trouble. He nodded to Hawkins, who released his hold.

Ogo began to wheeze for air and Hawkins stepped back just enough to avoid the smell. It was obvious he hadn't even wanted to touch the slimeball, but there hadn't been another choice. Manning knew they would have undoubtedly been wasting their time if they had tried to apply less direct methods. Despite his slovenly and unkempt appearance, Ogo was still a terrorist with ties to some very dangerous individuals. The Aum Shinrikyo was an extremist group from what Manning could tell, and they weren't shy about killing if it furthered their goals.

"Less than eight hours ago," Manning began, "an American aircraft carrier disappeared in the middle of the Pacific Ocean. What happened to it?"

"I no know," Ogo said, barely able to get it out as he rubbed his throat and fought to catch his breath.

Manning sighed, then turned to Hawkins and nodded. The younger man started to step forward but Ogo immediately protested, holding up his hands and begging Manning to keep Hawkins away. Manning raised one hand toward his partner, then looked at Ogo expectantly.

"I tell truth. I no know what happened to it," Ogo continued. "I know only where it going."

"And where is that? Where is it going?" Manning probed.

"I no tell you unless you make deal," Ogo said.

"Oh, for God's sake, let's just beat it out of him," Hawkins said.

"Hold up a sec," Manning said, taking a seat in front of the terrorist-smuggler and folding his arms. "I'm interested in what he has to say. Go ahead, Ogo, we're listening. What kind of deal do you want?"

"I tell you, but you take me out here first," Ogo replied.

"No way," Manning said, shaking his head. "There's no way they'd let us take you out of here without a fight, and we're not about to drop the hammer on the cops here."

"Yeah, we're on their side actually, in case you hadn't noticed."

"You tell lie," Ogo observed. "You need lie to get in here. You no friends of police here. You enemy, like me."

Manning could feel his face darken a shade or two. Quietly he said, "We're nothing like you. You thrive on the death of others for no other pleasure than enforcing your own will on others. Don't think for one minute that we're anything like that. No, I don't believe we can make a deal with you. We don't negotiate with terrorists."

Manning looked at Hawkins, who started forward, and Ogo began squealing in outrage. This time, though, Manning chose not to stop his friend. The younger man had been a champion wrestler for his Delta Force team in the Army, and while Hawkins wasn't the biggest dude in the world, Manning knew he was as strong as an ox. Some correct pressure applied in the correct places and he knew that Ogo would sing like a canary. But even as Hawkins continued to apply more pressure, Ogo didn't look any more conciliatory. It looked plain and simple like he was going to die.

Finally, Manning ordered Hawkins to cease, and as Ogo bent over Manning said, "This whole thing is pretty pointless. Are you sure that you don't want to reconsider answering my questions."

Ogo didn't answer for the longest time, and when he was finally strong enough to raise his head, he was staring daggers at Manning. The big Canadian simply sat there in stony silence, unaffected by Ogo's weak attempts to intimidate him. Manning had come up against much more powerful and terrible men and survived; he wasn't about to cower under this simpleton's attempt at a baleful stare.

"You know deal I ask," Ogo finally said. "You no deal, I no talk."

Manning considered the statement for a long while, but he finally had to agree that it was only the most logical course. He said, "All right, Ogo, I'll tell you what. I'll get with my people and see what they have to say. When are they taking you out of here?"

"I leave two hour," Ogo replied. "Go to Tokyo."

"Yeah, I know where they're taking you to." Manning rose and added, "If we decide to do this, then you had best be ready when we bring the hammer down."

"I be ready," Ogo said with a nod.

"And one other thing," Manning said, turning to Ogo as he reached the door. "Once we pull you out, *if* we pull you out, you're going to tell us exactly where the hell they've taken that aircraft carrier. Or you'll die the longest and most painful death I can think of."

And with that, Manning and Hawkins left the room.

As they were outside and collecting their briefcases from Wong, Ducamp made an appearance. They made some additional small talk with the guy for a minute as he escorted them to the exit, and as they reached the door Manning figured it was an opportune moment to get down to brass tacks.

"So, our client says that he's leaving later this morning," Manning said in as off handed fashion as he could manage.

"Yes," Ducamp replied, but it didn't seem he wanted to offer any more information than that.

Manning decided to risk pressing him. "Is it going to be soon? If so, I need to get home and packed. I don't know if I have a lot of time."

"You really don't have time," Ducamp said, looking at his watch. "I'm actually going off shift in about twenty minutes. I don't know *exactly* what time he leaves, but I can tell you that it's sometime this morning."

"I see," Manning replied.

"Er, do you know if it will be possible for one of us to accompany him to Tokyo?"

"Now that you'd have to ask the magistrate," Ducamp said. "I don't know anyone except him who can authorize that. I don't believe the day commander has the authority, and I know I certainly do not."

"All right, well thank you for your cooperation, Sergeant."

Ducamp nodded as he escorted them to the front door and parted with, "Good luck."

"I HATE TO ADMIT IT, but it seems like this Ogo has us over a barrel," Manning told McCarter and Encizo.

"Maybe," McCarter said, "but you're guaranteeing me that you didn't promise him we'd get him away from the police."

"I'm positive, David," Manning replied a little irritably.

McCarter shook it off as crankiness from being overtired. They were all tired, and McCarter had to admit that even *he* was beginning to feel a little punchy. This would take careful coordination. If they were going to effect this pseudo-rescue on Ogo, they were going to have to take some extra precautions to insure that nobody got hurt, particularly not the police or their prize.

"It would be fairly easy to keep bystanders out of it," Encizo said, as if reading McCarter's thoughts.

"We're taking an awful bloody risk," McCarter replied. "I'm not sure if I like this, gents."

"Well, we don't have a lot of time to make a decision and get a plan in place, so we probably need to decide quickly, boys," Hawkins said.

"He's right," Manning observed, looking McCarter square in the eyes and adding, "It's your call, boss."

McCarter mulled it over another minute. Brognola would be furious if they mucked it up. But he'd been even angrier if he found out they'd had a chance to find the *Stennis*. As far as he was concerned, their mission took precedence over U.S. public relations or some perceived error in judgment. What McCarter didn't have time for was to sit around in self-debate and wait so long to take action that he suddenly found himself unable to do the same. Sitting just on the other side of the walls of that center was a man who could very well hold the key to finding his friends, and McCarter wasn't about to let that opportunity slip away.

"Let's do it," he finally said.

THEY WOULD BE OPERATING on very little intelligence and a whole lot of dumb luck. Phoenix Force had no idea how the DPS would transport their prisoner, or at what time, which meant that from the moment McCarter decided to go with a rescue plan they had to put the place under continuous surveillance. Hawkins had noticed what looked like a door leading out to a garage of some kind, an observation he'd made through a small window on the heavy metal door.

McCarter stayed with Encizo so the pair could watch both sides of the building. He sent Hawkins back to the NEACP to alert Grimaldi that a sudden takeoff would probably be required, even without a flight control clearance. Manning had gone hunting for the closest car rental dealership.

The minutes seemed to tick by agonizingly. McCarter had warned the rest of Phoenix Force that they were to take all precautions in dealing with the police officers. It seemed the best plan would be to attempt the takedown of the transport vehicle and retrieval of Ogo as they arrived at the airport. To attempt to do it any earlier posed too many risks, both in the sense of by-standers that could get in their way as well as the pos-sibility they'd encounter the entire police force assigned to San Jose. There wasn't a lot of action in this town, and there was no question that all available law-en-forcement personnel would get involved if it came to pitched battle.

Not that McCarter planned to let that happen.

In some respects, McCarter wished they had Yakov Katzenelenbogen around to assist them, even if in only an advisory capacity. He missed the veteran soldier, an aged but entirely capable warrior who had fallen to the hands of terrorist Salim Zuhayr. Katz's death had reminded David McCarter of the mortality of each and every one of them. For a while—just for a short time—he'd forgotten what sacrifice really meant; he'd flirted with death, even cheated it on occasion, and he'd survived time and again. But now it was different, and McCarter realized that nothing lasted forever.

Manning's voice cut through his thoughts, filling the earpiece McCarter wore as he sat at a café directly across from the gated sally port exit. McCarter wasn't sure who or even what to look for, but he acknowledged Manning, who had announced he was positioned on the front side of the building. Encizo had taken up a similar view, and McCarter cautioned them both to stay cool and be as nonchalant as possible.

"It's likely if they bring him out, it will be from where I'm at."

While waiting for something to go down, McCarter had memorized a map of every street between there and the airport, and also taken note of the possible routes they could have taken. Fortunately, there were only two ways to the airport, and one of them was considerably longer than the other, so McCarter was counting on them taking the fastest and most direct route. Not to mention the fact they would probably do that anyway. After all, they had no reason to think that anybody could want Ogo that badly, or that other than a few locals even knew who he was or what was going on.

McCarter turned his full attention from the magazine he'd been pretending to read and watched as the garage door began to rise on the sally port. McCarter bent his head, turning it slightly away and directing his voice to the tiny microphone set on the inside of his collar.

"Get set, blokes. This could be it."

The door finished opening and a large white van slowly emerged from the sally port. McCarter couldn't make out faces inside, but he could tell there were only three in the van, two officers in the front seat and a prisoner in back. As the van rolled past his observation point, McCarter squinted to see if he could make out a face through the tinted window, but he couldn't tell if it was Ogo or not.

He had to make a decision, and to hell with it. If he was wrong, he was wrong.

"I think they're on the move," McCarter said. "Turned south on the Mariana Parkway."

"That would be in the direction of the airport," Encizo said.

"Move out," McCarter said as he dashed from his seat and sprinted down the sidewalk in the same direction the van had gone. It was stopped by a traffic signal, so McCarter decided to cross the street to the rear and head up on the opposite side. There was less a chance the van's passengers would notice him.

"I've got half the crew," Manning said, indicating that Encizo was now in the car and they were mobile. "What's your location?"

McCarter gave it to him.

"Hang tight, boss, we're thirty seconds away."

The Briton was beginning to get impatient, checking his watch, then glancing between the traffic signal and the van. Fortunately he was in such a position where he could keep an eye on the van but they wouldn't notice him. A few of the passerby saw his behavior and spared him a odd glance or two, but nobody really bothered to stop and make an official inquiry. Perhaps it was the hardened warning glance McCarter showed them any time they seemed to display more than simple curiosity.

The light went green and McCarter watched helplessly as the van started to move. He looked down the cross street and still didn't see Manning or the vehicle. Not that he would have known what it looked like anyway.

"Damn, where are you?" McCarter asked.

A squeal of tires right in front of him and a reply indicating as much from Encizo allayed his fears.

McCarter jumped into the front seat of the two-door, banging his knees on the dash. The pain jolted up his legs from his knees and the Briton let out a furious stream of expletives.

"You couldn't do better than a bloody compact?" he demanded.

"Hey, this was all they had," Manning said as he whipped away from the curve and burned the red light to turn onto the street McCarter had indicated.

The Briton switched to another band—this one long-range—and keyed the transceiver. "Team Leader to Eagle One, do you copy?"

"Loud and clear, Team Leader," Grimaldi replied instantaneously.

"We're behind the package and getting ready to receive it. Did you get the information I requested?"

"Copy, Team Leader," Grimaldi said. "It's Cathay Pacific flight 1742, departing at eleven sharp from Terminal Two."

"Received and acknowledged," McCarter replied. "Be ready and waiting."

"Roger and out here," Grimaldi said.

McCarter nodded with satisfaction and then checked his watch. He then looked over at Manning, who was concentrating on his driving. He was about to ask the big Canadian if he'd ditched the license tags in the trunk as instructed, but he decided against it. Manning had enough to worry about.

Within fifteen minutes they were seeing signs for the airport terminal. McCarter checked his pistol's load, insuring that the weapon was on safe and there wasn't a round in the chamber. His instructions had been clear to the rest of the team as well: no conflict. The last thing they needed was a firefight with Saipan police.

They reached the terminal Grimaldi had indicated and the van suddenly slowed and started for the curb.

"We don't move until Ogo's out and Manning's confirmed it."

"This two-seater isn't going to make it easy for a guy of his size," Manning said.

"We'll have to take our chances," McCarter replied.

"It's not too late to back out," Encizo suggested.

"No way."

Manning stopped the vehicle, then opened his door and immediately went EVA. Encizo came out Manning's side, giving himself a little extra time. Only the front seat passenger bailed from the van and as he started to open the side sliding door, McCarter got an idea.

"Forget the car," he told Manning and Encizo. "If it's Ogo inside, we'll take the bloody van."

The men nodded and Ogo was barely out of the van before Manning confirmed it. The men of Phoenix Force rushed the van, Encizo aiming his pistol at the guard, while McCarter pushed Ogo back inside the van and Manning went about the task of keeping the driver at bay. There were a few shouts as panicked onlookers watched the action, shocked by what they were witnessing.

A moment later Encizo and Manning were inside, the Canadian at the wheel once more, and McCarter felt the smooth acceleration of the van as they got the hell out

of there. McCarter wondered if Manning knew where
to go, but decided to let him and Encizo worry about
that. The Briton turned and studied Ogo, who was
staring at him with wide eyes.

"Well now, Ogo. We have a lot to talk about,"
McCarter said with a frosty smile.

But Mafnas Ogo only nodded.

CHAPTER TWENTY-ONE

Pacific Ocean

Hamid Adil stood in the center of the smoking ruins of the encampment and surveyed his surroundings with complete disgust. He could hardly believe his eyes. Someone had destroyed everything, *everything* that he had worked so hard to achieve. All of their equipment had been sabotaged. The tents were nothing but smoldering piles of debris, and reports were already coming in of bodies having been found in the nearby woods.

At least this debacle had been Shukan's sacrifice and not his own, so Adil took some solace in that thought. Still, this would set back their plans considerably, and he would seek some type of recompense for himself and his honor, and most assuredly for the honor of Ansar al-Islam.

One of Shukan's aides rushed to the Japanese scientist and spoke in tones too soft for Adil to hear, and

Shukan then replied. After watching nearly a full minute of this, Adil couldn't take it any longer.

"Stop your whispering!" Adil demanded. "What is going on?"

The aide looked startled, his eyes going wide when he realized Adil was shouting at him and his master. Shukan put one hand on the man's shoulder, obviously as a reassuring gesture, then whispered something in the man's ear. The aide rushed away, obviously intent on accomplishing some errand on which Shukan had obviously sent him. Adil knew it was probably more of a way of sheltering the young, inexperienced aide against Adil's violent temper.

"He was merely reporting to me that he noticed the generators were sabotaged," Shukan said, marching up next to Adil and taking in the scene in a fashion similar to what Adil had.

"Sabotaged how?" Adil asked.

"Apparently someone drained the tanks on the diesel-powered generators by cutting the fuel lines."

Adil nodded, understanding the simplicity and yet cleverness of the tactic. Whoever discovered the group had cut the power to the generators, using it as a diversion to draw their quarry into the open. Of course, they had apparently sent someone to investigate and that individual was taken by surprise. Somehow, though, the incursion had culminated into a battle.

"Something puzzles me in all of this," Adil said quietly to Budai.

"What is it?"

"A significant force would have been required to destroy that many men."

"Possibly," Budai said, "unless they happened to take them by surprise."

"I think it was they who ended up surprised. This force, whoever they are, did not just happen upon this base of operations, and they certainly weren't expecting to find a significantly armed force inhabiting this particular island. That's one of the reasons it was selected."

"What is your point, please?" Shukan's voice said behind them.

Adil whirled, about to lash out, infuriated that this minuscule subhuman had found the gall to eavesdrop on their conversation. Adil was learning to like Shukan less by the second, and he wasn't sure—particularly in light of these latest circumstances—how long he would be able to continue to tolerate him. He didn't trust Shukan, and the carnage now in front of his eyes gave him even less of a reason.

"What?" he snapped.

"I asked what your point was in pointing out that whoever attacked my people had not picked it randomly."

"My point is that someone is searching for us," Adil said, choosing his words carefully and holding back a very strong desire to reach out and strangle this very temporary ally.

"Well, of course they're searching for us!" Shukan cried. "Did you think that they would just give up their ship and its precious cargo as lost?"

"I thought nothing of the sort," Adil said. "And I find it insulting that you would even make such a suggestion."

"Spare me your attempts to make me believe you have any sensibilities," Shukan replied haughtily. "I've seen the way that you look at me. Do you think that I'm too stupid to discern a desire to murder in another man's eyes?"

He gestured to the area with a sweeping motion and continued, "You have lost nothing here. The loss is mine, and I expected that this might occur. I knew that United States would send someone after us, and that they would scour every part of the ocean until they found us. The people left here were sacrificial lambs and expected to throw them off the trail. And it would seem my ruse worked."

"So you sent a group of your people, those who trusted you, to their deaths," Adil said. He looked at Budai and purposely embellished the accusation with, "At least we can now see what kind of an ally we have. We might not as had any at all."

"You're still alive, are you not?" Shukan reminded him. "And whoever is aboard the *Stennis* stands little chance of accomplishing their mission, now that I have the ship under total control."

Adil could hardly believe what he was hearing from this spineless egomaniac. He was actually taking credit for having kept the resistors on the *Stennis* at bay, when it was his men that were slowly pinning them down, and closing the gap to the point where they would find and eradicate every last one of them. To think that Shukan was actually taking credit for this made him want to reach out and strangle the very life from the man.

"How dare you take credit for keeping at bay the terrorists aboard that ship," Adil said, not caring to hide the loathing in his voice. "It is *my* men who have died trying to keep the ship secure, and it's *my* men who have ensured that the ship continues toward its destination. We had a deal for you to deliver me here with the plane, and your people would assist me. Look at this place! Now what of your plans? Do you intend to leave additional men?"

"I never intended to leave you here with the X-51," Shukan replied.

"What do you mean?" From the corner of his eye, Adil could see that Budai had put his hands in a position that would allow him rapid access to his side arm. If there were a moment that Shukan would attempt to betray them, this would be it.

But instead Shukan smiled and said, "As I've already explained once, those individuals out there were a decoy. I had intelligence from those over me that each individual here had in some way performed in a less than satisfactory matter. We knew that this would prove an excellent way of disposing of them. They had orders to defend this location, and that I would return."

"You sacrificed them then," Budai noted.

"Only for the greater good," Shukan replied in a nonchalant fashion. "Yours as well as mine, and as you've already pointed out, there was no loss to you. I hope, gentlemen, that this will serve as an object lesson to you both that I am dedicated to completing my mission under any circumstances."

"We didn't need any such lesson," Adil pointed out. "And if we had, we certainly would not have needed you to teach it to us. From the very beginning of our agreement you have done a number of things that we would consider less than considerate, and you have repeatedly demonstrated that you are not a man to be trusted. I shall insure that my superiors discuss this with yours following completion of this mission."

"Phah!" Shukan said, waving him away and cackling loudly. "Do you think that my superiors really care about me? Or better even, that your superiors care about you?"

"How dare you—" Budai began.

"They care nothing for you! We're simply pawns in this little game. Why else do you think that the Aum Shinrikyo would have dared allied themselves with a group like yours? They are in this for profit. Do you know what my mission is? I am to take this vessel to our secret base and totally dismantle it. The nuclear reactors will be used to create bombs that we will use to make a statement heard throughout our world, and the remainder will be sold on the black markets."

"You don't honestly think that the U.S. government will let that happen, do you?" Adil asked disbelievingly. "The Americans are hopelessly fixated on their material possessions, and this is especially true on their military equipment. They will hunt you down and destroy you before you have a chance to disassemble a ship of that size. You mark my words."

"I will have faith in the expertise of my men and my superiors, and believe that the power of nature and the cosmic forces of our universe will do the rest, and provide me with the divine wisdom I require to complete my mission."

"There is only one force, and that is Allah," Adil said. "And I do not wish to hear any more about your pagan beliefs or ceremonies. I do not impart my religious viewpoints upon you, and I ask that you not attempt to contaminate my views or the views of any of my men with mention of your heathen rituals."

"If your men were more confident in this Allah of yours, perhaps you would not have to be so worried about their conversion." Shukan let a smile drift across his face.

Adil wanted to jam the muzzle of his pistol through those two rows of gleaming white teeth and break them out of Shukan's filthy mouth. Then he would pull the trigger and send Shukan straight to where he belonged: hell. Instead, Adil made a show of looking at his watch.

"It is time for us to return," he said. "Any more time spent out here could result in our discovery. We must proceed to this base of yours."

"It is not far...perhaps another hour of travel, if we proceed at maximum speed."

"Isn't there a risk of them discovering our wake?"

"There is always a risk, but I foresee it as a minor one. We do not have any more time, as you say. We must go."

And while Hamid Adil loathed having to spend one more minute with Shukan, he knew that the scientist was right. But he also knew that this wasn't over. Before he left, he would make sure that Jin Shukan died a slow and horrible death.

THE FIRST THING that Rosario Blancanales had noticed was that the ship had slowed. He could sense it more than hear it, as the bowels of the *Stennis* this far forward provided a significant noise barrier to the sounds of engines, screws or the ocean waves crashing against her as she displaced tons of water per second. Still, he knew that for some unknown reason, her captors had decided to slow her down.

He and his men had decided to hide in large supply closet for a quick break. Twice they had heard patrols move past them, but fortunately it sounded as if they were in a hurry, and so they hadn't bothered to stop and open the closet door. What Blancanales couldn't be sure of is how much longer their luck would hold out.

"What is it, Rose?" Hearst asked.

Blancanales recovered from his brief moment of transcendental meditation and turned to see the black man's eyes wide with concern and, perhaps, just a twinkle of fear.

"What's that? Oh, nothing. I'm just starting to feel the pressure of lots of shooting and very little sleep."

"Yeah, that's been a downside to this," Hearst remarked. "The enemy out there, whoever it is, probably has us outnumbered twenty or thirty to one, which means they can work in shifts. Us, we just have to pretend to be one big, happy family of insomniacs."

Blancanales couldn't resist smiling. Actually, the more he got to know Hearst the more he liked the young Marine sergeant. Hearst seemed well-spoken and educated, but he also had a very astute and biting sense of humor, not unlike David McCarter's own uncanny wit. The two would have probably hit it off under other circumstances, but as those didn't exist at this point it didn't much matter.

Hearst was certainly right about one thing, and that was the odds. It was sure as hell one big ship, but that didn't mean they could avoid the patrols forever. Eventually, they were going to run into their enemies and then it would be do-or-die time. The other thing bothering Blancanales was the sickness that had spread rampantly through the crew. While there was definitely an indication of decreased resistance in this part of the ship—and there were terrorist units on the move because so far they had avoided two of them—he was confident they wouldn't be able to hide forever. Eventually, they would either end up running out of ammunition or just get caught, and then it would be curtains for Able Team and the end to any chance of communicating with Stony Man.

"How much farther do you think it is to our quarters?" Blancanales asked Hearst.

"We don't have too much farther to go," Hearst replied. "The problem isn't going to be getting to quarters, as much as it will be the armory and the medical ward. I know your friend Irons there is in charge, but I sure wish he hadn't agreed with Dr. Danner about risking our hides to get to the infirmary."

"It might have seemed like a bad decision at the time," Blancanales said gently, "but I think Ironman's got it figured right. At least, the movement of roving enemy patrols toward the aft part of the ship is certainly a good indication."

"Yeah, so maybe getting to your equipment and the armory are good objectives, but what about lugging a bunch of heavy-ass medical references back to the doctor. Isn't the risk too great?"

"No risk should be too great when it means you can save the lives of hundreds...perhaps even thousands."

The Able Team warrior could see something change in Hearst's expression, even in the very poor light peaking under the closed doors of the closet, but he let his words soak in. There was no point in trying to add or detract from what he'd said now. He could see that Hearst was looking to the faces of the sailors with them, attempting to capture their reaction, and Blancanales realized that maybe Hearst had thought the comments were made for the purpose of embarrassing him.

"That wasn't my intention to make that sound like it did," Blancanales said quickly. "I'm sorry about that, Hearst. You deserve a bit more respect than that."

"Forget it. I knew what you meant."

"All right, rest time's up. Let's get moving."

The men rose, the Able Team commando opening the door just enough to insure that the corridor was clear and then encouraging the men to follow him. They were halfway down the hallway when trouble appeared. A group of at least a dozen terrorists were heading up the corridor toward them, and Blancanales saw the winking muzzles a millisecond before he heard the shots reverberating down the hallway.

"Down!" he ordered his team, but he knew it was too late even as he said it.

The first of the terrorist rounds caught Johnstone square in the chest, ripping through his heart and lungs. The petty officer staggered backward, tripping over a small protrusion from the wall and tumbling into Gornich and Norris. He coughed violently, audible even above the din of autofire. He turned his head a moment later as a glob of pink frothy blood landed on the deck.

Blancanales heard a shout coming from Hearst and risked a backward glance to the see the man's face gleaming with bits of Gornich's flesh, blood and brains. He'd apparently taken a round to the skull while trying to help Johnstone. Hearst pushed Norris down and that was when he took the first round. It punched clean through his throat, and his head snapped back with complete surprise.

Blancanales turned his head in the direction of the terrorists, opening up on them with full force. His first volley took a pair of terrorists in the chest, the tight but varied fire slamming them into each other. Blancanales figured his only chance of defeating a force that size was getting Norris to help. He could feel a body lying next to him, and he turned toward who he assumed was Norris. Instead he saw the bloodied profile of Hearst.

Apparently, through some twist of fate or luck or whatever one might call it, Hearst had lived through the ordeal. He was lying at an angle on his side, holding his Spectre M-4 ahead of him and shooting in the direction of enemy movement. Blood bubbled from a wound in his throat, a vicious tear with ragged flesh hanging, and a quick inspection showed the exit wound was just above the left shoulder blade. Somehow, Blancanales realized, the tough son of a bitch was hanging in there.

Instead of worrying about it further, he started to focus his fire on the terrorists. The heavy firestorm being laid down by Hearst was working well enough to keep most of the terrorists behind cover. Blancanales took careful aim on the area, waiting until a terrorist exposed himself long enough for a clean shot. The first one he caught with a short burst to the skull, the man's brains dousing those around him with a gory spray as the rounds took off the top of his skull.

The second terrorist fell with a quartet of white-hot lead to the midsection. The terrorist screamed, tossing his weapon aside as he noticed the sudden condition of his stomach. The scream died in his throat and Blancanales's fifth shot went through the terrorist's open mouth and blew out the back of his head.

The Able Team commando took a break long enough to notice that Norris, the only one who hadn't been armed and ironically had been the one to survive, had now joined the fray. The young seaman had procured the pistols of both his deceased friends and was dealing out his own brand of revenge. He fired the pistols alternately, taking one of the terrorists with a clean shot through the chest. The terrorist dropped to his knees, triggering his weapon and putting six rounds in the ceiling.

This isn't working, he thought. Over the noise and sounds of ricochets he said, "There are too many of them. We have to fall back!"

Norris stopped shooting long enough to try to register what Blancanales had said, then returned to firing at the terrorists. He had to admire the guy's guts. He knew that Norris wasn't being disobedient. This was his way of providing cover so Blancanales could escape with Hearst. But the young sergeant had other ideas as he slid his weapon to Norris, then grabbed the lapel of the Able Team warrior's fatigue blouse.

He reached out his hand, palm up.

Blancanales knew what it meant: the crazy bastard wanted one of his grenades. "No way, Hearst, I'm taking us all out of here alive."

Hearst furiously shook his head, then slapped one hand over his throat. With a hoarse whisper, he rasped, "Let…it…be…brother."

Blancanales could feel the agony welling up in his gut, but he knew that Hearst was right. The wound wasn't necessarily fatal, provided that they could treat it right away, but in this case that just wasn't going to be possible. He knew they would either have to back-track to the infirmary with Hearst, or leave him hidden securely somewhere—which wasn't likely to last—in which case he'd bleed to death.

Blancanales reached into his pocket and withdrew one of the M-33 frags. He pulled the pin, pressed the frag into Hearst's palm, then patted the young man's head. He turned and roared at Norris to retreat, climbing to his feet and expending the last of one magazine upon his withdrawal.

As they rounded a far corner in the cavernous hallways within the bowels of the ship and heard the grenade explode, Blancanales struggled to keep his vision clear. He mentally recited a prayer on the run.

CHAPTER TWENTY-TWO

Carl Lyons contemplated the door less than five feet ahead of him. Beyond that door was the engine room, and the one chance he thought they might have of bringing the terrorists' plans to a grinding halt. At first, Lyons had only wanted the terrorists to believe that they were going to try to sabotage the engine room, but now he was actually considering doing something to sabotage the ship's systems. Schwarz was trying to talk him out of it.

"You're crazy, Ironman," Schwarz told him. "You try going in there and blowing something up and you'll likely get your ass shot off and ours, too. It doesn't make any sense."

"Well, we can't stand around here with stinky-thumb syndrome while Blancanales and the rest of them make a break for it," Lyons said. "After all, we're only assuming that this plan will work. We don't really know it will, and worst-case scenario is that Pol's walking into a deathtrap."

"And what if he is?" Schwarz argued. "What could we really do about it at this point, huh? What could anybody do about it? Now I think the best thing we can do is keep as many of these buggers distracted for as long as we possibly can, and hope that buys Blancanales enough time to get his mission accomplished."

Lyons knew it was sound advice, although he didn't want to admit it. He was letting his emotions get the better of him, something he'd found himself doing with increasing frequency as of late, and that sure as hell wasn't going to help their situation. Of course he knew Schwarz was right—the place would be very heavily guarded and they had neither the ammunition nor the manpower to combat that kind of force.

"So what's our plan?" Sizemore chimed in.

"To stay alive and keep our asses from getting shot off," Lyons grumbled.

"Well, we can't just stand around here waiting for them to pick us off," Sizemore snapped.

"Keep your shirt on," Lyons told him with a warning look.

Sizemore turned to Schwarz, hoping for some help, but the electronics wizard simply shook his head as a way of warning the young petty officer not to push his luck. Lyons caught the exchange but pretended that he hadn't seen it. He knew that Sizemore was just reacting to the pressure. They had just seen one of their comrades cut down like it was nothing, and that wasn't an easy thing for guys like that to see. They weren't used to watching a friend shot to death, and they certainly weren't used to all of the elements of combat—the deafening gunfire and heat and smell of blood and misery.

"My friend's right, though," Lyons continued as if nothing had happened. "We'll need to make some noise if we've got a snowball's chance in hell of drawing the terrorists away the other team."

"What do you suggest, sir?" Lloyd Benson asked.

"Heh-heh... 'sir,'" Schwarz muttered. "Did you hear that? He actually called you 'sir.'"

Lyons scowled although it was obvious from the look that there was no true malice behind. "All right, quit the clowning. Now, you want to help me figure this one out?"

Schwarz shrugged. "This is your ball game. I'm fresh out of ideas."

Lyons considered their situation a moment. This wasn't going exactly as he planned, and before the whole thing got dicked up it was clear he'd have to come up with some quick answers. Since he'd taken out the remainder of those pursuers with a grenade, they hadn't encountered a single terrorist. That was odd indeed, considering that the closer they got to the engine room the thicker resistance should have been.

And then something dawned on him, and Lyons felt like being sick. He looked around conspiratorially and said, "I think we're in trouble."

"What is it?" Sizemore asked.

"We were so focused on pulling the terrorists away from Pol and his crew that I never stopped to consider the possibility we were walking into our own trap."

Schwarz looked perplexed.

"Don't you get it?" Lyons said. "We've walked into a stinger's nest, and I'm not sure there's any way out of it. This was a trap from the beginning. They were just hoping we'd get this far, so they could simply tighten it up."

"Like insects caught in a web. We're into the center of it before we realize we're in trouble."

Lyons nodded.

"Let's vamoose," Schwarz said.

The two men turned and saw that they were already too late. A group of four heavily armed terrorists were already approaching from one corridor, their weapons out and ready for action. Lyons let off a short, steady burst from his AKSU as he yelled at the others to head in the opposite direction. He followed them a moment later, rounding the corner just in time to avoid a maelstrom of autofire. The three of them had their backs pressed the wall and Lyons quickly mimicked them.

"They've upgraded to rifles," Lyons told Schwarz breathlessly.

"Probably saving the best for last," Schwarz quipped.

"We'll split up," Lyons said. "You take Sizemore, I'll take Benson. We'll meet back in the infirmary in—" he glanced at his watch "—twenty-five minutes. If we don't show up, you can assume we're dead and continue as planned. Same deal goes both ways. Cool?"

Schwarz nodded and shook his hand. "Good luck."

"You, too," Lyons replied, then gestured down the adjoining corridor they were using for cover. "Now you guys go that way, and we'll keep their heads down until you have a good lead."

Schwarz looked as if he wanted to argue, but then appeared to change his mind. It wouldn't have done him any good. Lyons had made a decision and everyone was just going to live with it. Combat wasn't the time to discuss issues in a committee, and Schwarz had learned long ago that it was the soldier who followed orders that stayed alive.

Lyons dashed across the corridor so he and Benson could pin them down from both directions. Once he was safely across, he nodded to Schwarz who turned and gestured for Sizemore to follow him. Lyons watched the two men retreat, unable to quell the sudden feeling of sadness and dread that overcame him. He silently wished the pair the best, then turned his attention to the task at hand.

"Keep your weapon low, and take only your surest targets," Lyons told Benson. "We're getting low on ammo, so make each round count. Do you understand?"

Benson nodded, the fierce resolve evident in his dark eyes. Lyons felt a pang of regret at the thought of losing Ericsson. They might already have seen the death of enough sailors this day, and it was entirely possible he was about to send another one to a similar fate. But at least these men had died with honor, and they didn't have to go down without a fight. Lyons would have much rather preferred going down fighting for what he believed in than lying in bed and rotting away from old age.

The first target presented itself and Benson dealt with

the terrorist, dispatching him with a single round to the chest. The terrorist flew backward from the impact, twisting somewhat before landing on his side as his weapon clattered to the deck. Lyons took the next one as he approached, causing the remaining pair behind him to take cover. The Able Team leader squeezed the trigger twice, catching the terrorist with a double-tap to the stomach. The rounds ripped through liver, stomach and exited at the kidneys. Dark stains immediately formed on the terrorists belly from the blood and at the crotch where his bladder released.

The other pair of terrorists now returned fire from cover, hosing the corridor with a wash of 7.62 mm slugs. The distinctive reports from the weapons told Lyons immediately that the terrorists were carrying AK-74s. The Able Team leader knelt, keeping his back pressed to the wall. The terrorists weren't really attempting to hit them as much as they were trying to keep their heads down. Lyons had seen the tactic before and he knew what it meant. They were stalling, waiting for something, and Lyons wanted to know what.

A quick glance to the right gave him his answer. Another quartet of terrorists was moving quietly toward him in leapfrog pattern up that adjoining corridor. Just as Lyons had suspected, the terrorists were trying to box them in. Clever, but it wasn't going to work this time. Lyons removed the one remaining M-33 fragmentation grenade from his pocket and primed it.

"Benson, get going!" Lyons commanded, shouting to be heard over the cacophony of weapons fire.

Benson obeyed immediately, jumping to his feet and heading down the corridor in the direction that Schwarz and Sizemore had gone. Lyons snap-aimed the AKSU one-handed and squeezed off a few bursts, keeping heads down as he considered the situation. He didn't want Benson getting too far ahead of him. The present situation made it quite apparent that there was safety in numbers.

Lyons kicked off another 3-round burst, striking a lucky hit on one of the terrorists. The rounds punched through the terrorist's face, which caused his head to explode like a grapefruit under a sledgehammer. Blood and bone erupted from the impact, spraying the walls around him. The terrorist dropped to the deck like a stone.

Lyons then exposed himself to the pair that remained in the adjoining hallway and lobbed the M-33 in their direction. The terrorists watched with interest as the grenade sailed toward them, and as it drew closer it became apparent these weren't rocks Lyons was throwing at them. The Able Team leader didn't wait around long enough to see curiosity turn to surprise on the terrorists' faces, or to see the devastating effects the blast had on the dumbfounded pair.

Even as the grenade exploded, he was already moving to catch up with Benson.

SCHWARZ FIGURED THAT he and his friends were in trouble.

So far, he and Sizemore had managed to avoid the enemy, but that kind of luck wasn't going to hold out forever. The terrorists had thrown a net around the area to catch some very little fish in a big pond, and Schwarz and Lyons had allowed themselves to swim into it. They had also led three others into that trap, one of whom was now deceased.

As he continued up the steps that would lead to the upper deck, Schwarz could hear Sizemore wheezing and trying to keep up with him. The younger man was a bit on the paunchy side, and unaccustomed to sudden bursts of energy, whereas Schwarz had been training for and doing this kind of thing most of his life.

He emerged from the stairwell onto the deck and immediately encountered resistance. A pair of terrorists were standing a mere ten feet away, their backs to him, and they heard the warrior's entrance. The hardmen reached for the their slung weapons, attempting to acquire a target, but Schwarz dropped to one knee and whipped his Glock 26 into play, which he'd taken back from Ericsson. The pistol seemed to jump to life in his hand of its own accord even as he squeezed the trigger.

The first terrorist took a 9 mm Parabellum round in the upper lip, the bone-crunching force of it smashing out his teeth and shredding his tongue. The bullet didn't actually penetrate the skull or vital brain stem, but it did cause the tongue to fall back into the terrorist's throat, and he fell to his knees with his hands on his neck. The second terrorist met a similar fate, but this shot was instantly fatal. The bullet ripped through the terrorist's aorta as it punched through his chest and exited below his left shoulder blade. He spun with the impact, letting out a cry of surprise before the sudden loss of blood overtook him. The terrorist slumped to the deck.

As Schwarz assisted Sizemore out of the hole and onto the deck, he could hear more terrorists approaching their position. "That did it."

He pushed Sizemore toward the nearest cover, then found some of his own. The Able Team electronics wizard switched the Glock for the AKSU. He quickly checked the action and verified the weapon was in battery, and then he popped over the top of the crate he was using for cover and acquired his first target in his sights. Schwarz waited until the terrorist was close enough before taking the shot. He knew once he unloaded on this guy, his position would be marked.

He squeezed the trigger. Flame spit from the muzzle of the AKSU as the high-velocity rounds struck their target. The terrorist's chest imploded under the assault of the AKSU slugs, and only a gaping hole remained where one of his lungs had been pulverized. A look of painful shock and terror spread across the terrorist's face as he realized he was going to die. A moment later, it fully registered as he toppled to the deck.

Schwarz turned to see Sizemore now had the Spectre M-4 up and ready for targets. The next terrorist appeared immediately behind where the first had fallen, and Sizemore took him. The young sailor was quickly learning, as he held the weapon tight and kept it low, now firing in short bursts rather than sustained ones. His aim was getting better, too. One of the bursts went from stomach to sternum and finally into the head. The terrorists convulsed under the 9 mm slugs slamming into him, and then dropped to the deck.

The two men stood ready to hold their position, even as they heard what sounded like an army of screaming terrorists headed straight for them.

BLANCANALES SLID TO a stop at the intersection of two corridors and peered around the corner: the area in front of their quarters was empty. He waited another minute, deciding that haste makes waste, and in his line of work it couldn't have been truer. The corridor remained silent, and he finally pulled his head back and frowned, trying to decide if it was truly clear or if they were walking into a trap.

"What is it?" Norris whispered. "What do you see?"

"Nothing."

Norris started to move past him. "Well, then, let's just—"

Blancanales grabbed him by the lapel of his uniform and pushed him back against the wall. "Hold up there, junior."

"But you just said you didn't see anything."

"Yeah, I did. And that's what bothers me." He mulled it over a minute, then said, "Listen, you stay here. I'm going to head down to our quarters and make sure it's clear. You watch for my signal. Got it?"

When Norris nodded, Blancanales took a deep breath and moved into the corridor. He moved quickly down its length, crossing one foot in front of the other so that he could move silent but briskly. It was a technique he'd learned during a training exercise—something that T. J. Hawkins had taught all of them. Hawkins had learned the fancy footwork while serving in the Army with Delta Force. The Able Team commando reached the door unmolested, checked his surroundings again, then fished a key from his pocket. He opened the door quietly and pushed inside without hesitation.

Once he'd cleared the quarters he leaned out the door and signaled to Norris. The sailor walked quickly down the hallway, keeping as close to the wall as he could; as soon as Norris was inside, Blancanales closed and locked the door. The Able Team warrior then turned and began lugging suitcases onto his bunk. He opened the first one and tossed clothes aside. There was a false bottom to the suitcase and he zipped it out. Beneath the clothes were three brand-new Glock 26s and a hundred rounds of 135-grain 9 mm Parabellum ammunition along with spare clips.

"Wow, you guys weren't kidding around."

"Start loading those clips with that ammo," Blancanales said in way of response. He handed the Spectre M-4 and the spare clip he'd lifted off one of the terrorists and added, "And don't forget the SMGs."

He turned and went to a wall locker, procured a second key for the padlock and opened the locker. Inside he found what Schwarz liked to call his "little black bag of tricks," which was actually an aluminum case lined with a thin layer of lead to prevent the contents from being exposed by X-ray machines. Blancanales brought

the case up to another bunk and after entering the electronic pass code for each latch, he opened it.

Inside the case were two boxes, each one about
9 inches cubed. They were flat and unremarkable on the
outside, but inside were sensitive electronics that could
transmit considerable ranges. Blancanales opened the
first box by removing an ink pen and pressing a recessed
button on the bottom of the box. The lid popped up
obediently. Inside was a coiled red wire capped with an
aluminum connector. He opened the second block in
like fashion, then plugged the connector from the first
box into a receptacle built into the second.

Once he'd completed his work, Blancanales reached
into the first box and raised a telescoping antenna that
reached nearly a foot high. He adjusted the settings on
the first box by using a pen to push another recessed
button in a specific sequence. Each series was actually
a sequence of numbers that translated to the placement
of ones and zeroes within a specific, sixteen-digit
format. This acted as a digital signature to tell Stony
Man that the signal was in fact being transmitted by
Able Team and not some enemy force hoping to lull
them into a trap.

Norris watched the entire process with fascination
until he could resist no longer. "What is that thing?"

"They're called comm-cubes. They're made of a
highly specialized material that's capable of boosting
and retransmitting signals. The first box acts as the
transmitter and the second, when keyed properly, acts
like a repeater to boost the signal."

"You mean you can actually talk to someone with that thing? Like a cell phone or something?"

Blancanales couldn't resist a smile. "Or something."

Actually he couldn't speak to anyone over the comm-cubes but it would definitely send out a homing signal on a special frequency owned by Stony Man, and licensed to some construction company according to FCC records.

"If this signal gets to its intended recipients, it won't be too long before help arrives. The only thing I can't be sure of is whether it can penetrate whatever kind of electronic net the terrorists have thrown over this ship."

"Well, if we—" Norris began, but Blancanales cut him off with a shushing noise.

"Did you hear that?" he asked.

"Hear what? Is someone coming?" Norris said, abandoning the weapons and swinging the muzzle of the Spectre in the direction of the door.

"No, but if I heard what I just think I've heard, we could be in for a lot of trouble."

"Okay, so what did you think you just heard?"

Blancanales didn't answer right away. He couldn't be absolutely sure, but he could have sworn he heard the noise, and he knew that if it was the same thing he thought it was, that this wasn't the first time he'd heard it. What he wasn't sure of was exactly what it meant. It was possible that Lyons had somehow succeeded in his crazy plan, and perhaps it was a sign that the terrorists had reached some intended destination. In either case, it wasn't in the original cards and if they had managed

to find some way to secure the ship then that meant
Lyons was going to need all the help he could.

Finally he said, "The engines just shut down. I think
we've stopped."

CHAPTER TWENTY-THREE

Somewhere over the Pacific Ocean

"We know where they might be, Hal," David McCarter announced.

"Are you putting me on?" Brognola replied.

"I might tease you about a lot of things, but definitely not something like that, gov'."

It looked for just a moment as if there was a flash of irritation on Brognola's face, but it was difficult to tell over the grainy resolution of the LCD. They were communicating with them from more than three thousand miles away, and there was about a five-second delay, so it wasn't easy to tie expressions to words, given that delay. Still, McCarter wasn't going to worry about it—Brognola's skin was plenty thick.

"Where are they?"

"We suspect on an island about 195 nautical miles from our present position. Jack's got the throttle wide open, so we should be there within the hour."

Price had been sitting next to Brognola, visible through the wide LCD monitor, but she now spoke up for the first time since making contact. "What do you mean, you 'suspect on an island'?"

McCarter hadn't really wanted to talk about that part of it, but he knew it was going to come out eventually. There wasn't anything they could have done about it once they had committed to snatching Mafnas Ogo from the authorities. Of course, they had happily turned him over to the Navy, advising them that he was caught trying to escape and that they should turn him over to the locals on Guam for extradition back to Saipan. Still, it wasn't going to look good.

McCarter quickly ran down what had occurred, how they had used role camouflage to contact Ogo, and how he'd told them about his mission to the island. With each passing minute, McCarter could see a vein in Brognola's forehead begin to bulge a little more, and he was sure that there would be some kind of flak to come out of it down the line.

When he'd finished his narrative, McCarter said, "I didn't really want to do it this way, but I didn't have any other choice. We were wasting time investigating personnel at the base on Guam. This made more sense."

When Brognola just sat and stared daggers at him, Price picked up the slack. "You could very well have created more trouble than you might know. I'm sure the President will have to issue some formal apologies for your, well, indiscretions we'll call them. But under the circumstances, I think the Man will understand."

"Next time you decide to pull a stunt like that," Brognola interjected, "I'd like to hear about it before you do it. Is that clear?"

McCarter nodded. "Like crystal, Hal."

Brognola nodded, then sighed deeply and said, "Okay, so what do you need from us?"

"Well, we don't know exactly what we're going to run into yet, but I could use some support from the *Fletcher* if it's still in that area. Some forward reconnaissance wouldn't hurt at all and some heavy firepower if it's needed."

"We'll notify Navy Command out of Pearl Harbor immediately," Brognola said. "Anything else?"

"We'll need some massive rescue personnel ready, as well. Our little bird told us that they neutralized the crew by contaminating the food and water supplies with ricin."

"We had wondered before if that wouldn't come into it," Price said. "We had intelligence that this isn't the first time terrorists, particularly the Ansar al-Islam, have experimented with ricin. We also considered the possibility that they had neutralized them with sarin gas, since it seems to be a very popular method of attack by the Aum Shinrikyo."

"Did your informant include any details on the reasons behind all of this?"

"As I believe the Yank saying goes, 'He sang like a canary,'" McCarter replied, giving them his best cheesy grin. "Sometime back, I guess Ansar al-Islam discovered through their contacts that Shukan was working on a secret project for the government. They didn't know exactly what it was, but they started digging around and I guess they somehow discovered that he was an Aum Shinrikyo sympathizer.

They then contacted some people inside and worked their way up the chain until they found out that the Aum Shinrikyo was quickly losing ground due to a lack of funding. Of course, they have a considerable amount of support through the al Qaeda network, so they agreed to pay top dollar for the prize and in return they would provide the *Stennis* and all of its equipment to the Aum Shinrikyo."

"Seems like a consolation prize compared to the X-51," Price said. "There's no way they'll be able to sell the *Stennis* on the open market. And most terrorist organizations aren't stupid enough to try stealing nuclear material from America. There's entirely too much risk involved."

"No, they can't sell the *Stennis* on the open market, but they can sell off her parts," Brognola observed. "And there's no question that the two nuclear power engines aboard that unit could provide enough of the significant raw material required to construct at least one atomic bomb if not several."

"Bingo," McCarter said. "Our little friend didn't really know what Ansar al-Islam had planned for the X-51, but he was sure that Shukan planned on dismantling the *Stennis* and scattering sales across the planet."

Brognola nodded. "It makes sense. They could refine many of the raw materials, and those things they sell outright could easily be modified until it was damn near impossible to tell if it came from the ship."

"Well, the military does serialize a vast majority of their parts," Price said.

"Nothing some acid etching couldn't take care of, Barb," McCarter replied.

"What did he know about this island?" Brognola inquired. "And how on earth didn't someone figure out what they were doing there by now?"

"As I understand, there are some natural barriers, huge caverns of some kind, where they planned on storing the ship. Once they're within that kind of geography, it would be virtually impossible to discover them."

Price nodded her agreement with McCarter, and said to Brognola, "David has a point. There are any number of uncharted and explored island chains between the Pacific West Coast and Micronesia. There's no telling what's on many of these islands, and even if the island surfaces had been explored, there's no reason to believe that there aren't numerous above-water caverns cut out from years of erosion or natural geological formations resulting from volcanic activity."

"It's still a significant undertaking," Brognola said.

"But not impossible," McCarter reminded them.

Brognola shook his head and replied, "I don't know. They would need some significant equipment to completely disassemble an aircraft carrier. Something about this tells me we still don't have the whole story."

"Well, you'll have the complete story soon enough," McCarter replied.

"What's your plan?"

"We doubt that they'll have any significant observation or counterintelligence measures on the island exterior. That kind of equipment has the potential to cause too much attention. They would want to leave the terrain as natural as possible."

Brognola nodded. "Makes sense. Go on."

"Our parachuting onto the island where we found that Aum Shinrikyo detachment seemed to go well, so we're going to try the same thing. My one concern is having some backup, since Jack can't exactly land and extract us and it's going to take some time to put down and then get back to the *Fletcher.* Doing it this way, we can move as a reconnaissance force and wait for reinforcements."

"It also serves as a good contingency since you don't know what kind of force you're going to be up against."

"We're estimating a force of somewhere around one hundred, give or take. There's no question these terrorists would have needed at least that many in order to maintain control of the ship, regardless of the fact they could have neutralized the majority of the crew."

"What about Able Team?" Price asked. "Did Ogo know anything about them?"

McCarter shook his head, a bit frustrated that he didn't have a better answer. "We can't know what their situation is until we get there. They might be alive, they might be dead. I won't feed you a bloody line and say that they're okay. It's just too early to tell, Barb."

Price nodded somberly.

"I want you to watch yourselves there," Brognola said. "Don't take any chances. Aaron tells me you've already delivered the coordinates of this island, so as soon as we know position and ETA of the *Fletcher,* we'll advise. But whatever the hell you do, don't take chances. You received my special instructions from Jack?"

McCarter nodded, cringing internally at the fact Brognola had mentioned something like that in front of the others. McCarter knew he'd have some explaining to do when the call ended. He wondered if he could drag it out long enough to reach the island so he wouldn't have to answer any uncomfortable questions."

"All right, then, I guess I don't have to impart to you how important the next six hours will be. It could be perhaps one of the most important assignments we've ever given you. Good luck."

"And come back to us alive," Price replied. "*All* of you. That's an order."

McCarter winked at her and said, "You can bet on it, Barb."

After the transmission ended, McCarter wheeled in the chair to see four expectant faces staring back at him. He knew it would come to this, and he'd hoped that his friends were so focused on the situation ahead that Brognola's statement would have simply sailed over their heads. No such luck—there was no putting one over on these guys.

Finally after a long silence Encizo said, "Well it seems nobody else is going to ask, so I guess I will. What are these 'special instructions' that Hal's talking about?"

McCarter decided to come right out with it. "We're packing a portable nuke. I had orders that if we found the crew dead and there didn't seem to be any hope of getting the *Stennis* back, we were to blow the bloody thing sky high and it would be put off to an accident."

A dead, weighty silence followed and McCarter found four pairs of eyes staring at him incredulously.

"Listen, I don't like it any more than you do, but those were my orders. I didn't even know about this until after we were airborne, so let's just say this is between Hal and me."

"You should have told us," James said.

"But I chose not to," McCarter said. "And if you want to hold that against me then you can go ahead and bloody well do it. But it was my call and I made it, and I'm not going to apologize for it, right or wrong."

None of them said another word, as the subject was now closed. And although the compartment had four other men in it, David McCarter was suddenly feeling quite alone.

Pacific Ocean

AS ROSARIO BLANCANALES and Jerry Norris made their way topside, the Able Team warrior became increasingly confident that he'd been right about the ship stopping. Still, the pair moved through the corridors of the *Stennis* with reserve, diligently watchful for trouble. Blancanales had learned over his many years in hostile situations that the enemy was most likely to do the least predictable thing, and he'd already promised himself that he wasn't going to die on this mission.

Due to their cautious movements, it took them nearly a half hour to reach the infirmary. With the assistance of Norris, Blancanales quickly located the medical texts needed by Dr. Danner, and slid them into a large pack he'd brought from Able Team's quarters. Once they were secure, Norris led him in the direction of the armory.

Blancanales checked his watch and realized they were quickly running out of time. The lives of thousands of sailors depended on him and Norris getting back to the infirmary alive with the medical books. Danner had insisted that with them he would be able to discover the reason for the shipwide sickness that had afflicted more than ninety-five percent of the crew, and perhaps come up with a cure.

In his opinion, the terrorists had made a critical error, and Blancanales was now hoping that Able Team would be able to capitalize on that and exploit the terrorists' plans. Whoever was running the show—whether Shukan or Ansar al-Islam or some other unknown entity—had solely counted on being able to take control of the ship based on whatever ailment the crew was suffering. That was a risky plan, and assumed that they would account for everyone. But blind dumb luck had prevailed for Able Team, and a few were well enough to fight. Unfortunately, they had been required to pay the ultimate sacrifice to save others.

Now, to Rosario Blancanales, each and every one of those men was truly a hero.

Once more to his surprise, they reached their objective without interference. He tried to remember not to let it spook him. After all, it had been Lyons's hope all the time to draw the troops away from the stern of the

ship. Blancanaleshad to admire him for being right;
Lyons was one of the ballsiest guys he had ever known.
Even from his earliest days as a young L.A.P.D. cop,
Lyons had been known to be a tough, no-nonsense kind
of guy.

Norris started to step toward the armory cage but
Blancanales grabbed his shoulder and held him firm.

"Hold up there a second, junior."

"What?"

"You go rushing into things that fast and you'll end
up blowing you *and* me to hell and back, not to mention
what kind of damage those munitions could cause under
the extreme heat."

"What are you talking about?"

"You don't see them?"

Norris looked back at the cage and stared for the
longest time, his eyes roving up and down, left to right
and back again, looking for something that was so
obvious to Blancanales. Actually, the Able Team warrior
was a little offended that the terrorists would have
insulted his intelligence so badly as to believe he
wouldn't suspect the armory was booby-trapped."

Norris finally shrugged. "I don't see what you're
talking about."

"All right, a quick lesson. First, it obviously didn't
occur to you that this armory is unguarded."

"Yeah, it occurred to me," Norris replied.

"When? Just now, when I mentioned it?"

Norris looked sheepish and began, "Well—"

"Never mind, it's not important. Look there, toward the top and bottom of the cage. See that long grayish line?"

Norris squinted his eyes before replying, "Oh yeah, I *do* see it now. Hell, I couldn't even tell because it blends into the color of the wall."

"That's by design," Blancanales replied. "What you're looking at there is det cord, my friend. Enough to cut that metal in two at the seams and blow that cage right off its mounts."

"Well, how are we going to get to it then?"

"By disarming the switch." The Able Team warrior reached into his pocket and withdrew one of the multipurpose tools he'd mooched from Schwarz's bag of tricks. The tool was made of solid, die-cast stainless steel treated to be nonconductive. It was about six-and-one-half-inches long when fully extended. Buried into the handle frames were hidden a pocketknife, pair of wire snips, carbide-coated file, serrated sheepsfoot blade and three screwdrivers.

Blancanales moved to the door. The simplest and most effective way of tripping the explosives would be to open the door. Thus far, the terrorists had proved themselves as rather predictable, so he was counting on a consistency in that pattern. He only hoped that the switch wasn't electronic, since he didn't have Schwarz here to lend expertise. Fate or something else was with him when he found a very simple mercury switch fashioned crudely to the gate, designed to go off when the gate was open and the switch was tripped.

He studied the three wires, finally nodded with satisfaction that the red and white intertwined wires was the mark, and quickly used the wire snips to cut through it. All remained calm. He then used the pliers to carefully extract the mercury switch and he held it up for Norris's inspection.

"Now if you had opened that door, we'd be little more than dust."

"Is it safe?"

Blancanales grinned. "I hope so. And let me guess, you don't have a key."

Norris shook his head.

"Guess will do this the old-fashioned way," Blancanales replied as he turned, drew his Glock 26 and put three rounds through the lock mechanism.

It did the trick. Soon, the pair was packing a score of M-16 A-3s with spare magazines. They loaded up on all the extra ammo and small arms they could carry, each with about four pistols and two assault rifles, and then left the armory and headed in the direction of the infirmary.

More than fifty minutes elapsed before they made topside, climbing up a ladder within a framed ladder well and opening a trapdoor at a stern portion of the flight deck. They took refuge near the left rear landing gear of an EA-6B Prowler. Blancanales was only slightly familiar with the sleek aircraft. He looked at Norris with as hopeful an expression as he could muster.

"Don't suppose you know how to fly this thing, huh?"

Norris shook his head. "Don't I wish. That would bump me up a few pay levels."

It was no joke. The Prowler was considered a protector of the rest of the eighty or so aircraft that compromised Carrier Wing Seven, and skilled pilots operated the plane. The EA-6B Prowler contained a vast array of electronic countermeasures equipment, as well as surveillance and jammers. It was capable of playing havoc with enemy aircraft while taking measures that ensured smooth coordination during aerial dogfights or air to surface attacks. It could even send phantom signals capable of throwing off antiaircraft guns and missiles.

A moment later they heard weaponsfire. "That would probably be our party over there. Shall we join them?"

"Lead the way," Norris said. "I fee like I'm ready for anything. I want some payback for my shipmates."

"Then let's go get it."

The pair rose simultaneously, then Blancanales took the lead crossing the deck as fast as he could while keeping low. They completed their journey and made it to a relative area of safety at the base of the bridge tower. The Able Team commando listened a moment longer, realizing that the battle had become more fierce. If his friends were trapped by the terrorists, they wouldn't fair well for long, given their limited ammunition. He also didn't know what their strength was, or whether they had lost anyone along the way, but if they had taken as many casualties as his team, they were in serious trouble.

"Follow me."

The Able Team warrior stood and entered a nearby door leading into the tower. He quickly located a set of steps and began to ascend them three at time. He passed the first tier, continuing on the second, and then navigated his way through the interior until he emerged onto the catwalk that led to open air.

Blancanales looked down and took in the horrific scene. Lyons, Gadgets and two of the three men they had taken with them were hunkered down behind aluminum deck crates filled with storage equipment while a band of terrorists slowly but steadily advanced on their position.

As he brought his M-16 A-3 into target acquisition, Blancanales shouted, "Here's your chance for payback!"

It was a reminder to the terrorists below that they had chosen to hijack the wrong ship.

CHAPTER TWENTY-FOUR

"Rasam, we have a situation," one of the guards reported.

Budai and Adil turned from the technical information Shukan had provided them on the X-51. Budai cringed at the thought that one of his men had used his first name in front of Adil, but a quick look at his master confirmed that Adil had been too engrossed to give the minor infraction any thought. He deeply respected Adil, but sometimes his friend could take things a bit too far.

"What do you mean 'a situation'?" Budai demanded. "Stop speaking in riddles and start giving me information. What have you to report?"

Shukan's voice interjected, "I would enjoy hearing more specifics about whatever you're discussing, given the worried looks on your face, but I would appreciate it if you spoke English while I'm here. It is somewhat of an inferior language, as I'm sure you'll agree, but it is neutral to us all."

VANISHING POINT

The man looked uncertainly at Shukan, then sought approval in his leader's eyes. Budai merely nodded and the man continued his report in English. "I do not have all the possible details yet, but our men are engaged in heavy combat with armed men on the flight deck."

"I would like to know how a few men with some pistols could possibly constitute a heavy combat situation," Shukan chimed in, not giving either Adil or Budai a chance to respond.

The Japanese scientist turned to Adil. "What's the meaning of this, Hamid? I thought you guaranteed the security of our operations. You assured me that you could take care of this paltry force of Americans, and now it would seem that they have duped you once again."

"Begging your pardon," the young Ansar al-Islam warrior who'd delivered the report said, "but our people say this is not a small force. It's estimated that there are at least six and possibly more men firing on our people, and they are *very* heavily armed. Assault rifles and grenades were reported."

Budai's face began to redden and he kept looking toward Adil, waiting for the nearly inevitable cursing and berating he was certain to undergo, but to his surprise it never came. Adil sighed, exchanged haughty glances with Shukan, then turned to face his trusted commander.

"Rasam, you are the most brilliant military tactician I have ever known," Adil said quietly in Kurmanji, which Budai knew to be an act of spite against Shukan.

"I expect you will deal with this situation effectively and permanently. Not a single American can leave this ship alive. Am I making myself clear?"

"Yes, of course it is clear, Hamid," Budai said with a bow. "I shall deal with this immediately."

"Then go forth to victory, my friend," Adil replied, putting a hand on his long-time friend's shoulder. "And may Allah be with you."

"May he be with us all, brother," Budai said politely, and then he turned and ordered his man to lead the way.

The two made their way down the long corridor and jogged in the direction of a stairwell that would lead them up to the deck adjoining the ship's tower. Budai had decided that he could direct the battle best from above, which would also present a more secure post from which to command. He wasn't in any way afraid to the die for their holy cause, but a leader couldn't lead if he was dead, and effective leaders were difficult to replace. Budai had no intention of leaving his master unsecured.

In a single respect, he had to admit that Shukan was right. The Americans were a paltry force, and the reports he'd received—some he'd chosen to keep from Hamid for the time being—were disturbing. He'd lost nearly a third of their force or more to just a few tenacious Americans. These men that had been providing Shukan's security, the same men that he understood first "rescued" Shukan, had proved to be formidable enemies. They had demonstrated an uncanny ability to move around the ship and avoid the constant patrols, and when it came to confrontation he understood they were fearless, inventive and resourceful. But Budai reminded himself that it wouldn't matter ultimately; they were still a minuscule force easily dealt with. They were a sheer nuisance like the insects of his country.

Still, Budai knew that his assessment didn't negate the potential threat these Americans posed. He'd learned very early in his career as a jihad fighter that to under-estimate an opponent could lead to a notably early death. They wouldn't be able to withstand a force of forty or fifty men once Budai had mustered his forces, but they did stand a chance of causing significant damage. He couldn't have cared less about the ship now that they were docked in the natural island stronghold of hardened volcanic rock, but he had a duty to his men and ensuring the safety of the X-51.

On the level above, the pair was required to pass through one of the areas where the guards had been manning the sickened crew members. For the most part, they had done the same thing shipwide, keeping the officers and senior noncommissioned officers in one particular compartment of the ship and leaving the enlisted men leaderless in scattered groups throughout the ship. By count, they had all but maybe one hundred men accounted for. Rumors had been working their way back that the ship's hospital was sealed up tight and probably hiding those missing per the roster—which they knew was kept with meticulous accuracy—but those individuals hadn't seemed to pose any kind of security threat. Moreover, they couldn't get to arms or radio for assistance from that area, so all they had accomplished was to seal themselves into what would ultimately become a mass grave.

The stench of the sick and dying was beginning to nauseate his men. One of the chief effects of the ricin poison they had perfected was its effects on the intestinal system. Some of its action on the blood had proved quite nasty on their test subjects, and Budai was considerably surprised that there had been no reports yet of death from the poisoning. Of course, it was expected that ricin could take anywhere from one to three days to kill a healthy adult. Still, all of the crew members affected were too weak to resist.

"Lock them up and follow us," Budai ordered as he passed the guards. "Our brothers above need us."

The two men nodded, unable to keep the eagerness and relief absent from their expressions. Budai couldn't say he blamed them. The smell was nauseating him already, and he was only passing through. Along the way, Budai encountered eight more of his men and ordered them to join him, too.

The small force he'd procured followed Budai on his heels. It took them only a few minutes to reach the tower. They began climbing the stairs, Budai now ordering six of his men to take point and the other five to maintain a rear guard. He would have to clear each deck of the tower before proceeding to the very top. He didn't really want to expend the extra time, but he couldn't afford to chance that some of these resistors were hiding on the decks and waiting for an opportunity to ambush him or his men.

They reached the first deck and Budai waited at the steps, instructing his men to fan out. He kept one man with him just in case they encountered the enemy. Budai stood there uncomfortably, anxious to help the men below. He could hear the yelling and the sporadic gunfire that always accompanied a battle. Of course, it didn't sound as heated as his man had originally reported, that was possibly a sign that they were close to victory.

Within a minute, his men had returned and assured him the first tower deck was clear. He turned immediately on his heel and headed for the stairs, his men fighting to keep pace with him. If there was anything they didn't have time for it was to waste precious seconds discussing what they hadn't found. The thought occurred to him that they could clear the decks much faster if he assigned four to take each deck, with him and the sentry that had been given the unlucky task of informing him of the battle.

He decided he would do that for the next deck, but they would stick to the routine on this. There was just something gnawing at his gut, telling him to split up his men. Budai listened to instincts, always, and he wasn't about to change his habits for the sake of mere convenience.

"Split up and search," he told the men as soon as they reached the second floor. "And use caution. I can practically smell the enemy. They are very near to us, I'm sure."

The men nodded, five proceeding in one direction of the corridor that led to the exterior catwalks, the other five taking the opposite side. Budai checked the AKSU that he carried, insuring that a round was chambered and the action unhindered. He could taste the impending conflict as he kept vigil.

He swore a solemn oath at that moment to bring the heads of the three Americans back to his master.

LYONS HADN'T COUNTED on meeting up with Schwarz under the present circumstances, but he was able to take enough satisfaction in the fact his friend was still alive. But it wasn't a moment too soon. Lyons and Lloyd Benson reached the flight deck in time to see the terrorists rapidly closing in on their allies' position, and Lyons decided to handle it the only way he knew how: he opened up with his AKSU on the nearest bunch using short, controlled bursts, and standing fully exposed to attract their attention.

The Able Team leader managed to drop the first terrorist with a triple burst to the side. Two of the bullets punched through the ribs and punctured a lung, while the third ripped open the terrorist's throat. The impact sent him spinning into one of his comrades, and Lyons got that man a moment later with two taps to the chest. The AKSU bolt locked back. Lyons decided he'd actually managed to accomplish what he'd intended, calling attention away from his friend. The undesired effect was that they shifted their weapons in his direction and opened up en masse.

He dived for nearby cover in a crew pit that Benson had already been smart enough to seek out. The young sailor managed to squeeze off a few rounds at what he could see, but Lyons wasn't sure if Benson hit anything because he was too busy trying to avoid becoming a bullet sponge. He landed in the crew pit, biting back the pain as he whacked a knee on the hard steel sides. The pit wasn't that wide or deep, and it would only provide adequate cover until the terrorists were on top of them. Then they would have no place to go and it would be time to cash it all in.

"Remind me to have a plan next time before I do something like that," Lyons said breathlessly.

"I'm worried about us not having a next time," Benson said as he exposed himself long enough to send another burst in the general direction of their opponents.

The Able Team leader dropped the empty magazine and quickly reloaded. It was the last one for the AKSU. He still had one of the Spectre M-4s, but he was certain that wouldn't last much longer than the AKSU, and there were still at least two dozen terrorists for them to deal with. Lyons popped his head over the border of the pit and began assisting Benson with the defense. It probably wouldn't be too much longer before the young seaman was out of ammo, as well, and Lyons wasn't at all sure how long Schwarz and Sizemore could hold out.

Benson got one as Lyons acquired his own target. Two 9 mm Parabellum rounds punched through the terrorist's skull. The gunman pitched forward, hitting the deck at the same time as his weapon and Lyons briefly glimpsed that the entire back of the terrorist's head was missing.

Lyons took the next one, putting a quartet of rounds

through a terrorist's gut and nearly eviscerating the man. The terrorist danced backward, his hands immediately going to his stomach, his weapon forgotten. Lyons could hardly take comfort in the sight, as four more terrorists came in behind those men as replacements. If the number of attackers was going to continue increasingly exponentially like this, there was no way in hell they would get out of it alive.

Lyons put his sights on the terrorist closest to him as the man raised his own weapon. Before either man could squeeze the trigger, the terrorist suddenly arched his back and his eyes went wide before he let out a shudder and collapsed. Lyons had seen the signs before—it was a death shudder where the body's autonomic nervous system sent a message along the neural pathways that read the equivalent of something like, "Hey stupid, you're dead."

Lyons didn't know what had happened, and at first he didn't see how Sizemore or Schwarz could have taken the man from that position. It wasn't until the other terrorists fell before he or Benson could squeeze off another shot that Lyons looked the only direction he hadn't yet: up. He smiled broadly at the sight of Rosario Blancanales and one of his team pouring down a serious firestorm on their enemies with the comforting report of assault rifles. Even from that distance, the profile of the M-16 was unmistakable.

The remaining terrorists looked wildly in all directions, attempting to ascertain the point of the ambush, but they were just a heartbeat too late. The distraction was enough for the men on the deck to take their targets, and the air support they were getting would more than finish the job.

This time, the targets would be few and cheap.

AS SOON AS Blancanales and Norris began raining destruction on the terrorists below, Lyons, Schwarz and their teammates seized the advantage.

Schwarz immediately broke from cover, as did Lyons, and moved in for a squeeze play, triggering their weapons on the run. The two sailors seemed shocked at first, visibly surprised by the near-suicidal gesture, but Blancanales simply smiled. It was the psychological effect they had needed, and the terrorists were dazed and confused enough that what would normally have resulted in instantaneous death suddenly turned into the most effective tactical maneuver.

"Look out!" Blancanales roared suddenly, shoving Norris back as the man was sighting on another target.

Blancanales barely knew what hit him as something warm and wet suddenly doused his face and clothes. He felt the muscles on Norris's arm convulse and tighten. The man suddenly became deadweight and the Able Team warrior had to let him go. He went down with him, sickened by the fact he would have to use the man's body as cover, but also unwilling to die without a fight.

Norris had been so focused on getting his payback that he hadn't seen the five terrorists who emerged onto the catwalk until it was too late. Blood still spurted from the vicious wounds he'd suffered, including a severed carotid artery, quickly slowing as his heart began to die. Fortunately, Norris wouldn't have to experience the pain and horror of his life ebbing away as half of his skull was missing.

Blancanales opened fire on the terrorists, full-auto, the M-16 A-3 spitting 5.56 mm rounds at a muzzle velocity of 3,260 feet per second. The high-velocity slugs punched through the first two terrorists, blowing holes in one's stomach and ripping through the chest of the man next to him. One terrorist stumbled forward, but the other was slammed backward, surprising the trio of survivals. One man tripped over the falling body and fell, which was probably the only thing that saved him.

The Able Team warrior triggered another sustained burst and blew the head off a third terrorist. The fourth man's upper torso erupted in a bloody pattern of shredded flesh as he took rounds to his abdomen, chest and throat. Blood exploded in a gory shower from the dual hits, the flesh and blood showering the terrorist who had ended up stumbling over the corpse of his comrade.

Blancanales took one more look at Norris, nodded in recognition of the man's bravery, and then he rose and immediately walked toward the terrorist with purpose, much like a tiger intent on finally partaking of its kill. The terrorist was obviously stunned by the approach of the bloodied, seething warrior and tried to bring his weapon to bear.

He was too late. Blancanales leveled the M-16 A-3 and shot the terrorist with a 3-round burst in the face at nearly point blank range. The force of the rounds shattered the man's skull, crushing bone and sending blood and brain matter flying in every direction. The man's headless corpse fell forward with a dull thump.

He returned to Norris's body, mumbled a quick honorific, then took Norris's weapon plus the spare he'd been carrying. It took some effort to get the weapon slung across his back out from under where he'd pinned it with his body. But Norris certainly wouldn't need it now, and they had to conserve all the weapons and ammo they could. The grisly task accomplished, Blancanales turned and headed for the stairwell.

All he could do now was keep the faith that Phoenix Force would arrive in time.

CHAPTER TWENTY-FIVE

The men of Phoenix Force reached the island successfully, and quickly assembled at McCarter's predesignated point following their jump from the NEACP. They were going to have a difficult time locating the ship, that much was certain. They weren't even sure if Ogo had told them the truth, although McCarter believed the smuggler. And while he knew he'd still have a lot to answer for when returning to Stony Man Farm, he also knew he'd done the right thing and he wasn't going to apologize for that.

They were about to begin a search of the island when T. J. Hawkins said, "Hold on there a minute, guys." He was looking at his watch, which they all knew doubled as a signal net. This was currently a prototype engineered by Wethers and Kurtzman, and Hawkins had agreed to field test it. It looked and worked like an ordinary watch but the sweeping second hand was actually designed to tune into different Stony Man frequencies.

"What is it, T.J.?" Encizo asked, standing next to the man and looking at the watch.

"We're getting a signal."

"From where?" McCarter asked.

"Is it one of ours?" James chimed in.

"Could be from Able Team," Manning said.

"Just ya'll hold on to your drawers a minute, will you?" Hawkins shook his head and went back to looking at the watch. Once he saw the signal again, he stopped the second hand, which in turn caused the watch to lock on to the signal. Depending on the chip put inside the watch, it could detect and track Stony Man's specialized high-frequency scrambles, radar signals, or even listen to local radio stations. It was indeed a powerful device.

"What's the story?" McCarter finally asked, growing impatient to get moving.

"It's a comm-block. Definitely a signal and *definitely* unique to Stony Man. They're calling for help." Hawkins turned and pointed in the direction of a nearby island peak. "It's coming from that direction."

"Well, then, what the hell are we doing standing around here?" McCarter snapped. "Let's get our bloody arses moving."

The men of Phoenix Force gathered their equipment and set off for the mountainous hill Hawkins had indicated. McCarter estimated it was about a klick from their present position, which meant it might take them some time to reach their friends if the terrain were rough. The Briton pushed those thoughts from his mind, pressing onward and determined to accomplish their mission.

A quick look at his watch confirmed that the *Fletcher* would probably be in firing range within the hour. He hoped they wouldn't have to use the military might of the destroyer. McCarter also hoped he wouldn't have to use the weighty piece of equipment in his pack. He hadn't wanted to even take the thing, waiting to see the ship and what condition its crew was in.

"You *have* to take it, David," Jack Grimaldi had told him. "Those are your orders and you don't want to be down there without it at the time you really need to use it."

"Yes, but if there's a chance that even one of those crew members is alive, then I won't use it, and if they don't bloody well like it then they can kiss my limey arse just before they cart it off to a firing squad."

"There's the remotest chance someone's alive, and I don't like this any more than you do, but that's what we've been ordered to do and I think we owe it to Hal and them to insure we carry it off," Grimaldi had replied. "And by the way, we don't have firing squads anymore. Now they just stick a needle in your arm, and there's nothing manly about dying that way."

McCarter couldn't help but consider the possibilities of what they might find. The comm-block signal was definitely good news, since it meant without a doubt that Able Team had signaled them, but he had no way of knowing whether any of his friends were still alive. It was possible they had generated the signal before being discovered by the terrorists. Still, he had to consider that in their searches they hadn't seen the signal before, which meant that this activation would have been more recent.

And all David McCarter could do was hope it was recent enough.

THE SUN HAD JUST STARTED to rise when Gary Manning discovered it. Behind a waterfall the big Canadian found an entrance to a vast, cavernous trail of aged volcanic rock covered with lichen and moss. The natural passage-way was very narrow, forcing them to walk in single file. McCarter decided to keep twenty meters between each man—the effective killing range of most hand grenades—with Manning on point.

At first it seemed like their trek through the darkened caves, the way ahead lit only by the red-lens flashlights each man carried, was going nowhere. But McCarter realized quickly enough that wasn't the case at all. Slowly, surely, faint echoes reached his ears. He pressed Manning to pick up the pace. If there was shooting, then that meant two sides in conflict, and that probably meant Able Team was a live and kicking.

Kicking ass that is, McCarter reminded himself.

Manning increased the pace but continued moving cautiously. It was entirely possible this cavern trail—wherever it led—was protected by the same parties re-sponsible for taking the *Stennis,* and they wouldn't be good to Able Team or anyone else if they rushed too quickly in what sounded like an already hostile situa-tion. They would have to plan and coordinate their movements carefully to get aboard the ship, if there still

was a ship, and it was too early to tell what kind of resistance they might encounter along the way.

Still, Phoenix Force was prepared to deal with a very
large force, and Brognola had advised that the *Fletcher*
planned to send in their complement of amphibious
assault Marines as soon as they were within range of the
island. McCarter had thought about arguing the point,
not wanting to risk the chance they would be mistaken
for hostiles, but then he decided against it. If terrorists
had been responsible for capturing the *Stennis,* then they
would have needed significant force to do so, and that
meant Phoenix Force could use all the help it could get.

Whatever they found, McCarter and his men would
be ready. And if they found that their friends had been
maimed or even killed over this, it would be a terrible
day of retribution indeed.

BLANCANALES HADN'T EXPECTED the kind of trouble he
encountered after just battling nearly a half dozen terrorists, but he dealt with it all the same. He rounded a
corner in the corridor leading from the exterior of the
tower to the stairs and spotted two men waiting near the
entrance to the stairwell. He could have taken an alter-
nate route, but it would take time and he didn't want to
risk hooking up with Lyons and Schwarz. It would go
a lot easier if they could stick together in getting back
to the infirmary.

This part of the tower was poorly lit, so the first
few rounds the pair fired at him were high and wide.
Blancanales didn't plan on giving them a second

chance. He went prone, aligned the M-16 A-3 on the nearer terrorist and squeezed the trigger. He'd readjusted his weapon to 3-round-burst mode, and it proved effective. The weapon vibrated under his tight grip, although the majority of the kick was absorbed by the stock buffer spring. The rounds struck the terrorist in the chest, knocking him backward into his partner.

Blancanales was about to drop the second one before he could recover but he suddenly found his hands full with another five terrorists racing from the opposite end of the hallway. The other terrorist forgotten, the Able Team warrior concentrated on the new group, keeping his weapon sights on the lead target while switching from 3-shot to full-auto mode.

He took the first one with a short burst that struck the stomach and chest. The impact sent the terrorist reeling, unable to control his forward movement, and he actually somersaulted once before coming to a rest on the deck. Blancanales got the second one with two rounds through the thigh. The terrorist dropped his weapon and emitted a horrific scream that was audible even above the weapons reports. The other trio obviously realized that they had underestimated the abilities of their opponent because they immediately scattered to find cover.

Oddly, the other terrorist from the pair he'd first encountered in this hallway had departed, probably through the stairwell entrance. Blancanales quickly pushed it from his mind and got back to the business at hand. This wasn't going to be easy with the terrorists now having some cover. He'd been in this situation before and lost two of his team members.

He hoped he wasn't next on the list.

LYONS AND SCHWARZ, along with Benson and Sizemore, had caught a brief glimpse of the trouble Blancanales had encountered, along with the death of a young sailor.

"We need to help him," Lyons said, turning and heading in the direction of tower.

The deck was now growing more visible as dawn sunlight streamed in from the cave entrance. They had been so busy fighting the terrorists that they hadn't noticed the vessel had stopped and was inside a large water cavern carved out of what Lyons assumed to be some type of land base, probably an island somewhere in the Pacific island chains.

"Ironman, hold up," Schwarz said.

Lyons stopped and looked back at his friend. "We can't worry about Pol now. He can take care of himself."

"No," Lyons said firmly, shaking his head. "We're not leaving him up there by himself. For all we know the terrorists are just waiting to ambush him."

"For all we know," Sizemore cut in, "they're waiting to ambush *us*. Your friend may just be the bait."

"Stay out of this," Lyons snapped. The Able Team leader locked eyes with Schwarz and said, "We're not leaving Pol alone. He had a bad feeling about all of us splitting apart to begin with, and I didn't notice any of his team with him outside of the poor dude who bought the farm. Not to mention the fact that Blancanales risked his life to get us more weapons and those medical texts for Danner. So we're not going to argue about this. We're going to just nut up and help him, end of story." He looked at Sizemore and added, "And we're *not* going to do out of some sickening desire to be heroes. We'll do it because he'd do the same thing for us. You got that, Sizemore?"

As they reached the steps, a terrorist was already halfway down, moving very quickly. Lyons whipped his Glock 26 into play and the hardman stopped short.

"Hold it," Lyons said. "Put your weapon down or you die here and now."

"Then I die," the terrorist said, although he did comply with Lyons's request.

For one long moment, something went cold in the pit of the Able Team leader's stomach, then in the next moment he realized they had indeed been duped. He recognized the man's voice. He wasn't sure how he'd managed to do it, or even if mere fate had simply put the two men together in this moment, but there was no question about that voice.

"You," Lyons said quietly. "You were the one who called me with the ransom demand. Except Shukan wasn't really in any danger, and you didn't really want money. You simply wanted to make sure that Shukan was above reproach."

"Yes," the terrorist replied. "And *you* are the infidel who has led this absurd raid against my people."

"Aw, you're breaking my heart," Lyons replied. "What's your name?"

"Rasam Budai," he answered with hesitation.

"Are you in charge of this little operation?"

Budai shook his head.

"And who is?"

Budai remained silent. Lyons wanted to squeeze the trigger at that moment and simply execute the worthless bastard standing in front of him, but he figured the guy could provide them with information that would be vital if they were to have any hope of thwarting whatever this group was up to, and that meant Budai was more useful to them alive at that moment.

"What are you planning?" Lyons asked.

"You know that I will not tell you. I *cannot* tell you that. I will not betray my master or our cause. The Americans oppressed us when all we did was defend our borders from the Turkish. You would not heed our warnings to stay away, and instead you allied your-selves with our enemies. That makes you our enemies, too. And I will not cooperate with our enemies."

"Sure. Whatever you say," Lyons replied. He turned to Sizemore and Benson. "You two think you're capable of keeping this guy under lock and key until we can come to retrieve him?"

The two men nodded eagerly, a keen expression on their faces. Lyons knew they were in a hurry to find someone on whom they could take out their frustra-tions. Given the deaths of their shipmates, Lyons wasn't sure that Budai would make it to the infirmary alive.

"No, better yet, you had best wait here with him. We're

going to find Agent Rose and we'll be back. You don't move from this spot until we come get you. Understood?"

The disappointment was evident, but the two men promised.

Lyons and Schwarz continued up the stairs. As they drew closer to the second deck they could hear the shooting. Sporadic autofire could be heard coming from either end of the corridor, which probably meant the terrorists had pinned Blancanales down while he was on his way to rendezvous with his friends.

As soon as they reached the relative safety of the door, Lyons turned to Schwarz. "On count of three, we go through. I don't know who's on which side, so we'll have to play it by ear."

Schwarz nodded as he double-checked the action on his Spectre M-4.

On three, the two men burst into the hallway, each one taking a direction. Lyons immediately saw Blancanales wave to him so it didn't take a brain surgeon to figure out where the enemy was positioned. Lyons whirled just in time to avoid a swarm of rounds that buzzed past his head like angry hornets. Lyons heard Schwarz open up with the Spectre even as he triggered his own weapon.

One round from Schwarz punched through a terrorist's lower jaw, smashing bone and ripping out a part of his throat. The terrorist dropped his weapon and clawed at his mangled neck, which was now spurting blood. This distracted the attention of the terrorist next to him; it also cost the hardman his life. In the moment where he stopped firing, Lyons put a bullet through the side of his head, effectively neutralizing any further threat.

The final terrorist realized very suddenly that he was outgunned three to one. He rose and tried to escape, but Schwarz leveled the Spectre M-4 and triggered a short burst that caught the terrorist and drove him to the deck.

Lyons and Schwarz turned to see their teammate trot toward them with a thumbs-up. When they were within reach, each exchanged high-fives with him. He was covered in blood, which concerned Lyons at first, but he didn't' see any apparently external injuries or signs that Blancanales was in pain.

"You all right, pal?" he asked.

Blancanales looked startled by the question, but then his expression changed and he nodded in understanding, obviously having remembered he was blood-soaked.

"Yeah," he replied. "Not mine."

"Well, that's good news," Schwarz commented.

"One of the terrorists got away, Carl. I don't know who he was—"

"Is he short and thin with a long, dark beard?"

"Yeah," Blancanalessaid. "Obviously you've already met him."

Lyons nodded. "I think he's a ranker in Ansar al-Islam, but I'm not sure where. He's definitely Iraqi. There's no mistaking the accent and he did mention that because we befriended the Turks during the war that we're now their enemies, too."

"Sure sounds like al-Islam," Blancanales added.

"Well, we're not out of the woods yet. What happened to the rest of your people?"

Schwarz explained quickly as he handed out the spare M-16 A-3s and magazines, apparently quite happy to be rid of the excess weight. He also explained about how he'd been able to activate the comm-blocks. When he'd finished, Lyons gave their situation some serious thought.

"We're going to have to dump those medical books on what's left of our team," Lyons said. "We'll take this Budai character and see if we can't commandeer us some sort of communications equipment. We need to get support here and fast. We aren't going to be able to hold out like this much longer."

"Yeah, but where are we going to find a communications array?" Schwarz asked.

"Well, let's go ask Budai," Lyons replied with a knowing grin.

CHAPTER TWENTY-SIX

"We must leave here immediately," Shukan told Hamid Adil. "My instrumentation indicates that there is a fully armed American destroyer within twenty minutes of our position."

Adil turned on his heel and pinned Shukan with a cold and merciless gaze. "We do not leave until my men and I have launched our attack against San Francisco."

"Your men—" Shukan spit. "It would seem you don't have any men left, or at best very few. Why the very idea is absurd! They appear to be dying against a numerically inferior force with handguns. Do you actually think that you can launch the X-51 against the United States now? They will shoot it down before it has gone a single nautical mile."

Adil reached to the holster he'd donned earlier and withdrew a 9 mm pistol in one smooth movement that was too fast for Jin Shukan to follow. "And I will shoot you down if you don't help me accomplish this."

Shukan appeared unaffected, as if having guns pointed at him was an everyday experience. Adil wondered if behind the thin veneer of scientist and scholar there was nothing but a black void; an ice-cold heart that had never learned to enjoy sunshine on his face, or the touch and fragrance of a beautiful woman. In fact, Adil wondered if there was anything there at all, even the slightest shred of humanity.

""I cannot help you if you kill me."

"I have no intention of killing you, unless you will not cooperate with me. If there is a chance that this will fail, I can't afford the liability you will cause. You may decide to make a deal with the Americans, and they might consider it for all you've done for them. They will show me no mercy."

"Those men above," Shukan said. "If they have done the kinds of things that your people have reported, mercy is something neither of us will obtain."

"Then that is why we must not delay this operation any longer. It was your idea to bring us here after your little scheme to throw the Americans off our track. It would seem that your plan didn't work, and I will not allow all of my men to suffer and die needlessly. You will configure the X-51 to launch now, or I will kill you. The alternative is much better as I may be able to escape in the submarine and deliver you back to your country unharmed. And there our alliance shall end forever."

"Very well," Shukan said, shrugging and returning to his laptop. "I suppose it will also help to cover our escape."

"Precisely," Adil said, not wanting to admit that he hadn't thought of that.

Shukan began entering the sequence that Adil figured would start the preflight checks on the X-51.

At most, they only had twenty or thirty minutes to put the plane in the air. Adil was confident the X-51 would get past the destroyer. In fact, that's partly what it had been designed to do. The X-51 was capable of traveling at phenomenal speeds, and cloaking itself. Of course, he had no intention of taking the Japanese scientist with them—the scientist wouldn't live that long. As he watched Shukan work, he wondered when he should kill him.

Finally, Adil decided he would wait until Budai returned. And then he would have the pleasure of killing an ally that he hated.

"WHERE'S THE COMMUNICATIONS area?" Lyons demanded.

"I do not know," Budai replied.

The Able Team leader withdrew his Glock 26 pistol and for the second time in less than fifteen minutes, he pointed it at Budai's head. "I'm not one for killing a guy in cold blood. But know this—I will kill you where you stand if you waste any more of my time, or lie to me, or tell me you don't know something I know you do."

"You can kill me, infidel, but it will avail you nothing. The scientist, Shukan, built this place. Or he had it built. I don't know anything about it or where anything is."

"Well, then, we'll just take a look around and you can act as insurance," Lyons said, turning Budai so his back was to him and grabbing the back of the terrorist's neck. "Move out."

As they emerged from the command tower and began proceeding across the deck in the direction of a large gangplank leading from the carrier to the cavern mouth, a pocket of terrorists began firing sniping shots. Lyons could tell immediately that the shots were meant more to keep them contained than to actually produce injury. The terrorist snipers could have shot them all dead by now, but their less than perfect aim got Lyons thinking that perhaps their prisoner was a bit more important than they thought.

Suddenly, the area to their left erupted in a blast of orange-red flame immediately followed by an expanding shower of white-hot sparks. Lyons immediately sensed the sulfuric-like odor of molten iron and could see the incendiary effects on a couple of the terrorists that could only be the result of an exploding AN-M14 TH3 grenade. What surprised him the most was that it wasn't directed at them.

A moment later he discovered why as the members of Phoenix Force charged down the gangplank and immediately began taking up positions to lay down covering fire. As the special ops team opened up on the Ansar al-Islam terrorists with unerring accuracy, Lyons paused only a moment to exchange glances with McCarter. The fox-faced Briton signaled him with an exaggerated wink and Lyons nodded his acknowledgment.

The two leaders then continued with their assigned tasks, Able Team going for the makeshift gangplank and Phoenix Force dealing out certain hell.

"There are plenty of ill and wounded belowdecks!" Lyons shouted at McCarter in passing. He jerked his head at Sizemore and Benson and added, "These guys will show you where!"

The Phoenix Force leader nodded, gesturing for the two men to get behind cover as Able Team continued onward with his prisoner. At the last moment, McCarter tossed something in his direction and Lyons's quick reflexes were the only thing that kept him from missing it. It was a radio, McCarter's way of telling them to keep in touch.

When they finally stepped on dry land, the first time in nearly four days, Lyons breathed a sigh of relief. With Phoenix Force now here to assist them, he was actually beginning to feel like they might succeed in turning the tables on the terrorists. The thought strengthened him, and he realized how exhausted he was at that point. He'd been pushing himself for nearly twenty-four hours straight. His teammates provided cover, keeping on either side of Lyons, sweeping the area with their weapons to insure safe passage. Soon they found themselves in a maze of rock and moss, with the sounds of battle quickly fading.

Whether by dumb luck or fate, they soon found what they were looking for. The building was small and squat, maybe one-hundred-foot square, with wires protruding through one of the walls and leading in different directions. Lyons shoved Budai aside, leaving him in Schwarz's care before stepping forward and examining the door. It was locked. Lyons muttered a few curses, then turned his eyes away as he held his .45-caliber Glock 26 close to the lock and squeezed the trigger. The cheap padlock immediately separated from the hinge, and Lyons kicked the door in. He felt on the wall and to his surprise found a switch. He flipped it and the room was bathed in a soft, yellowish light. Even despite the dim lighting, the gleaming panels glowed. There was a very expensive communications array set up against one wall.

Lyons looked back at his friends and said, "We've hit pay dirt, boys."

"I'll be damned," Schwarz said as he moved forward to stand next to Lyons. "You were right all along, Ironman. How did you know?"

"Simple," Lyons replied with a smug, self-satisfied grin. "There was no way they could keep this place running without the ability to communicate to outside areas, and an operation this large would definitely require a significant system. Knowing that, it just came down to finding it."

Blancanales nodded. "Very sharp, buddy."

Lyons nodded before looking at Schwarz. "Time to go to work. See if you can raise the Farm on that thing."

"I don't know if I can," Schwarz replied. "I don't have any of the communication codes to get into this thing. And I'm sure our friend here isn't going to be any help."

"Well, do your best," Lyons replied. "I've got faith in you."

The electronics wizard merely nodded, and while he appreciated the sentiments, he could only hope that faith was enough.

IT DIDN'T TAKE LONG for Phoenix Force to dispatch what few terrorists remained above deck. McCarter knew they might encounter additional resistance below, but the most important thing at the moment was to secure the ship. McCarter and the rest of them had briefly studied plans of the ship while on the NEACP, but they didn't know it like the pair Lyons had left with Phoenix Force. McCarter was happy for any help he could get, and the guys who introduced themselves as Sizemore and Benson had obviously met with Ironman's stamp of approval. That was the only endorsement McCarter needed.

"Where are these men at?" McCarter asked Sizemore.

"In the infirmary, three decks below."

"Do you guys have that area secured?" Encizo asked.

"Secured?" Benson asked with disbelief. "You have to be kidding me, man. The majority of our crew is either dead or dying."

"What are you talking about?" James asked. "Are you saying that a few terrorists slaughtered your entire crew?"

"No," Benson replied, shaking his head. "They're all sick. The guys who were with us think that these terrorists contaminated the food and water supplies. We had maybe fifty at most who weren't sick. The others are either so ill they can't even stand up or they're just plain MIA."

"Take us to the infirmary," McCarter said. "Right now."

Before anyone could say another word, the sound of jet engines firing suddenly demanded their full attention. All eyes turned in the direction of the flight deck and noticed that the X-51 was beginning to visibly vibrate as her engines suddenly ignited. They could feel the vibrations between the soles of their shoes as the X-51 moved out from the flight line and into launch position.

"That blooming thing's going to take off, ya'll," Hawkins observed with some measure of shock mixed with excitement.

"They must be planning to launch a strike," Manning said.

"Yeah, but against whom?" James asked.

"Only Shukan has the knowledge to do something like that," McCarter said. "Not that it will even bloody matter if we don't find the bugger."

"We'd better alert the *Fletcher.*"

McCarter nodded and reached for the radio on his belt. He keyed the transmit button twice, then called for Lyons. "Phoenix to Able, do you copy?"

A small burst of static, then Lyons came back with, "Loud and clear, pal. What's up?"

"Someone's launching the X-51. I don't think our transmitters can deliver enough of a signal to advise counteroffensive forces. Do you think you could get to the outside with a transmitter?"

"I can do one better," Lyons replied. "We found a communications array. Wizard says two minutes until it's up and humming."

McCarter turned one eye back at the X-51 that was growing steadily noisier as he clicked the transmitter and said, "I don't think we've that much time, mate."

There was a long pause before Lyons replied, "The Wizard says sorry, best he can do. You want to give me the info?"

It made McCarter nervous communicating frequency and password information across the open airwaves, but it was a risk he'd have to take. The commander of the *Fletcher,* Streator, had given McCarter a specific code to use so that he could positively identify any requests coming from him as valid. Well, this was their one chance and they'd have to risk it.

"I copied your information, Phoenix. We'll do our best."

"Roger, and we'll do our part to keep any heat off your backs. Phoenix out."

As McCarter replaced the radio on his belt, Encizo asked, "Now what?"

"Schwarz will do his best to get us up and running as fast he can," McCarter said. "In the meantime, we need to find as many able-bodied men as possible to get this ship up, running and the bloody hell away from here."

McCarter stopped to think about it. He really didn't want to split his team up, but he didn't see that they had much choice. They had a lot of ground to cover and very little time to cover it in, and it wouldn't do to get their asses blown sky-high before they were clear of the caverns. They would just have to rely on Lyons to get the job done on that end. The best they could do was to find some support aboard the ship. There *had* to be more men somewhere.

"Here's what we'll do," McCarter said. He looked at Encizo and Manning. "You two go with Benson here and get to the infirmary. See what kind of help you can render. We need to get this ship out of here and quick, because when they bring down a fire mission from the *Fletcher,* we don't want to be around. So the rest of us will go with Sizemore who'll take us to the most likely hiding places of other sailors. They couldn't have gotten everyone with this contaminant."

"How do you know?" Benson asked.

"Odds plain and simple, sailor," Encizo replied. "When you have more than forty-five hundred people on a ship of this size, there's no question that where there were fifteen or twenty who managed to avoid getting sick, there have to be more. They've just decided not to expose themselves."

"Cowards." Sizemore spit.

"Bullshit," James replied. "They're just trying to stay alive."

"No more talk like that, mate," McCarter snapped.

Sizemore's shame came on him when his face reddened. He'd been slapped down by men that were obviously much better trained than he was, and it was obvious to the Phoenix Force warriors that the strain of the past twelve hours had taken its toll on both men.

Still, they would have to rely on these men with their lives. None of them knew the layout of the ship well enough to navigate on their own, so they'd have to go with on-the-job training.

The roar of the X-51 increased and McCarter gestured for them to split into their groups and get to a safe location. As Sizemore led them away from the flight deck and toward the command tower, the X-51 emitted a high-pitched whine before shooting down the runway and into open air. It quickly banked and turned to avoid smashing into a cave wall, then disappeared from view, heading toward the cave entrance.

And McCarter hoped that Lyons's estimates had been correct.

"WHAT'S TAKING SO long?" Lyons demanded.

"Ironman, will you chill out?" Blancanales snapped as he stood over Budai. "He's doing the best he can."

Lyons started to open his mouth in verbal retaliation but the warning glint in his teammate's eyes, something he saw rarely in Blancanales, told him it was simply better to shut up and let it go. Of course, he realized Blancanales was right. He'd been treating Schwarz a bit too harshly ever since they'd argued about helping out Blancanales and he needed to let that go for now. There were other times, much better times, to worry about that.

"We're up!" Schwarz cried with elation, slapping his hands together and rubbing them.

"All right," Lyons replied, looking at his hand where

he'd scribbled the information, "send a signal priority-coded on this frequency."

Lyons read off the information and Schwarz dialed it into the advanced communications array. A high-pitched signal was followed by a low-pitched signal that ended with a long burst of static. An unfamiliar voice came through, probably that of a communications controller.

"United States Naval Command, this is a secured and priority frequency. You have contacted the U.S.S. *Fletcher.* Please state your emergency and declare your authorization. Your signal is being tracked visually."

Lyons picked up the microphone transmitter, a bit hesitant, but a quick smile and wink from Schwarz put his mind at ease. He cleared his throat and said, "Attention U.S.S. *Fletcher*, I say, code name is Cinnamon, message is Priority One for the CO of your ship. Fall down on this signal and confirm. Again, I say again that code name is Cinnamon, message is Priority One for the CO."

Only silence followed, and Lyons wondered if he'd done something wrong. Nearly a full minute elapsed, and then another minute, and just as they were going on their third a clear, crisp voice broke through. "Brown, you've got me. What's your situation?"

"Commander, this isn't Brown," Lyons replied. "My name is Irons, and I'm a federal agent that was providing security aboard the *Stennis* when she was hijacked. Understand that we have pretty much secured the ship and are now taking measures to get her out of this island cavern and clear.

"I don't know your present position, but be advised that there's an aircraft headed away from this signal of origin and bound for who knows where. Whatever happens, Commander, that craft is not to make its destination. Is that understood? I say again, the aircraft that originated from this signal is *not* to make its destination."

"In other words," Streator replied, "you're telling me to blow it out of the sky."

"You're correct, sir."

"Consider it done," Streator said. "And good luck to you boys."

Lyons signed off and then turned to his teammates. "Well, we've done our part. Now it's up to Phoenix."

"Somehow," Blancanales replied, "I don't think they'll disappoint."

"YOUR PRECIOUS X-51 is now airborne," Shukan announced, inclining his head in a conciliatory fashion. "And now, I think it is time we depart."

"As do I," Hamid Adil replied, then shot Shukan in the head.

Adil went to the Japanese scientist's mobile computer, quickly powered it down and disconnected it from the wall, then headed for the upper decks. There was no way he would leave anything behind that would allow the Americans to figure out exactly what happened. Within a day, this ship would be filled with rotting, stinking dead bodies and that would keep their hands plenty full.

All Adil had to do was to avoid the Americans long

enough to get to the submarine that waited just off the shores of the island. He brought the microphone to his lips and whispered the code that would advise his troops to be ready to retrieve him. They would pick him up by boat on that back side of the island, transfer him to the submarine, and then they would be on their way.

Adil was just below the top deck when he suddenly found himself faced with an army of sailors rushing toward him. These men weren't sick; in fact, they were just the opposite and appeared to be in quite good health. Alarms and sirens suddenly began to sound throughout the ship and Adil could feel the vibrations through the walls as she rumbled to life.

The sailors stopped dead in their tracks at first sight of the terrorist. He stared at them as they stared back, then he turned and ran in the opposite direction. There were a number of other ways to the top deck, and he knew all of the routes. He'd studied them carefully. He'd wished there had been enough time to wait for Budai to return and escort him to the opposite end of the island, but he was out of time. That was fine, however, because Budai knew the escape route.

Adil was stopped suddenly in his tracks once more, finding himself faced with more sailors who also seemed to be in perfect health. He turned in retreat but the sailors he'd first encountered were now closing in. Slowly he watched them approach from either side, the looks in their faces telling the tale of what was about to happen. He could understand their hatred, and he knew that only one choice remained.

He would end his reign of Ansar al-Islam with honor. As the men continued to close in on him, Hamid Adil slowly withdrew the his 9 mm pistol, pressed the barrel to his head and begged Allah's mercy as he squeezed the trigger.

Nothing in the set of the set

EPILOGUE

Stony Man Farm, Virginia

There was an air of solemnity mixed with excitement in the War Room, and Harold Brognola had to admit that it felt good.

The men of Phoenix Force and Able Team had arrived safely less two hours earlier, and the weariness and intensity of the ordeal clung to the faces of every single one of them. Most particularly weary, and looking older than Brognola ever remembered, was Rosario Blancanales. Of course, it was no surprise to him when he'd heard how the man had lost all three of the sailors assigned to accompany him through the bowels of the *Stennis*.

Each of the sailors who had directly contributed to the success of the mission was to receive the Navy Cross in a ceremony at Arlington later this week. It would follow the funerals of four serviceman that would be buried there, men who had paid the ultimate price to save their countrymen and their ship.

"According to the preliminary reports I've already received, sixteen other sailors are in critical condition at a variety of hospitals in San Francisco as well as Tokyo and the Marianas Naval Station at Guam," Brognola said. "Sadly, they're not expected to survive."

That announcement added to the solemnity on the somber faces around the table. Such sacrifices were sometimes necessary to sustain the greater common good. Everyone sitting at that table understood that, and yet it somehow didn't make it any easier.

Brognola continued, "We're going to have a hell of a time keeping this out of the press. For now, the Oval Office has been working with the Pentagon to keep this as quiet as possible. They're calling it a training accident."

Carl Lyons snorted. "Yeah, that'll hold water for about thirty seconds."

"Either way, it's not our problem. We're not in the damage control business. Let the military and the Man hammer it on their own terms."

Lyons fell silent, and the solemn mood increased throughout the room.

"On another note," Brognola said, turning his attention on McCarter, "we *are* going to have to explain how a prisoner in the custody of public safety officers is taken from them and suddenly returned a few hours later to the custody of the authorities on Guam."

McCarter grinned and replied, "And no worse for the wear the bloke was, eh, governor?"

"Cut the crap," Price said. "There's nothing funny about this. And there will be no more sucker plays like that without telling us first, David, or I swear you'll be out on the street collecting unemployment."

Brognola was surprised that Price would come down that hard on the cocky Briton, but he allowed the mission controller to speak her peace. It had caused them some considerable trouble and exposed them to risks other than embarrassment with the Oval Office. They were supposed to keep as low a profile as possible during operations, and this latest stunt hadn't even come close to following protocol.

The Stony Man teams were just exhausted, and Brognola decided to change the subject. "Okay, that's all of the ass chewing out of the way. Now, I want to express on behalf of the President how proud we are of you, and what a great job you did. You saved thousands of lives, men, and you recovered military property with very little damage. You're to be commended, and the Man has authorized me to send all of you a long and mandatory vacation. And you're encouraged to all strike out on your own."

"In other words," Encizo said, "take a little vacation from each other, too."

Price replied with a grin, "Well, they say distance makes the heart grow fonder."

The entire group burst out laughing on that one, and as the laughter died down Brognola said, "Again, good job. Now get the hell out of here. You're to report back in two weeks. Unless something goes to hell somewhere in the world."

"David," Lyons said, "I didn't thank you for coming to save our asses. We owe you."

McCarter appeared to brighten at the suggestion. "Oh, really? And when can we expect our return?"

Lyons exchanged glances with Schwarz and Blancanales, then grinned. "The check's in the mail."

A long-lost sword.

A willing heroine.

A quest to protect humanity's
sacred secrets from falling
into the wrong hands.

Her destiny will be revealed.

July 2006.

GOLD
EAGLE®

TAKE 'EM FREE

2 action-packed novels plus a mystery bonus

NO RISK

NO OBLIGATION TO BUY